Farewell My Herring

By L. C. Tyler

a&b

Farewell My Herring

L. C. TYLER

Allison & Busby Limited
11 Wardour Mews
London W1F 8AN
allisonandbusby.com

First published in Great Britain by Allison & Busby in 2021.
This paperback edition published by Allison & Busby in 2021.

A CIP catalogue record for this book is available from the British Library.

10 9 8 7 6 5 4 3 2 1

ISBN 978-0-7490-2745-2

Typeset in 10.5/15.5 pt Sabon LT Pro by
Allison & Busby Ltd

FSC
www.fsc.org
MIX
Paper from
responsible sources
FSC® C020471

The paper used for this Allison & Busby publication
has been produced from trees that have been legally sourced
from well-managed and credibly certified forests.

Printed and bound by
CPI Group (UK) Ltd, Croydon, CR0 4YY

For Lizzie and John

THE FIRST PASS

CHAPTER ONE

Ethelred

'If I were to kill you somewhere like this,' said the taxi driver cheerfully, 'it would be months before they found the bits the buzzards didn't want. Every time I drop a passenger off round here, I think: now, there's a good place for a quiet murder.'

I nodded. Much the same thought had already occurred to me. During our drive up from the station, the valley had progressively narrowed and coarsened. Broad, orderly fields of winter wheat had given way to rough sheep pasture, then sheep pasture to dead bracken and wind-smashed reeds that even the sheep didn't consider to be food. The bare limestone crags and the fan-shaped sheets of scree had a strangely industrial air, but were as natural here, and as grim, as the sky above – a billowing grey-black that presaged snow, though a few incongruous patches of bright blue still gleamed through.

'No phone signal, of course,' he continued, turning

suddenly and heart-stoppingly from his view of the road to address me. 'Not after Butterthwaite. Even if you were certain I was going to bump you off, you'd have no way of letting anyone know. Not even a final, desperate text to the family. Perfect crime, eh?'

'Butterthwaite? Where's that?' I asked. My gaze was fixed on the road ahead – a single-track thread of dark tarmac with passing places at scarcely adequate intervals. The drystone walls, which had lined the road most of the way up, were no longer there for us to hit, but the steep and unguarded slope down to the stream on our left spoke of even better opportunities for premature death.

'Three mile back,' he said. He looked ahead again, perhaps curious to see how far we had come. 'It was the last village we passed through, if you want to call it a village. School closed in 1911. Pub in 1963. They finally finished vandalising the telephone box in 1980. Just the farm and a row of holiday cottages now. The farm sells ice cream and cans of drink in the summer. That's all it is. Walkers don't come up this way much. That's peat bog down there by the beck, that is. Never dries out in the summer and never seems to freeze in the winter. You'd be up to your knees in it if you went more than half a dozen yards. A man vanished without trace, a year or two back. His wife said he'd fallen behind as they both came down from the fells – he stopped to look at some peregrine falcons, she said. She was never that interested in raptors herself. Anyway, she just pressed on down to the main road and waited for him there. Eventually she caught the bus into Harrogate and had a cream tea at Betty's.

Plenty of people saw her there, but they never did find out what happened to the husband. The jury believed her story though. Or, like as not, they just thought he deserved it.'

'They often do,' said Elsie. She had taken the front passenger seat, though she had no need at all of the additional leg room it afforded, leaving me to fold myself into the back of the taxi as best I could, with her hard suitcase on the shiny, red fake-leather beside me. It bounced sharply into my thigh whenever we hit a bump.

'As for Fell Hall at the top of the valley,' said the driver, now speaking to me via the rear-view mirror, 'well, nobody had lived in that for years and years until the Golden Age Trust took it over to run these writing courses.'

'I suppose it's called Fell Hall because it is right up in the fells?' Elsie asked.

'No, it's named after Dr Gideon Fell. A detective. Apparently this chap, John Dickson Carr, wrote about him. Crime writer, you see. All their courses are crime writing up there. You'll be crime writers yourselves if you're going up to the hall today? I usually take the tutors up on Wednesday evening, then the students start to arrive on the Thursday morning, so I'm guessing you're both writers.'

'Do I look like a crime writer?' asked Elsie pointedly.

'Yes,' said the driver, who was hopefully not expecting a tip from her.

'*He's* a writer,' she said, jerking a plump thumb back in my direction. 'That's what writers look like. If they're not careful. I'm his agent. And, fortunately, also the agent of a number of other writers, or I wouldn't be able to afford the fare up here.'

He nodded. That was an important consideration.

'So, would I have heard of you, sir?' he asked me.

'Probably not,' said Elsie.

'He might have,' I said.

'I'm sure he only reads bestsellers,' said Elsie. 'Most sensible people do.'

'No. I read all sorts of stuff,' the taxi driver replied. 'I get them from charity shops mainly. Books people don't want to keep, like.'

Elsie shrugged. It was then perfectly possible that he knew me well.

'What name do you write under?' he asked.

'Various names, but mainly as Peter Fielding,' I said.

'Come again?'

I repeated the name.

'Who else?' he asked.

'J. R. Elliot?'

'Thrillers?'

'Historical mysteries. Reign of Richard the Second. The detective is called Master Thomas. He's one of Chaucer's clerks.'

'Chaucer, eh? Sounds a bit too clever for me. Who else?'

'Amanda Collins?' I said.

'Yes – definitely. Amanda Collins. I'm sure I've read some of them. Police procedurals, aren't they? Set in Worthing? Really gruesome murders?'

'No, they're romantic comedies. No murders of any sort. I do those occasionally too.'

'Not any more,' said Elsie. 'Your publisher's dropped you.'

'You didn't tell me that.'

'I was waiting for the right moment.'

The last small trace of blue sky had vanished. Mist was ominously rolling down the valley, or perhaps we were climbing up into the clouds. It was difficult to say. The driver crunched a gear change. He swore, switched the windscreen wipers on and peered with narrowed eyes at the road that rose in a long, sinuous curve, following the line of the valley. Large flakes of snow had started to fall. Down amongst the winter wheat, it was late for snow, but not up here. Up here, you felt, it would never be too late.

'So, you teach them how to write crime novels, then?' he asked me. 'How to create red herrings, and so on?'

'The course is for writers of traditional mysteries,' said Elsie. 'So, yes, it's really all about herrings. Misdirecting the reader is the most important tool in their box. That and locked rooms. And railway timetables. Oh, and these days you're also allowed at least one cynical, hungover detective fighting their own personal inner demons as they track down yet another serial killer.'

'I bet there's a bit more to it than that, though?' he said. 'Am I right?'

'Absolutely,' said Elsie. 'You have to get somebody – somebody with a knowledge of the real world – to sell the book to a publisher – not an easy task, because publishers have been sold duds before and are now less and less trusting of the assurances of decent, honest agents. They want to check actual sales records these days, which can be inconvenient. Then you have to come up with a better title than the author's one and design a really good cover with a blurb on the back that describes a book that somebody might actually want to read rather than the one the author wrote. Once the hard work's done, you add the author's eighty thousand words, minus the clichés, repetition, contradictions, dull bits, split infinitives and non sequiturs, and – if there are still any words left – you've got a book.'

'She's joking,' I explained.

'Ah,' he said. 'Is she now?'

'That's Fell Hall over there?' asked Elsie.

The driver nodded and changed gear again. The road had finally ceased to climb, but the tarmac had given out as we passed between some massive stone gateposts, and we bumped the last few hundred yards over a rocky track that merged imperceptibly, in every direction, into the broad, misty moorland.

Ahead of us, an irregular black outline pierced by narrow, dimly lit windows could now be discerned through the enveloping septentrional gloom. Slowly the character of our destination became clearer – the slick slate roof, the rough-hewn stone walls, the randomly placed gables, the motley collection of outbuildings. Only the practised eye could have told which bits were medieval and which had been added in the nineteenth century by somebody with a morbid imagination; but it was clear that it had grown cautiously over the years, like the stunted trees we had passed on the road, keeping its own counsel but missing nothing that went on around it.

'I think you've made it just in time,' the driver said. 'Another hour and there'll be a couple inches of snow. Not good on these gradients – or not with my tyres, anyway. Do you want a hand with that suitcase, love?'

'No,' said Elsie, who knew that she didn't have to tip me, however large and heavy the bag. 'Ethelred will carry it. Under one *nom de plume* or another.'

'I'll do it as Amanda Collins, shall I?' I said.

'She doesn't have anything else to do, poor cow,' said Elsie.

CHAPTER TWO

Ethelred

'You must be Elsie Thirkettle,' said the course director, shaking her hand. 'I'm Wendy Idsworth.' She checked a list on her clipboard. 'And you are Peter Fielding?'

Wendy's voice was southern, middle class. Though I'd been only a couple of hours up here in the North, it already sounded incongruous, foreign, affected, though it was much as I spoke myself.

'It's one of the names I write under,' I said. 'My real name is Ethelred. Ethelred Tressider.'

'Really?' She raised her eyebrows.

'After King Ethelred the First – not Ethelred the Unready. My father was always very clear on that point. It was an important distinction for him, and he could never quite understand why it wasn't one for other people.'

She nodded. She was definitely with other people on that.

'So, would you like us to call you Peter or Ethelred?' she enquired.

I paused for a moment too long.

'Call him Ethelred,' said Elsie. 'Peter makes him sound almost normal.'

Wendy mouthed all three Anglo-Saxon syllables of 'Ethelred' as she amended the list of tutors on her clipboard. That was that, then. I was not to escape being Ethelred, not even for the weekend. She tapped the metal clip with her pen and nodded again.

She was a short, thin woman with dark hair. Her face seemed prematurely wrinkled, as do the faces of many who spend a lot of their time out on the fells. Wendy was resident director – she remained summer and winter, organising courses, overseeing repairs to the ancient structure of Fell Hall, walking the trails whenever the opportunity arose. She must have sat out many lonely, snowy nights and days. But apparently she enjoyed her solitude. She was in fact something of a legend in the writing world, though a rarely seen one. I'd run into her once in Harrogate, when she'd visited the crime writing festival for a day, but she'd been back up in the fells before most of us hit the bar, which was pretty early. The fliers advertising the Fell Hall courses were written by her, but never featured her photograph, not even in the background of some cheerful group of writers and would-be writers. It was as if she were the ghost in the machine of the Golden Age Trust, to which she was wholly devoted.

'You're in Ripon,' she said, passing me two keys. 'Ripon's a small single room but quite adequate for a short stay. The second key is for the front door if you need it, though I imagine you won't be going out much after dark in this weather. Elsie, we've put you in the Malham Suite, as you requested. I think you'll find it very comfortable indeed. The various settings for the bath are quite complicated, but there is a manual in the bathroom, next to the towel heater. Both rooms are up on the first floor – Ripon's some way beyond Malham, at the very end of the corridor. Try stuffing a flannel or something in the gap in the window, Ethelred, if it gets too cold for you. Are you both OK with your bags?'

'Ethelred can manage everything,' said Elsie. 'We'll be fine.'

Wendy noticed a presence hovering at her shoulder. A large young woman with a ruddy face and untidy blonde hair. 'Yes, Jenny?' she said.

'I've put the two girls in Giggleswick,' Jenny reported. She wiped her hands on her apron – a reflex action indicating a completed task, unless the girls had been particularly wet. 'I've also prepped the veg and the pie's done and ready to go in the oven whenever you like. If that's all, I'll go back down in the next taxi.'

Wendy shook her head. 'All of the tutors are now here. Unless there is another wholly unauthorised arrival of participants, there's no way of getting back into town tonight. I can't drive you; I'm needed at the Hall. And obviously there's no way of phoning for a taxi.'

'But you promised . . . my mum's birthday.'

'I need you here tomorrow, Jenny, bright and early.'

'My car might be fixed by tomorrow. If it's not, I could have got a lift from Dad, first thing in the morning. He wouldn't have minded a break from the farm.'

'The road may be blocked with snow by then.'

'In that case nobody will get here and there's no course

to run. You wouldn't need me.'

'Don't be pert, Jenny. I've warned you about that before. There are no more taxis coming up and no way of getting one for you – even if a driver was prepared to come up here so late and in the snow.'

'But I told you—'

'You did tell me, but I don't believe I promised anything.'

'With no phone reception up here, I can't even call Mum to wish her happy birthday.'

'I don't have time for this now, Jenny. Just scamper along to the kitchen, there's a good girl. That pie won't put itself in the oven, will it? I'll join you as soon as I can.'

Jenny looked at Wendy as if she could happily murder her, but just said 'I'll get on with dinner then, shall I?'

'Thank you, Jenny. That would be very kind. I'll come and check what you're doing in a moment.' She turned to us. 'Everyone will muck in tomorrow when all of the participants are here, but the first evening, with just the tutors, we cook for you.'

'Did Jenny say the participants had started to arrive though?' I asked.

Wendy rolled her eyes theatrically. 'Yes, two of them. Claimed they'd got the wrong start time. I've put them together in the smallest double. I suppose they'll have to join us for dinner. We can't actually let them starve to death, can we?'

'Starve to death?' I said. 'Definitely not. They should join us.'

Wendy looked disappointed at my wimpish response. You could always get more participants. There was usually a waiting list for each course.

'They'll be in the way when we're discussing the programme tonight. That's the whole point of the tutors arriving ahead of the participants. To finalise what you will all do, without any distractions. I suppose we can send the girls to bed early. I have some decent whisky I was planning to open later – for the tutors, not the participants. And I've told them firmly to stay out of the way until it's time to eat. Now, if you'll excuse me, I need to go and see what sort of mess Jenny is getting into on her own.'

'I'm glad I don't work for her,' I said, once she had gone.

'I'd employ her though,' said Elsie. 'She won't let unimportant things like people or common decency stop her meeting her targets.'

'Efficient,' I said.

'An administrative legend,' said Elsie. 'The goddess of timetabling and booking systems.'

'She's been director since the centre opened,' I said.

'Indeed. Appointed by the founder of the trust.'

'Who is or was a fan of John Dickson Carr? The name of the trust and the hall are a bit of a give-away.'

'To be honest nobody knows a lot about the founder. He's an American called Hiram Shuttleworth. He was in finance apparently, and he'd traced his family roots back to this part of the world. He decided to use a few millions of his accumulated wealth to buy High End Hall, as it was called then, renovate it and turn it into a study centre for teaching and for research into crime fiction written during the Golden Age of the 1920s and '30s, including but not limited to the Anglo-American John Dickson Carr.

The post was never advertised, much to the annoyance of several writers with a love of both classic crime fiction and the great outdoors. Wendy was just given it. But not many people would have stuck it up here with the wind and the rain and the snow. If you didn't love it, no money on earth would make it worthwhile. She wasn't such a bad choice. They say that she's never taken a whole day off since she arrived here.'

'That would be contrary to the Working Time Directive,' I said.

'Not on this side of Butterthwaite, apparently.'

'She's a writer herself?' I asked.

'Publishing background, did somebody say? Editing? Another John Dickson Carr fan certainly – I've heard her lecture on him. She's not a bundle of laughs but she's thorough.'

'You've met her before then?'

'Once. You don't get to see her much unless you come up here.'

'Did you ever hear the rumour she used to be a spy – that she still is one?' I asked.

'Everyone's heard that one. CIA, somebody told me.'

'But you don't believe it?'

'Even the grimmest of CIA operatives occasionally allow themselves to break into a half-smile.'

'Good point,' I said. 'I'll drop your bag off on my way to my room, shall I?'

CHAPTER THREE

Elsie

I was already in the main sitting room when Ethelred came back down, having unpacked his little bag. I had been enjoying the ambience – the diffused light from the table lamps scattered round the room, the old and comfortable sofas covered with faded William Morris fabric, the low beamed ceiling, the roaring fire in the vast stone fireplace, the storm rattling the narrow casement windows. It was a picture of England drawn by somebody who clearly loved it but hadn't been there lately.

Sadly, though this was Ethelred's natural habitat, his arrival did nothing to enhance the charming representation of a bygone era. He was one of the unhappiest bunnies in the North. Ripon, he said, had proved even smaller and colder than he had feared, and the ceiling height was inconveniently low. There was no desk for him to work at, because there was no space for one. And blah, blah, blah. After a bit, I started listening again.

'Did I ask you to be as tall as you are?' I asked. 'I don't think so. Don't complain to me about ceiling heights. I am responsible for negotiating your book contracts and the payment of advances and royalties after very reasonable agency deductions. Anyway, some bits of the room must be over six foot high.'

He looked mournful, though he does that even when things are going really well. 'The ceiling is mainly sloping,' he said. 'I think it must have been a storeroom originally. I can only stand upright in a couple of places.'

'There you are then. How many places can you be in at any one time? I mean, you're not God. You're not obliged to be omnipresent. You have a place to stand up and a spare one if you feel like moving around. And you can lie down, can't you?'

'Yes,' he said. 'I can lie down, though a longer bed would also be helpful.'

'You wouldn't want a long bed in a room that small. And, as I said, it was entirely your decision to be tall. It's not a mistake I ever made.'

'How is your room?' he enquired, with only partly justified suspicion.

'My suite, you mean? I haven't had time to explore it all yet,' I said. 'Ask me in a day or so.'

'How . . . ?' He frowned, as he often does when things puzzle him.

'How did I get a better room than you? Forward planning, Ethelred. The moment I agreed to do this gig, I checked on the internet for reviews of the courses . . . have I ever explained the internet to you?'

He looked even more mournful and said that he used the internet all the time, as I knew well.

'Then,' I continued patiently, 'you could have easily discovered on Tripadvisor that Malham was the master bedroom suite of the former owner of the house and much in demand. I emailed at once, and my small and very reasonable request was granted, while you were probably still sharpening your quill pen and looking for a sheep to kill in order to make parchment.'

'Actually I emailed too, though I'm not sure how she gets emails up here. There isn't a landline and there's no mobile reception at all.'

'I suppose she drives down to Butterthwaite,' I said. 'You can get a signal there. She downloads everything and comes back here to draft replies. Then she goes back down again a few days later to send them. I think modern technology impacts on her life even less than it does on yours.'

'I'm surprised you can do business like that in the modern world.'

'Ethelred, trust me, you know nothing about the modern world. It's not somewhere you've ever been.'

'Well, I wouldn't want to be this cut off myself. What if she had an accident?'

'If she really wanted an accident, she'd have to drive down to Butterthwaite to have it. Otherwise, she'd have to manage without. Generations must have lived up here, when you think about it, contentedly cut off from the rest of society. It's only the twenty-first century that thinks it has to be online twenty-four seven in order not to miss out.'

He nodded. He didn't doubt for one moment that the

past had been a better and happier world, and that the 1950s had been the best of all. In a way he was right – I mean, those skirts! Those elbow-length gloves! Those pillbox hats! Those crazy sunglasses! Wall-to-wall rock-and-roll in cafes made entirely of red and cream vinyl! But I'm not sure that's the side of it that he was thinking of.

'I suppose she must really like the isolation,' he said eventually.

The door opened, so we immediately stopped talking until we'd checked it wasn't Wendy. It proved to be a writer whom I knew quite well, dressed in his usual black jeans, black T-shirt and leather jacket.

'Good to see you, Jasper,' I said, kissing him an inch or so from both cheeks. He possessed one of those untrustworthy faces that you didn't want to get too close to, in case you caught deviousness. And anyway he always had a covering of itchy dark stubble on his chin. The gap between his front teeth, endearing in most people, simply added to the impression he was a disreputable minor character from a black-and-white movie. All he was lacking was the pencil moustache and the ebony cigarette holder. In that sense at least, he and Ethelred were blood brothers. 'You two know each other, I take it?' I asked.

'Yes,' Jasper Lavant replied, showing the classic Mid-Century incisor gap to perfection. 'We were on a panel together at Bristol last year.'

'I think not,' said Ethelred.

'Well, it was somebody very much like you. We had a conversation about royalties. You were saying you were earning so little, you might as well give up writing. Only tutoring was keeping you going.'

'Not me,' said Ethelred.

'Are you sure?' I asked. 'It sounds very much like you, Ethelred. Was it said in a really self-pitying way?'

'Yes,' said Jasper.

'It still wasn't me,' said Ethelred.

'*Murder Unlimited* is selling well,' I said, turning to Jasper. 'Number two in the *Sunday Times* last weekend. Well done, you!'

'Yes, it's had a bit of a resurgence since they announced the TV series.'

I caught Ethelred's eye for an instant. We both knew that Jasper's next four books had been complete dross, but his debut, *Murder Unlimited*, had made him a packet. And his first post-TV book would probably be quite profitable too. He was still worth having as a client if I could prise him away from his current agent, whoever that was. I had two and a half days to butter him up.

'A truly great book,' I said, as sincerely as I could manage without actually sicking up.

'Thank you.'

'A classic.'

'You are too kind.'

'The sort of book you can't put down. A real page-turner.'

'It had some good reviews,' he said, with a very poor attempt at a modest smile.

I decided to stop there, never having read it. You can get badly caught out by being too specific about a book you've merely considered reading if you run out of other stuff. Now I realised I should have promoted it up the to-be-read pile and glanced at the opening chapter. Of course, I couldn't download it onto my Kindle here. But maybe there would be a dog-eared copy on the bookshelves. It was the sort of book you regularly found abandoned on the bookshelves of guest houses and holiday cottages, treated as some reader's plaything, then cruelly tossed aside. Still, if you keep telling an author his books are wonderful, he rarely tests your knowledge chapter by chapter.

'You came up by train?' asked Ethelred conversationally.

'That was the advice, wasn't it?' said Jasper. 'Reduce the centre's carbon footprint. The comment about the state of the road up here was also an inducement to leave the Porsche at home.'

Other writers might have just said 'car'. Jasper had however spotted an opportunity to remind us that he normally drove the sort of car that people like us only ever saw as a puff of exhaust vanishing down the fast lane. I suspected he'd driven one for years. He'd been in banking or something before he became an author. Financially, he probably needed a TV series less than any other writer I knew. But he had the contract, signed and sealed, with a household name already recruited to play the lead. That life might be fair has never been an assumption of my agency's business plan.

'I wonder why Wendy does it?' said Jasper. 'Living up here, I mean. Rumour has it that she never leaves.'

'I've met her at Harrogate,' said Ethelred.

'Yes, I mean obviously she gets away for a few hours

now and then, but not for long apparently. I've heard—'
Jasper looked quickly towards the door. 'Word on the street
is that she's part of some MI6 operation, based here at the
hall. The whole courses thing is just a front.'

'Why would MI6 want a base in the middle of nowhere?'
asked Ethelred.

'That's the point of it,' said Jasper. He tapped the side of
his nose to tell us that what he was about to say was both
in confidence and undeniably true. 'It's a sort of safe house
where they can hide somebody when they need to. No one
sees them come or go. And if it gets too hot here, they can
head off to some shepherd's hut close by.'

'You know that, then?' asked Ethelred stiffly. He didn't
much like Jasper, in spite of the shared nostalgia thing.
Not many people did when they got to know Jasper well.
Too smug. Too full of being Jasper. Too obviously rich in a
profession that mainly isn't.

'Research, dear boy,' he said. 'I have a few contacts who
happen to be in that line of work. They tell me things.'

'I would have thought that the Official Secrets Act would
have limited what they could reveal.'

'You'd be surprised. I've reached the stage when pals
from my university days have got themselves quite high up
in all sorts of organisations – some of which Joe Public has
probably never even heard of. Insider knowledge and good
solid research is what distinguishes the best fiction from the
mediocre.'

'Hmm,' said Ethelred, who probably hadn't updated his
police procedures since he started writing crime fiction, at
a time when you could still have a good night out for five

shillings and listen to Arthur Askey on the wireless when you got home.

I wondered if Jasper really knew anything we didn't, or even believed what he was saying. Jasper practised bullshitting in the way a violinist practises scales. And I didn't rate Jasper's research that highly if the best he could come up with was a shepherd's hut. I mean, honestly? Hadn't they all been sold off to former cabinet ministers to write their memoirs in? But then I remembered the buttering-up thing and the fifteen-per-cent-of-the-advance thing relating to his next TV-tie-in book, which would sell so much better than the recent shit ones, even if it was shit too. I took a deep breath.

'Absolutely, Jasper,' I said. 'Insider knowledge and good solid research. You are so right. I mean – *Murder Unlimited* – the background research that must have gone into that! *So* impressive.'

'In what way?' he asked.

I revised my assumption that writers never cross-examined you when you were giving them ridiculously lavish compliments.

'In *every possible* way,' I said.

'But you mean a particular part of the plot?'

'The ending,' I said. It seemed safe. Most books have endings. His probably did too. I'd check when I could get hold of a copy.

'That's odd. The one criticism I've had of the book was the ending. The TV people want to change it.'

'Do they? Idiots! It's a great ending. Trust me.'

'I'd do it differently if I were writing the book now.'

'Well, I think it takes tremendous skill to do it *your* way,' I said. 'So, tell me about the TV—'

'What do you mean exactly?' Jasper was understandably puzzled, having read his book himself and knowing how it ended. 'You liked my making it obvious who the killer is early on, and then not putting in the final twist that everyone was expecting?'

'Yes. That's it. A masterstroke. It's the sort of thing Christie might have done.'

'But actually didn't. So – let's get this right – you really have read the book?'

'Obviously. Cover to cover.'

'And you say you quickly realised who the killer was?'

'Yes.'

'Wasn't there one of the other characters you suspected along the way? I mean there must have been somebody?'

You really needed to have at least read the blurb on the back to have a chance of getting that one right. Of course, I could make an inspired guess. What were the chances of a suspect called Smith? Quite good? Or I could randomly plump for a name like Juliet. No, better not risk it.

'Nope,' I said. 'I didn't suspect any of the others.'

'Not even Juliet?' he asked. 'I mean she had a pretty good motive, didn't she?'

'Juliet! Ha! You almost had me fooled there,' I said with a care-free choking noise. 'I admit that. But I've read a lot of crime fiction.'

'You do actually like crime fiction then?'

At first sight, this was a much easier question to answer. But my brain was no longer functioning at that basic level.

A simple 'yes' would no longer satisfy its overwhelming need for evasion and ambiguity.

'Like it?' I said. 'Hell, does a rat catcher like rats?'

'OK. Fair enough . . .' He was looking at me oddly. We were both wondering exactly what rat catchers did think of rats. Plague-spreaders but totally essential to their business model? Maybe that.

It was then that the door opened, and we all turned towards it, which was fine with me because I was done with buttering up and wanted to quit while I was ahead.

'Hi, Hal,' said Ethelred to the young man who had just arrived.

'Hi, Ethelred,' he replied.

'Do you both know Hal Compton?' Ethelred asked us.

Jasper didn't, though he had heard of him and congratulated Hal on the success of his latest book. I did know him and, this time, had actually read the book in question, because he'd sent it to me and I'd turned it down. These things happen. Still, I had good reason to have noticed that *The Spy Before Yesterday* had been number one on the same *Sunday Times* list that had featured Jasper as number two. The course participants were, if you ignored Ethelred, getting value for money this weekend. Hal Compton's career had been the mirror image of Jasper's. His early books – humorous crime fiction with G. K. Chesterton as the detective – had scarcely been noticed by reviewers and had not sold well. Then he'd switched, suddenly and unexpectedly, to thrillers and now *The Spy Before Yesterday* looked like being the crime novel of the year. That was why you hung onto people like Ethelred – however bad their current sales were – you just never knew when they might suddenly make their breakthrough. Of course, I'd chosen the wrong one to keep and the wrong one to reject, but the principle was still sound.

I placed a hand on the sleeve of Hal's pale blue cashmere sweater. It felt of vastly increased royalty payments. 'I'm really pleased that your book is doing so well,' I said. I hoped Jasper didn't notice the difference between what I'd said to him earlier and what I was saying when I was being genuine, because I *was* pleased for Hal, in spite of his being with another agent. Of course, I'd stolen clients from Francis and Nowak before, and there's no legal quota on the number of writers you're allowed to steal from a rival agency, but from what I knew of Hal he was too decent to desert Janet Francis when she'd sold his most successful book for him. I respected that totally. Obviously I was still going to try though.

He looked slightly embarrassed in a way that Jasper had not and said 'Yes, it came at exactly the right time. My last publisher had dropped me, we'd just had a baby and I was getting fairly desperate about cash flow. I thought I might actually have to get a real job. Then I suddenly seemed to hit on the right idea . . .' His voice tailed off and just for a moment I thought he was actually going to blush. 'Well, there it is. There's a lot of luck in these things. Well done on the television series, by the way, Jasper.'

'As you say, there's often a lot of luck in these things,' said Jasper. He placed a slight but significant emphasis on 'often'.

Hal flicked away a boyish lock of blonde hair and

smiled. 'Did any of you hear the row from the kitchen just now? Wendy and her minion were having a bit of a disagreement.'

'Jenny Cosham,' said Ethelred, who must have been interested enough to ask somebody what Jenny's surname was.

'I overheard a bit,' said Jasper. 'As I came past the door. Jenny wanted to go to her mother's birthday party tonight, but the snow has stopped her. Tough luck for the girl.'

'I think Wendy was always planning to keep her here tonight, if she could,' said Ethelred. 'I don't think that not telling her our taxi was there was any sort of accident.'

This was probably true. Wendy did not tolerate randomness of any sort. I'm not saying that she'd already planned out the rest of her life day by day, but she'd established the general principles of how it would be, both for herself and for others – especially others.

'Her entire existence is devoted to the centre,' said Jasper. 'She thinks everyone else's should be too. She's – what do you call it? – a bit obsessive-compulsive. Everything has to be in exactly the right place – things and people. I tried to rearrange the seating plan one evening on another course. I think she'd have been hurt less if I'd kicked her on the knee.'

'Maybe that's why she likes it here,' said Ethelred. 'It's a place where she has complete control over every little detail. When we're here and, even more so, when we all go away.'

Hal looked towards the door. I already knew what he was going to say.

'Don't breathe a word of this,' he said, 'but I have heard

the Golden Age Trust is just a front for a Mossad operation in England. And Wendy is running it for them. They say that the founder, this American called Shuttleworth, has Israeli connections and that—'

The door opened again, and Wendy's face appeared round it.

'Why are you all looking so startled?' she asked. 'Dinner will be served in exactly five minutes. Please check the seating plan as you go in. There's nothing worse than people who don't stick to the plan.'

CHAPTER FOUR

Elsie

The two girls were already there. Wendy had placed them at one end of the table – the end furthest from the door. The rest of us took our places according to the Famous Plan. Hal was next to one of the girls, Ethelred next to the other, Wendy at the top of the table, me and Jasper facing each other across it in the remaining two seats. I couldn't see any logic to where we all were, but it clearly pleased Wendy, and Wendy was actually queen regnant of obsessive-compulsive. Nobody doubted that. One of the girls, the smaller and – I'm being totally upfront with you here – mousier one, proved to be called Claire Rowland. She scarcely occupied a space at all, thinking about it. It was as if she'd been given a chair that was six inches lower than everyone else's, though Wendy would have made sure all of the chairs in the dining room matched perfectly. Her brasher friend, with the crimson hair, burgundy lipstick, purple headscarf and denim dungarees was Fliss Verity.

Draped diagonally across Fliss's chest was the even more colourful strap of a large shoulder bag that she must have purchased in Bhutan or possibly Hoxton. She had not forgiven Wendy for confining them to their rooms for an hour and had not forgiven Claire for her mistake.

'Well,' she said, with a cheerfulness that she wished us all to know was forced, 'I'm so sorry you're having to put up with our company tonight, but my very good friend here was convinced that we had to arrive this evening for an early start tomorrow. We'll stay out of your way as much as possible.'

Like a lot of people these days, her accent was difficult to tie down – Midlands certainly, but overlain or underlain with the other places where she'd lived and worked.

Jasper leered at her, showing the tooth-gap in its full glory. 'No need to stay out of my way,' he said. 'Delighted to have your company, my dear. I'm Jasper Lavant, by the way.'

'Yes,' said Fliss. 'So you are.'

Jasper blinked, unsure whether he had been firmly put down or simply had his name confirmed for him, a service that Fliss was happy to provide for older people who might otherwise forget.

Ethelred chose this moment to tell the girls that he was Ethelred. 'Writing as Peter Fielding mainly these days,' he added. He sounded more apologetic than he really needed to be.

'I like your J. R. Elliot books best,' said Claire. 'You must know a lot about the period. When I read the books I really feel I'm back in the fourteenth century. You can almost smell what it was like.'

We all turned to her because, apart from introducing herself, this was the first thing she'd said. Our gaze alone was enough to make her dry up completely. Several of us were also wondering whether smelling the fourteenth century was actually safe.

'Thank you,' said Ethelred, with a self-deprecating smile that a Victorian maiden could not have improved on. 'That's very kind of you.'

'She's read all your books, Ethelred,' said Fliss, stifling a yawn and looking for the wine bottle. 'A big fan. Aren't you, Claire?'

There was honestly only one possible answer to that question, in view of her earlier statement, but Claire was now reluctant to commit herself one way or the other in case we all looked at her again. She smiled shyly, at least not denying it.

Ethelred's big fan was dressed that evening in a brown sweater over a brown, floral patterned blouse, which strengthened the impression that she was, in real life, a mouse, who had stumbled in from the cold outside and was hoping not to be noticed as she scurried around picking up literary crumbs.

Though Fliss had stepped quickly into a gap that she saw developing in the conversation, the gap had appeared anyway. Somebody needed to say something.

'Well, I may as well introduce myself too,' I said. 'I'm Elsie Thirkettle.'

This time, Claire decided to respond, even though it might give away her location to a passing owl. 'Yes, I know,' she squeaked. 'You're Ethelred's agent. It says so in several places on his website. He obviously admires you enormously.'

I glanced over at Ethelred to see whether he was about to reveal that I had designed his website for him, but a look from me convinced him that now was not a great time.

'And this is Hal Compton,' said Wendy, indicating the other bestselling member of the party.

Hal smiled weakly.

'Hello, Hal,' said Claire.

'You know each other already?' asked Wendy.

'We met at a conference last year, didn't we, Hal?' said Claire.

Her rather assertive tone took everyone by surprise, Hal as much as any of us. He swallowed hard before saying. 'Yes, that's right. Up in Scotland. Great fun. I'd forgotten . . . I mean *hadn't* forgotten – how could I? – the very interesting chat that we had. For such a long time. Good to see you again . . . Claire. How's the writing going?'

'I've got something ready to show you, if you're still willing to read it. I thought it was OK, but now I'm sort of having doubts.'

Hal swallowed hard again. 'Of course. Of course. I'd be delighted. Delighted to read it.'

Well, if his plan had been to lie low for the whole conference and hope Claire wouldn't shove a crap manuscript in his direction, he had clearly failed miserably. That's the trouble with male writers – put them in a bar full of girls for long enough and they'll wake up the next day trying to remember how many draft first novels they've promised to read.

At that moment Jenny arrived with a trolley, on which was a tureen of soup, some rustic blue and white striped bowls and a giant ladle, suggestive of limitless Yorkshire hospitality. A pleasant mushroomy smell filled the room – next to chocolate, one of the best smells you can get. She cautiously manoeuvred the trolley beside Wendy, who proceeded to fill each bowl and pass them down the table, as if we were one happy family. Jenny, merely a distant cousin in this context, fetched some baskets of bread from the sideboard. The thought occurred to me that the bread had not be placed on the table earlier so that we did not eat it at the wrong time. Which we totally would have done. The baskets were emptied rapidly, and Wendy gave her rather reluctant permission to Jenny to refill them.

'So, tell us about your book, Claire,' said Ethelred, who'd promised to read a few manuscripts himself in his time, though not when I was keeping an eye on him.

'Oh, it's based on a real-life murder some years ago,' said Claire. Her voice had grown stronger and slightly louder now that she no longer had to admit to being a fan of Ethelred's under any of his aliases. 'The Emily Tomsitt case.'

Jasper frowned, as if summoning up an impossibly obscure fact from the very depths of his memory. 'She killed her boyfriend, right? Strangled him?'

'Her partner. That's right.'

'Jailed for it, wasn't she?' he asked, buttering some bread. 'Five – no, must be ten years ago?'

'Yes. A lot of people thought he had it coming to him,

though. A nasty character.'

'How long did she get for it?' asked Jasper. 'I mean, murder's murder, however unpleasant he may have been.' He was keen, for some reason, to establish that obnoxious males could not be bumped off with impunity. Ethelred gave him a reassuring nod: when the time came, Jasper could die happy in the knowledge that it would still be murder.

'I can't remember,' said Claire. 'There was an appeal later anyway. And I was only interested in the murder itself. And it's a fictionalised account. In my version she may be found not guilty. That's what should have happened anyway.'

She looked round the table, at each of us in turn, as if asking our opinion on this plot development. Her gaze fell last on Wendy, who, if she had previously been in publishing, might have had some view one way or the other. But Wendy simply looked startled. Narrative arcs were well outside her comfort zone. Still, the opportunity to interfere in somebody's else's life was always welcome.

'You say it's not going well?' she said eventually.

'No.'

'Maybe you've got the wrong subject, my dear. I think that's it.'

'You reckon?'

'Yes. Definitely.'

'So, what should I do instead?'

Wendy swallowed hard, as if this was the last response she had expected, but she quickly recovered herself.

'If you want a case of a spouse murdering their other half, there have been a couple round here in the last twenty years or so. Maybe it's something in the air.'

'Sounds good,' said Hal. 'Which one are you suggesting?'

'Well . . .' said Wendy.

'Go on,' said Hal. 'You must have one in mind.'

I wondered if Wendy would relate the story that the taxi driver had told us on the way up – where the wife had in fact been found not guilty of any crime other than inattention – but it seemed that the valley was well-populated with spouse-killers, because she began to relate another case entirely. 'I was just thinking of a murder about twenty, maybe twenty-five, years ago,' she continued. 'That was a husband killing his wife, of course. Down there at the farm in Butterthwaite. Oh, for goodness' sake, Jenny! That is the last straw!'

Jenny, re-entering the room with a fresh basket of bread, had dropped it on the stone floor. She was scrabbling around, apologising and trying to put the bread back in the basket piece by piece.

'No, no, you silly, silly girl,' Wendy exclaimed. 'It's no good now it's been on the floor. Throw it out, then wash your hands before you touch anything that's to go on this table. Do you hear me? Back here with clean hands. Jump to it!'

'Yes, I'm sorry, Wendy. I'm so sorry,' said Jenny, almost in tears.

'Just go. You've spoilt the bread. Crying over it in that silly way merely makes it worse. It's bread not . . .' She paused, unable for a moment to think of anything of greater value that might fit into a standard-sized wicker basket. Pain au chocolat, possibly. 'Come back when you've cut some more and pulled yourself together.'

Clutching the basket, Jenny almost ran from the room.

I thought that was a bit harsh, bearing in mind that it wasn't actually patisserie of any sort, but Wendy simply said to us: 'I'm sorry about that. Stupid girl interrupting us in that clumsy way. But I shouldn't have snapped. I do apologise. Now, where was I? Oh yes, the Butterthwaite case . . . No, perhaps that wouldn't be such a good idea either. Very straightforward. There are much better local cases. I'll think of one later.'

'No, that sounds really interesting,' said Hal. 'We came through the village, didn't we? Not a great deal of it left, but very pretty. So, what happened there?'

'I don't think you would find it that entertaining,' said Wendy, scanning the table, perhaps in the hope of locating the last piece of undropped bread.

'Why don't you let us judge?' said Jasper, happy to move on to what he considered to be the much safer subject of wife-killing. 'The Butterthwaite murder? I think I've heard of that somewhere. Remind us what happened.'

Wendy drew a deep breath. 'Very well, then. The husband, down at the farm in Butterthwaite, was having an affair and his wife found out. Nobody knows exactly what happened next, but the wife was discovered dead and the husband vanished. Literally vanished. Never seen again. The girl – the one he was having an affair with – well, a lot of people said she was looking after him, that he had a little den somewhere up here, hidden away in the bracken, and she brought him food and other things. Certainly she took to fell walking at the time, and she'd never done it before. Then she suddenly stopped. Nobody knows why. About the same time, she got married – to somebody completely unconnected with the killing.'

'Now, there's a mystery for you, Claire,' said Hal. 'Better than the Tomsitt case.'

'But I've researched the Tomsitt case,' said Claire uncertainly. 'There was a serious miscarriage of justice. They failed to take into account the abuse she'd suffered. She should never have been jailed.'

'No, Wendy's right,' said Hal. 'It's too well known. And there's nothing to it – I mean the crime itself. She'd put up with a lot for a long time, I grant you, and then one night she just lost it for no particular reason and killed him. She phoned the police straight away to tell them what she'd done. Not even a proper police investigation. Just a murder and a confession. On the other hand, Wendy's case – well, you can let your imagination run wild. Where did the husband get to? What happened to him? Is he still living somewhere under a false identity? Might he kill again? Maybe he does kill again – then somebody from his past recognises him? Or maybe the person he kills is his former girlfriend's new husband?'

Wendy looked at Hal uncertainly. Perhaps she felt that it would be wrong to move too far from the reassuring comfort of established facts and dive into this heady stream of speculation.

'Possibly,' she said. 'I mean you could do something a bit like that – with imagination. Set up here in the fells, of course. You wouldn't want to change that. But if Jasper knows of the case, then maybe that one is too well known too.'

'I don't know that much,' said Jasper. 'I'd forgotten a lot of it. Very interesting though.'

'Wendy could help you on all sorts of detail, Claire,' said Hal. 'Historical stuff. Plants. Geology. Wildlife. Local dialect. People like that stuff.'

I wondered if Hal thought that the Butterthwaite case in some way let him off the hook – that he wouldn't have to read the crap draft. If so, I could have informed him he was gaining only the most temporary of reprieves. I could already tell that Claire was not somebody who let things go easily. But, equally, if I'd been her agent, I would have said to press on with what she had and not listen to the siren voices. Those that always call to writers about two thirds of the way through any novel, hinting at the wondrous possibilities of a totally different plot but not bothering to mention at this stage the treacherous rocks that lay just below the surface of the sparkling blue literary waters of which they sang.

'Well, maybe . . .' said Claire, neatly summarising my reservations.

'Think about it,' said Wendy. 'Perhaps not that one exactly, but definitely not the Tomsitt case. Too well known. We're agreed on that?'

Claire sort of nodded, but she'd clearly read Homer, if only in a cheap paperback translation, and didn't trust sirens one little bit. Anyway, I could tell she felt some sort of affinity with Tomsitt that went beyond just providing her with a convenient plot. Many women must have looked at their other halves after reading about the case and wondered whether, if you didn't make the mistake of phoning the police straight away, you could actually get away with it.

'Well done!' Wendy continued, though Claire would have been aware that she had not actually done anything that Wendy approved of. 'We can talk later. But there are lots of local crimes. I have a book on them somewhere.' She nodded as if it was a problem that she had neatly laid to rest on our behalf. Something had happened that was briefly out of her control and ours, but now it was safely back in its box. We had her to thank.

For a while we slurped soup, not silently exactly but without talking. Then Fliss said: 'Claire's a big fan of yours too, Hal.'

'Ah . . . is she?' He looked up cautiously, like a deer who has just noticed a lion-shaped shadow on the far side of the pool.

'You bet. After we all met in Glasgow, she read most of your Chesterton books. But she liked *The Spy Before Yesterday* best of all, didn't you, Claire?'

There was an uneasy silence, as we each remembered Fliss's earlier attempt to get Claire to lighten up a bit.

'Well . . .' said Hal.

'I really do like your earlier stuff,' said Claire with unexpected enthusiasm. 'It's very funny. But *The Spy Before Yesterday* was brilliant too. It reminded me of something else I'd read—'

'*Really?*' said Ethelred incredulously. This interjection caused most of us to abandon our mushroom soup for a moment, but fortunately he went on. 'Yes, of course, it's a fantastic book, but one of the things that everyone's agreed on is that it really breaks new ground – it's not like *anything* that's come before. That's what's so amazing about it. That's why I'm so envious. I'm sure Jasper is too.'

Jasper smiled in a way that suggested that he was never jealous of another writer's well-deserved success.

We looked at Claire, hoping that she might say what it had reminded her of, but Hal was more interested in the general principle of the thing.

'To be fair, there's nothing absolutely new,' he said, frowning. 'Aren't there supposed to be just seven basic plots? I mean according to Christopher Booker. The Quest, Rags to Riches, Overcoming the Monster, Voyage and Return . . . and some others.'

'Romeo and Juliet?' suggested Jasper helpfully, now that the question of his possible jealousy had been safely negotiated.

'I don't think that's one of them,' said Hal, 'but seven basic plots is hardly a scientifically proven fact. You can have as many or few as you wish, up to a point.'

'I've just remembered: Comedy's another one of the basic plots,' said Jasper. 'It's the one where everything gets more and more confusing, then a single final event clarifies and makes everything right again.'

'That's crime fiction,' said Hal. 'At least, the way I used to write it.'

Claire reached out and touched him on the arm, possibly out of sympathy or possibly because she just wanted to touch him. It's also the way Ethelred still writes crime fiction of course but nobody sought to console him.

'Then there's the Rule of Three,' said Ethelred. 'Three

passes at everything – the three little pigs, the Three Billy Goats Gruff, three ghosts visiting Ebenezer Scrooge, the Three Wishes, Goldilocks's three bowls of porridge.'

'And three beds,' said Jasper with a smirk. 'She jumps from one to another.'

'But not quite in the way you imply,' said Ethelred, for whom a bed was, sadly, just somewhere he slept when not writing books. 'And there are also three chairs at the bears' house. Three times three, if you like, for Goldilocks. But three is the general rule. At the first two passes you are checked, but at the final one you make it through to the other side – and sometimes back to where you started.'

We seemed to have lost sight of the uniqueness or otherwise of Hal's bestseller. I tried to remember who had started this thread of conversation. Hal himself probably, so that was his fault. Writers don't often get praise and need to milk every opportunity to the full.

'You'll have used the rule of three yourself, Jasper, in your old job,' said Hal, taking us even further from the adulation he was due.

Jasper frowned. 'The mathematical one? Not really. When I trained as an accountant, we were still taught about "casting out nines" to check our addition. There's your three times three, if you like. I'm not sure the technique is much used any more, not now everything is added up by computer.'

'Computers don't always get it right,' said Claire. 'Though a great deal depends on what people put in them.'

Jasper turned slowly and blinked at her. 'You think so?'

Fliss laughed. 'Claire's a trained accountant too,' she said.

'Are you?' Jasper asked with minimal interest.

'Yes, I'm a forensic accountant,' said Claire. 'I deal with fraud cases. That's always been my line – from way back.'

I looked at Claire again. At first I'd got her down as being in her early twenties, but her size and her child-like features had wrong-footed me. That and sitting her in this middle-aged group of writers, agents and administrators, beside whom most people would have looked young. She was at least thirty, maybe thirty-five, as was Fliss. Indeed, much the same age as Hal, who was the youngest of the three writers on offer by at least fifteen years.

'From way back?' said Jasper. 'When's that exactly?'

'I mean before you wrote your first book,' said Claire with a laugh. 'That far back.' Just as she had in talking about her writing, Claire had grown in confidence again in discussing the day job. Less shy. A much bigger, braver mouse, capable of teasing a bestselling author. I thought she'd probably make a very good forensic accountant. Hot on detail. Ready to put in time casting out nines or whatever was needed to track down the fraudster.

'Maybe you should write about fraud rather than murder, Claire,' I suggested.

'I might,' she said. 'That's not a bad idea. It depends which is most profitable. What do you think, Jasper? You know all about profit, don't you? And losses.'

'Ah,' said Jasper. He still seemed to be trying to recall the years before he wrote his first book – a much happier time for most writers.

I'd expected Wendy to drag us back to a local fraud that had occurred back in the days when a hedge fund meant money to buy hedges. But she too was thinking of other things. I suspected her mind was on Jenny in the kitchen. She had not returned with bread. Perhaps Jenny didn't trust herself anywhere near a sharp knife at the moment. I wouldn't have done. At this moment I would still have been savagely hacking my third loaf into breadcrumbs.

'So you were an accountant?' Ethelred said to Jasper. 'I thought you were a banker.'

His dark jaw worked for a moment, as if chewing something tough and not altogether pleasant. 'I have an accountancy qualification. I worked for a bank,' he said tersely. 'But I've left all that well behind, thank goodness. Let's talk about something more interesting, if you've no objection.'

Well, many books ago, Ethelred had worked for the Inland Revenue, as it was then, so he was in no position to criticise anyone at all. Actually, working for the Inland Revenue is probably the most exciting thing Ethelred has ever done.

Jenny eventually returned, not with bread, but to collect our soup bowls and to deliver the next course – a steaming steak pie and two serving dishes filled with potatoes, cauliflower and peas. There was no vegetarian alternative since the only vegetarian in the room had no right to be there.

'I can manage with the vegetables,' said Fliss, helping herself, by way of compensation, to more wine from one of the opened bottles.

Ethelred asked Jenny when she got to eat, but she said she'd already had something in the kitchen. I wondered if she got to dine with us later in the programme, when we were all mucking in. I suspected Wendy might still send her to the servants' quarters. There was a sense in which Jenny was essential to the operation and a sense in which Wendy deeply resented her presence – perhaps precisely because she was so essential. You could tell that relinquishing even a small amount of control of anything was painful for Wendy and that somebody would have to pay the price for it sooner or later.

The wine was good. At least according to Ethelred, who likes that sort of thing. I'd already noticed Jasper take an appreciative sip, look at the label on the bottle and nod thoughtfully. We all relaxed, a little or a great deal, depending on our respective ability to do so. Jasper continued his attempts to chat up Fliss, occasionally leaning across Ethelred to do it, in spite of the fact that Fliss was clearly up for nothing Jasper-related. Hal actually said a few words to Claire, though I got the impression he would rather she hadn't been there. Wendy explained why the Butterthwaite valley was superior to any other valley anywhere on earth and gave us a summary of the history of Fell Hall.

'It is one of the highest permanently occupied farmhouses in the country,' she said proudly. 'It was monastic originally, then owned by a local farmer. It had been abandoned by 1600 – too cold, too bleak – though it must have still been a family house just before that, when a Catholic priest, Father Speedwell, was caught hiding here and taken to York to be burned at the stake. They say his ghost still haunts the kitchen, close to where they arrested him. Later, the place was used just as a barn for a farm down the valley – bits of it were kept watertight, but the rest was allowed to go to ruin. In the late nineteenth century it was done up by a recluse who wanted to live as far from his neighbours as he could. It slowly fell into disrepair again after his death, until the Trust bought it and restored it to what it is now. It's an amazing mixture of styles. I can show you some twelfth century stonework tomorrow, if any of you would like to see it. And the priest hole where Father Speedwell hid – amazingly it survived through all that neglect and rebuilding.'

Jenny reappeared to clear the second lot of plates and then brought in some apples and cheese. She said not a word to Wendy other than to ask, when clearing the third and final course, whether that would be all.

'I think so,' said Wendy. 'You can go to bed once you've finished the washing-up, Jenny. You have a busy day tomorrow.'

Ethelred offered to help wash up, since there did seem to be a lot to do, but Wendy said she needed Ethelred in the sitting room to discuss the programme. And so we dispersed and proceeded one by one to the sitting room so we could do whatever Wendy wanted us to do next.

As we walked along the corridor together, Ethelred said to me, 'Wendy seems determined to publicise the charms of Butterthwaite. She won't rest until Claire has changed the setting of her book to North Yorkshire. I bet she makes her do it too.'

'Not if Jenny kills Wendy first,' I said. 'If I were Wendy,

I wouldn't let Jenny anywhere near the carving knives for the next week at least.'

But strangely, when the murder did eventually take place, it wasn't Wendy who was killed at all. And it wasn't even done with a knife.

CHAPTER FIVE

Ethelred

The snow was still falling when I looked out into the dark night through a gap in the thick woollen curtains. A lancet of yellow light spilt from the sitting room onto the crisp white surface beyond. I'd have said we already had two or three inches on the ground, with a lot more up in the sky.

'Well, none of us is going anywhere any time soon,' said Jasper over my shoulder. 'The road will be impassable by morning. I think Wendy's briefing will go to waste if none of the other participants can make it up here.'

This was true enough. Wendy had however insisted that we run through the programme in a companionable circle by the fire, because that was what she'd always planned to do. The girls had not been dismissed to their room – Fliss had simply refused to budge, saying it was too far and too cold to go and sit around in a draughty attic. But they had been sent to a remote corner of the sitting room, Fliss clutching her large embroidered bag, where they arguably could not influence Wendy's plans in any way.

In the end we might as well not have bothered. What Wendy told us was largely what we already knew and had agreed by email. I was still covering research and dialogue, which was as well, because that was exactly what I had prepared. Hal was focusing on opening chapters, plotting and maintaining tension. Jasper was doing character and place. Wendy was to talk about the history of the crime novel with particular emphasis on John Dickson Carr's undoubted legacy to the world. Elsie was repeating her very popular 'how to submit your manuscript', which always had people making frantic notes, though much of it could be summarised as 'look at the agent's website and just do what it says'. We did admittedly learn where the fire exits were and the arrangements for meals, but Wendy could have told us that the following day, when she told everyone else. If there was to be anyone else. Unseen and unheard, the snow outside was continuing to soften a harsh and rocky landscape.

'I hope we'll be paid our fee, whether the course goes ahead or not,' said Jasper. 'It's a long way to come if we're not. I have to say the wine was rather good. Vosne-Romanée. That was unexpected.' I doubted that Jasper needed the relatively modest fee, but, with his finance background, not chasing any debt owing would have irked him. He was right about the wine though. I couldn't remember being served anything quite that good on any previous course I'd taught on.

'I suppose we could run it just for Fliss and Claire,' I said, glancing over to the far side of the room, where Fliss was in conversation with Elsie. 'I mean, we're all here anyway.'

Jasper grinned. 'Fancy a bit of one-to-one tuition, eh, Ethelred?'

'That wasn't quite what I meant,' I said.

'Claire's taken already, I think,' Jasper persisted. 'If that's who you had your eye on. She and Hal have just slipped out of the room, if you know what I mean. I think there's a bit of past history between them, judging by Hal's response at dinner.'

I looked round. Neither was there.

'They're probably talking about Claire's manuscript – and no, that's not a euphemism for anything.'

Jasper gave me a knowing grin. 'Isn't it? You must have noticed that look on Hal's face – the "didn't I sleep with you at the last conference?" look.'

'I think that's a bit unfair on both of them.'

'Oh, wake up, Ethelred. These conferences are like a literary speed-dating event. For most of us, anyway. I mean, who'd come all the way up here just to listen to you droning on about getting early fifteenth century dialogue right.'

'Fourteenth,' I said. 'Late fourteenth.'

'Are they very different?'

'Different enough,' I said, though probably only to contradict Jasper, who was beginning to annoy me. Language changes constantly, but slowly and irregularly. I'd have had difficulty, if pressed, in proving that 1400 was a decisive linguistic turning point.

'Well, Ethelred, I'll have to take your word for it,' said Jasper with a crooked smile. 'But I fear there may be some things for which life is just too short. I can tell you Fliss isn't here for that sort of detail. I doubt she'll even show up for your session.'

'If you say so.'

'I do say so. I chatted with her as we were leaving the dining table. She told me she gave up any idea of writing a novel years ago. But her mate Claire hasn't, so she trots along the way she did when they both had literary ambitions. They agreed to support each other, see? That's what girls do. It's quite sweet, really.'

'So she wishes Claire well. I agree, that's nice.'

'Not really,' said Jasper. He glanced again at the other end of the room, where Fliss was still occupied. 'I think she's actually hoping, deep down, that Claire will fall flat on her face. I mean, Fliss has abandoned all hope of being published. Can you imagine how nauseating it would be for her if Claire turned out to have written a bestseller? The bestseller she herself might have penned. Receiving the adulation that might have been hers. OK, you and I know writers don't get anything like the adulation we deserve, but Fliss doesn't know that yet. In the meantime, she's enjoying watching her best friend make a fool of herself, scribbling away into the night, attending overpriced seminars, shamelessly chatting up writers who might help her. I bet Claire succeeding big is Fliss's worst nightmare.'

'You have a very cynical view of how the world works,' I said.

'Writers do,' he said. 'Successful writers anyway. They look at things the way they are and write tragedy. Lesser writers look at things the way they wish they were and write comedy. Hal was very wise to switch away from comic crime. Nobody gets anywhere with that.'

'That last book of his was brilliant,' I conceded. 'It's the sort of book that you read and are immediately envious of. I was almost at the end before I worked out that what had really been happening was nothing like what you'd believed for the first twenty chapters. He'd completely hoodwinked me. I remember a similar trick in *The Spy Who Came in From the Cold* – but this was even better. Maybe the best thriller I've ever read.'

'So, do you think that was the book that Claire meant when she said it reminded her of another novel?' asked Jasper. 'I suppose I could just about see some similarities.'

'Who knows? People see different things in different books. I'll ask her when I get a chance.'

It was at that point that Claire and Hal re-entered the room, bringing with them a brief gust of cold air from the hallway. Claire was smiling happily. Whatever favour she'd asked Hal for, she seemed to have got it. Then I looked at Hal's face. It was white. His eyes were the nearest thing to hollow pits I had ever seen in real life. He saw me looking at him and tried to grin, but his mouth wouldn't do it. Breaking away from Claire, he headed straight for the sideboard, grabbed a tumbler and helped himself to a quadruple malt whisky. Then he downed it in one.

'So what was that all about?' Elsie asked me a little later.

I checked we would not be overheard then replied, 'Hal and Claire? No idea. She wanted advice on her novel.'

'Then she must have written the scariest thriller ever. I ought to sign her up.'

'Perhaps Hal had some bad news – I mean nothing to do with Claire.'

'How does he get that in a house with no phone reception or Wi-Fi?' asked Elsie.

Wendy came over to join us. 'What are you two naughty people plotting over here?' She wagged a schoolmistress's finger at each of us in turn. 'Whatever it is, I'm sure it can wait. It's much warmer by the hearth.'

In spite of the superficially jovial tone, there was a note of irritation in her voice. She had clearly envisaged the group sitting round the blazing log fire, drinking whisky and swapping literary anecdotes into the small hours. Claire's abduction of Hal and now our whispered conversation on the far side of the room was not part of the plan. Her dislike of the 'girls' had intensified. How right she'd been to try to send them back to the distant attic where they belonged.

'We'll be over in a moment,' I said.

Wendy decided not to budge. We were sheep who needed rounding up for our own good. She knew what happened to sheep who wandered off on their own over the fells. She'd seen their blanched bones plenty of times.

'It's a lot nicer on the sofas,' she insisted. 'Though that Fliss girl is drinking far too much whisky. I bought it for the tutors. I don't know why she's here. She really doesn't seem that interested in crime fiction. She's never read a single book by John Dickson Carr – not even *The Hollow Man* – can you believe that? Said all of the Golden Age writers were snobbish and predictable. I won't be accepting her on future courses.'

'Jasper said she was only here to support Claire,' I said.

'Well, she's certainly drinking for both of them,' said Wendy tartly.

'Apparently Fliss used to have ambitions to write,' I said. 'But she's given them up.'

'Very wise,' said Elsie. 'Writing is a cruel business. You know at the age of twenty you'll never play football for England. You know when you're thirty that you'll never become a film star. But most people never realise that they can't write to save their lives. Trust me – I have to read their manuscripts. Like Roman galley slaves, only death frees them.'

'Thirty or thirty-five isn't old to have a first novel published,' I said. 'Some people don't even start writing until then.'

'Did Jasper say exactly why Fliss gave up?' asked Elsie.

'No,' I said. I looked round the room. 'Where is Jasper?'

'He was here a few minutes ago,' said Elsie.

'And where's Claire?' asked Wendy. 'She's vanished again. If she's taken Jasper this time, it's really too bad.'

The door opened, and Claire and Jasper came back in. Claire was as happy as before – happier if anything. Almost radiant. Jasper's face was drawn and haggard. He saw me and swallowed hard. Then he too headed for the whisky decanter.

'I'll say one thing for Claire,' said Elsie. 'She certainly knows how to work the room.'

CHAPTER SIX

Ethelred

'Numbers are important in fiction,' said Wendy. 'Think of Agatha Christie. *The Big Four. One, Two, Buckle My Shoe. Three Act Tragedy. The Seven Dials Mystery. Five Little Pigs.*'

'Or Dorothy L. Sayers,' said Hal. '*Five Red Herrings. The Nine Tailors.* And then of course there's John Dickson Carr's *The Eight of Swords.*'

'To be fair,' I said, 'there are far more Christie titles without numbers in them. And no Allingham titles are numeric. You could probably find more crime novels with Shakespearean titles.'

'Or Webster quotes,' said Fliss. 'A lot of crime writers have given revenge tragedy a nod.'

'A good title helps sell a book,' said Wendy.

'Not as much as a good cover,' said Elsie.

'I like to think that the content counts for something,' I said.

Claire nodded enthusiastically, and then looked round to check that nobody had noticed her do it.

We were back on the topic of numbers and having the light literary conversation that Wendy had scheduled for nine-fifteen. For the first time that evening she looked relaxed and happy. We were doing what we were supposed to be doing, showing off our knowledge of classic crime fiction, tying it all in to the broader flow of English literature.

'What do you think, you two?' asked Wendy, turning to Hal and Jasper. 'You're both keeping very quiet. And you've both written bestsellers, so you ought to know.'

'What?' asked Jasper.

'We're talking about what sells books,' said Wendy. 'We were on the number thing, but we drifted a bit.' Her words were slightly slurred. She certainly knew how to drink whisky, but then she'd had many dark, solitary evenings during which to practice.

'No idea,' said Jasper, shaking his head.

'And you, Hal?'

'Sorry – what were you talking about?' he replied.

'You both seem very preoccupied. Actually you look quite ill. I hope you haven't got flu or something. There's nobody else to take your sessions.'

'Flu? Not that I know of,' said Hal. 'It's just that this fire is a bit soporific.'

'It isn't usually,' said Wendy, running as ever to the defence of anything connected with the valley or inter-war detective fiction. 'Most people find it very cheerful. A lot of them mention it in their feedback forms.'

'Well, I may just go to bed in a moment,' said Hal. 'It's been a long day.'

But whatever time we were supposed to go to bed, this wasn't it.

'Just pour yourself another drink,' said Wendy. She didn't add 'and be a man', but that was what she meant.

Hal shook his head but stayed where he was. He was too deep in thought to want to argue with Wendy. If she'd given him a whisky, he'd have probably drunk it to avoid having to say 'no'.

'Do you think we should ask Jenny to join us?' I asked. 'I don't like thinking of her all alone when we're here.'

'She's quite happy as she is,' said Wendy. 'She has to be up early anyway.'

'She lives over towards Harrogate?' I asked.

'Well, in that direction,' said Wendy. 'She spends a few nights up here, of course, when conferences are running. She has a perfectly comfortable room when she needs it, even though that reduces the number of participants we can cater for. Normally she drives up – it takes about forty minutes – but her car is in for repair at the moment. Entirely predictable. She never gets it serviced when she should.'

'Has she always lived there?'

'Her family has always lived in the area. They're local,' she said with distinct approval. 'I wouldn't have employed an outsider if there was a local girl to do the job.'

'Well, I think I'm going to bed anyway,' said Jasper. 'If you will all excuse me.' He stood up.

'Me too in that case,' said Hal. He rose slowly, clutching the arm of the sofa.

'But surely . . .' said Wendy.

'I'll help you clear the glasses away,' said Claire.

'Oh, very well,' said Wendy. She was not happy. 'Yes, please, Claire. If you really don't mind.'

That left Elsie and Fliss and me round the fire.

'Shame to quit while there's whisky in the decanter,' said Fliss, rising and taking a clean glass from the tray. 'Oh, don't worry, I'll rinse this under the tap in our room – Wendy'll never know.'

'I bet she does,' said Elsie. 'I bet she gets up in the middle of the night to check that nothing has managed to get out of place while we are all sleeping.'

'You don't drink whisky, Elsie?' asked Fliss. 'Or wine?'

'Waste of calories,' she said. 'I've got a stash of chocolate in my suite.'

'Can I get you one, Ethelred?'

I shook my head. I was very tempted but didn't want a hangover for the first day of the course. 'So where did you and Claire meet?' I asked.

'At uni. We were both reading English at Bristol. We swore we'd each have written a novel by the time we were thirty and we'd see each other through, whatever happened. Literary sisters for ever united. Think of the Brontës but with more interesting hair.'

'And?'

'I didn't write mine – or nothing worth showing to anyone. I thought we'd call it a day, but Claire had got the bug.'

'Have you read the book she's writing now?'

Fliss paused. 'A bit.' She looked around to see if Claire

had returned. 'All she's done so far.'

'Any good? Or is that an unfair question?'

'No, that's fair. The book – it's great actually. I mean, the first thirty thousand words anyway. Really, really good. Not like the others we'd both written before. The Tomsitt character – she really comes to life. Claire absolutely empathises with her. I'd almost say she was in love with Emily Tomsitt. So she may just have cracked it. She's got talent and she's worked at it. Fair play to her, I say.' She gave a long sigh.

'It doesn't inspire you to go on?'

'No, quite the reverse. It fills me with despair. I'll never be as good as that. She's Shakespeare, I'm . . . I don't know what. Robert Greene maybe? That's the advantage of an English degree, Ethelred. It gives you a wide range of obscure authors to compare yourself to.' She took a heroic gulp of her drink that would have qualified her to be Dylan Thomas twice over and looked across at the decanter.

'You don't know until you try – I mean really try,' I said.

'Don't patronise me, Ethelred. I have really tried. But I overheard what Elsie was saying to you earlier. You have to know when to quit or it drives you crazy.'

'Ignore me,' said Elsie, in a wholly unprecedented act of charity towards an aspiring author. 'Bestsellers come out of nowhere. They do it all the time. And nobody really knows what they've written until it's published. Do you want me to take a look at the last thing you wrote?'

'So you can tell me it's complete shit?'

'Only if it is,' Elsie said encouragingly.

'No,' said Fliss. 'I already know how bad it is. I don't

64

need you to confirm it. Thanks all the same.'

She returned to the decanter and was filling her glass again when Wendy and Claire came back.

'Right, I think I'm ready for bed too,' said Claire cheerfully.

But Wendy was so distracted that she didn't even notice Fliss attempting to forget she was Robert Greene.

'Yes, we'd better all go to bed,' Wendy said weakly. 'It's been . . . it's been a trying day. Not what I foresaw. I don't know when I've had a more difficult one.'

'Yes,' I said, 'We'd better get some sleep in case the other participants do make it up here tomorrow.'

'Tomorrow?' asked Wendy, as if it was so far ahead that it was scarcely worth planning for.

'You never know,' I said. 'They might make it. If the snow stops.'

'What?' said Wendy, looking out at the dark night. 'Yes, of course. It's snowing, isn't it? But you never know what may happen. Everything is possible.'

With that she turned on her heel and departed without any further goodnights or even instructions for switching off lights. Claire and Fliss followed, Fliss slightly unsteadily, clutching her outsized bag. As she left the room, Claire turned and gave us a final, shy smile. It had apparently been the sort of quiet, cosy evening that she enjoyed. She was looking forward to tomorrow.

'Well, I don't think Wendy managed to persuade Claire to write that Butterthwaite murder thing,' said Elsie.

'No,' I said. 'I don't think she did either.'

THREE UNEXPECTED
INCIDENTS

CHAPTER SEVEN

Ethelred

The moment I opened my curtains it was clear that life had changed for all of us. The snow stretched away, smooth and untroubled, to every horizon, a vast white wave, reaching from the highest available summit to the lowest point I could see. The room was every bit as cold as Wendy had predicted and, perhaps temporarily warmed by the whisky, I had omitted to locate a spare towel last night to deal with the draught from the ill-fitting frame, though a small snowdrift on the windowsill was plugging the gap quite well without my help.

Fortunately I had packed a thick, heavy Norwegian sweater. I put it on over my pyjamas and walked quickly along the freezing corridor to the nearest bathroom, in which I spent the minimum amount of time shaving and washing.

The other inhabitants of Fell Hall were clearly not early risers. As I proceeded through the house my footsteps echoed in the empty corridors. The ticking of the grandfather clock, which I had not noticed the night before, followed me insistently. Only when I reached the sitting room did I discover another living soul.

'So there *is* somebody else around,' said Claire, looking up from the book she was reading. She looked fresh and bright. Perhaps like Elsie she had avoided alcohol the previous evening. The pages of her book were, conversely, looking yellowed and ragged. When she put it down, I saw that it had a badly drawn white skull on the cover. It was neither classic Golden Age nor by one of the more literary modern crime writers. I was slightly surprised that Wendy had allowed it on her shelves, though Claire might of course have brought it with her. 'I think it's a while until breakfast, though,' she added. 'I've been into the kitchen and instructed Jenny to bring some coffee to the sitting room. She doesn't need to start cooking yet.'

'Doesn't she? I can't believe Wendy will have Jenny anything other than fully occupied.'

Claire laughed. 'Well, we need coffee, so Jenny can make it for us. We're paying well enough for the course. Look, Ethelred, since we're the only ones here, could we have a quick chat?'

'Yes,' I said cautiously. I hadn't forgotten the faces of those who'd had a quick chat with her the evening before – Wendy's least of all.

'It's like this,' she said. 'I think Wendy may be right about my book. I reread some of it last night and it still feels . . . well, a bit flat.'

'Don't worry,' I said. 'All manuscripts do when you've

read them and reread them over and over. Leave it for a few weeks – then you'll be able to see it again as somebody would when they read it for the first time. Fliss says it's great. She says you're Shakespeare. That's quite good as these things go.'

'Fliss! What would she know?'

'Well, she may have given up writing, but that doesn't mean she can't judge the quality of a book.'

'I don't think she even likes crime fiction any more.'

'A lot of people don't,' I conceded. I wondered whether to add 'it doesn't make them bad people', but Claire responded before I could decide whether it did.

'I don't even know why she came here,' she said with some feeling. 'I told her not to bother, but she insisted.'

'Well, if you're good friends . . .'

'We see very little of each other these days, since she got married and had a kid. Different interests now, I guess.'

'I didn't know she was married. Or that she had a child. She said nothing at all to me about her family last night.'

'She says plenty to me though,' said Claire resentfully. 'I don't want to know every little detail of her life. We're not twenty any more – girls gossiping. Counting cherry stones to see what sort of husband they will find themselves.'

'No,' I said. The cherry stones thing offered a fairly limited range of trades and professions to the prospective bride. 'Rich man' was still what you really wanted, though 'thief' might be OK, if he operated at a corporate level.

'*She* married Ollie. Her decision entirely. It's hardly my fault, is it?'

'No,' I said.

'She could have married James if she'd wanted to.'

'Ah,' I said. 'Would that have been better?'

'Well, it would have simplified her love life a great deal.'

'Right,' I said, hoping to clarify this rapidly emerging cast of characters. 'So, Ollie . . .'

'Knows nothing at all. That's the worst bit. He thinks everything's fine. He'll find out sooner or later of course. He's bound to. I said to Fliss somebody's going to tell him – you'd better decide what it is you really want, my girl. So, she then starts on about how she totally loves Ollie and would be devastated if he left her, which was news to me, I can tell you. You'd better finish with James pretty quick, then, I said. You're a mother now, for God's sake. It's disgusting.'

'Perhaps then, the least said . . .'

Claire laughed. 'Obviously that's all in confidence. I mean, you won't say any of that to anyone else here?'

'Of course not,' I said. 'But, in the meantime, don't worry about the book. It's always like that.'

'Wendy's still right that a lot of people know about the case I'm using. There have been two or three books based on it already.'

'What was the name of the woman again?' I said.

'Emily Tomsitt.'

'Sorry – of course,' I said.

'No, it's interesting you have to ask. Most women writers wouldn't. But the case did split opinion a bit. Most of the men I spoke to at the time of her appeal thought it was quite right she'd been jailed. Most of the women thought she was the real victim. After her conviction, it was mainly women who campaigned for the retrial.'

'I'll look it up,' I said. 'Once I can get access to the internet again.'

'Anyway, when I started the book, it didn't worry me other people had used the case, but now I know what I've written is rubbish . . . so, I wondered whether I should write about this local murder after all. Or maybe a fraud case – write about what you know, eh?'

'It's not the subject but how you deal with it,' I said. 'At one point in my Buckford series, I decided to give Sergeant Fairfax an interest in music. One of the things he talks about is *La Folía*. Also known as *The Follies of Spain*. Does that mean anything to you?'

'Should it?'

'It's a fairly simple tune but it's one of the oldest surviving musical themes. The most famous version is Handel's *Sarabande*, but it's been used by Lully, Corelli, Vivaldi, Scarlatti, Salieri, Liszt, Rachmaninov. Somebody told me about a hundred and fifty composers have written variations on it or quoted it. It's even hidden somewhere in Beethoven's Fifth. That somebody's done it before, doesn't mean you shouldn't. Salieri's *Twenty-Six Variations on La Folia* is probably the best thing he ever wrote.'

'I suppose,' she said. She possibly wasn't a big Salieri fan. 'You just need to make it fresh.'

'That's what I've tried to do. I've just lost sight of how you do that exactly. That's sort of why I came here. A new start.'

'Did you ask Hal's and Jasper's advice last night?' I asked.

'And Wendy's. Yes, they were useful. But what you say is helpful too. Maybe I'll stick with Tomsitt for a bit then. I'm still not sure.'

So, Wendy, Jasper and Hal had just been consulted on her book. There was nothing in her tone to suggest that anything she'd said would give any of them the slightest cause for concern. But it clearly had. She sounded completely convincing, there talking to me, but Jasper could not have faked the look of terror last night, however hard he had tried.

Later I wished I had asked her more about those conversations, but at that point Jenny bustled in with some cups and a large thermos flask of coffee, of the sort that you often find at conferences and meetings, with a spout and a big round button at the top.

'Ah, two of you now, is it?' she said, more kindly than we had any reason to expect. 'Lucky I brought these extra cups. Breakfast will be another half hour. It might have been earlier but I had to make coffee.'

'That's really kind of you,' I said. 'You and Wendy are looking after us well. I don't know what Wendy would do without you.'

She raised her eyebrows and smiled for the first time. 'Well, Wendy gives the instructions and I follow them,' she said. 'Between us we don't do so badly after all. As madam keeps telling me, "We must look after our guests, Jenny."'

I smiled. The last phrase could have been Wendy there in person. Jenny was a good mimic and had caught her tone and accent perfectly. When not being reprimanded, she was bright and funny. But then Wendy's actual voice echoed down the corridor, Jenny's face fell. 'I'd better go,' she muttered. 'Her ladyship wants me. I don't want to be in detention again.'

'How much do you know about Wendy?' I asked Claire, when the door had closed.

She frowned. 'What do you mean by that?'

'Oh, just that a sort of legend has grown up round her, sitting in splendid isolation up here.'

'Really?' she said. She took a cup and fiddled briefly with the flask to produce a hissing stream of hot, viscous black coffee. She passed it to me.

'Well, the whole thing about the centre being secretly run by the CIA or MI6 or the KGB or some other intelligence agency.'

'Oh, I think that's very unlikely,' said Claire, starting to fill a second cup for herself.

'I don't mean that I believe it,' I said. 'It's just that almost everybody here is talking about it.'

'That doesn't make it true,' said Claire rather severely.

It felt like a reprimand – that I had considerably exceeded the bounds of good taste. Claire had gone from being startling indiscreet about Fliss's love life to being very proper – almost protective – over Wendy.

'She just likes it up here,' said Claire. 'You shouldn't assume that a woman who decides to isolate herself from men is weird.'

'I hadn't,' I said. 'She seems to be isolating herself from everyone – not just men. And, actually, she's invited more men than women to speak at the conference. Almost all men in fact.'

'Men are just trouble,' Claire observed.

I assumed she was thinking primarily of Ollie and James, in spite of her claim to have no interest in Fliss's domestic arrangements. What I couldn't understand was her sudden support for Wendy and how it fitted in with Wendy's discomfort the night before.

Later we were joined by Hal, followed by Jasper and Fliss. All three looked a bit the worse for wear and gratefully accepted the offer of coffee. But I noticed that Claire did not relinquish control of the button. She arranged things so that anyone who wanted coffee had to ask her for it. Wendy would have approved of her approach.

Elsie still had not emerged when Jenny, precisely half an hour after her first appearance, announced that breakfast was ready. I let the others proceed to the dining room and I climbed the stairs to alert Elsie. Breakfast was never something she liked to miss. Or lunch. Or dinner. Or tea. Or a small but tasty snack between any of the above. She'd thank me for waking her.

CHAPTER EIGHT

Elsie

The problem with snow – obvious when you think about it – is that it is far too white. It looks great when it's new, a bit like the pale lemon skirt I bought a couple of years back, but you spill just a tiny bit of chocolate on it and it has to go straight to the dry-cleaners *every single time*. If I were designing snow from scratch I'd make it burnt orange – cheerful enough but more easy-care. And not dazzling when you draw back the curtains and look out on twenty square miles of the stuff in the early morning sunshine. Of course, it must have been worse for anyone with a hangover. I really hoped Fliss had brought her sunglasses with her.

I closed the curtains of my bedroom again and wandered into my bathroom. I'd scarcely been in the bath for twenty minutes when there was a banging on the door and Ethelred shouting that breakfast was ready. I reluctantly switched off the side jets, which I'd only just got to work, and grabbed a large fluffy towel. Then I selected suitable attire from my modest suitcase and followed the smell of bacon.

'It looks as if we have the day off,' said Hal to Wendy hopefully, as he pushed his now empty plate away.

A day off actually sounded rather dull for most of us, but I wondered if he really wanted to get on with the sequel to *The Spy Before Yesterday*. As an agent, I approved of any author who delivered their manuscript before midnight on the day prescribed in the contract.

Wendy paused, her natural desire to run courses at any cost contending with her equally strong inclination to punish Fliss and Claire for their early arrival. 'I agree. If nobody else arrives, then I can't see any point in starting.'

'Fine by me,' said Fliss. 'We can play games. Claire's good at playing games.'

'I've no idea what you mean,' said Claire. 'I don't even like games especially.'

'No? Seems to me that you love them,' said Fliss.

'I'll have some more coffee, Jenny, if you please,' said Claire.

'It's on the dresser over there, love,' said Jenny. 'If that's not too far for you to go.' She'd taken a dislike to Claire – maybe something to do with disturbing her in the kitchen earlier. Or perhaps she'd picked up, as I had, that Claire was in some way part of Team Wendy and that put her on the wrong side of the fence in a much longer running conflict. Jenny collected some dirty plates, though not Claire's, and went off to the kitchen with them.

'There's really no way of contacting civilisation?' asked Hal. 'I mean what if one of us went outside and slipped in the snow and broke their leg? You must have some way of calling an ambulance? Signal flares?'

'I have some crepe bandages and a couple of packets of paracetamol,' said Wendy. 'The snow doesn't last long, not this late in the year. We'd have you down to the nearest hospital by next Tuesday at the latest. And, if the worst really came to the worst, I could have a go at setting the bone myself. I can do that sort of thing – in theory. And CPR of course. But my advice would be not to go out if you are at all unsteady this morning.'

She had clearly noted the empty whisky bottle and for some reason was blaming Hal – perhaps because he had been so keen to have the day off.

'What about food?' asked Fliss. 'I mean if we're all stuck here for days?'

'Well, we've catered for fifteen participants, of which only two are here. We shouldn't go short.'

'And you've included plenty of nutritious chocolate in that?' I said.

'There's chocolate mousse one evening, I think.'

'And the other evenings?'

'Other things,' said Wendy. 'Too much chocolate is bad for you.'

'I wasn't asking for too much. I was asking for just enough. Like Goldilocks.'

'Well, the menu for the weekend is already planned. It can't be changed.'

I wondered how I could best ration the three bars I had

brought with me, bearing in mind that I'd already eaten two and a half of them.

'Croissants?' I asked.

'No.'

'Jam doughnuts?'

'No.'

'Custard doughnuts?'

'No.'

'Chocolate doughnuts?'

'No.'

'Doughnuts with no filling – just lots of nice crunchy sugar on the outside?'

'No doughnuts of any sort.'

So, there it was. As an organiser of courses, Wendy was rubbish. Her status as a conference legend had just been totally trashed.

I looked out of the dining-room window. The snow was still the same; it was just that I resented it that bit more than I had earlier.

'What are the odds of anyone else making it up here, do you think?' asked Hal.

'I wouldn't bet on it,' I said.

'Tell you what, Elsie, I'll give you odds of ten to one,' he said.

I paused, wondering if he was able and willing to do that in chocolate. That would be five whole bars. On the other hand I couldn't risk losing the half-bar I had.

'No chance,' I said.

But I should have accepted those odds, because, a little before eleven o'clock, Fliss bounced into the room. 'You won't believe this,' she said, 'but there's somebody coming up the road.'

'In what?' I said hopefully. 'A snowplough?'

'No,' she replied. 'On foot.'

We gathered at the window and watched the small speck get larger, swaying as it struggled through the snow. It gradually became a man, carrying a rucksack, dressed in a ski jacket, thick trousers, gaiters and heavy walking boots. It was difficult to say at this distance whether the rucksack contained emergency chocolate, but it was difficult to see how it wouldn't. He was aided in his mission of mercy by walking poles, which he planted and lifted with a slow but determined rhythm. It was another ten or fifteen minutes before he fell through the front door, dropping his pack and a great deal of snow on the polished oak floor in the spacious entrance hall, where we had all gathered to discover who it might be.

'Dean!' said Claire.

'I bet you didn't expect to see me here,' he said with a smile.

'Bloody hell,' said Fliss.

'Good to see you too, Fliss,' said Dean.

'You young people all seem to know each other,' I said.

Dean held out an icy hand for me to shake. 'Dean Marden,' he said. 'You are Wendy, I assume?'

'No, I'm Wendy,' said Wendy, quickly reasserting control. 'How on earth did you get here?'

'I drove from London this morning as far as Butterthwaite. The road's clear lower down. But, just beyond the farm, it gets bad, so I left the car by the side of the road and walked.

I always keep my boots and poles in the car, just in case. It's only four miles and not that steep a road. There were one or two moments when I didn't think I'd get through, but I have and here I am.'

'That was very foolish of you,' said Wendy. 'If you'd strayed at all from the line of the road . . .'

'Oh, that was clear enough,' said Dean. 'I could see where I was going. But there are pretty deep drifts. It's a good job I keep myself fit.'

Well, that too was clear enough for anyone to see. Compared with the other males we had – all older than Dean and with a fitness honed by long hours sitting at a desk, drinking coffee and eating Jaffa Cakes – Dean was certainly the hottest man present. And, though Wendy's sparse frame spoke of a level of athleticism that I had no intention of achieving, Dean was much larger and more muscular. I decided there and then that if one of us had to be sent down the mountain on some genuinely life-saving errand, then I'd prefer Dean to Ethelred. Actually thinking about it, I'd have preferred Jenny to Ethelred. No disrespect to anyone, but she was also solidly built and had local knowledge.

'How much chocolate did you bring with you, Dean?' I asked, cutting to the chase.

Dean looked puzzled, being for some reason unable to guess any of my innermost fantasies.

'None,' he said. 'I thought all meals were included?'

'Of course they are,' said Wendy, a little huffily, I thought.

'Can I get you some coffee, Dean?' asked Jenny. 'You must be—'

But initiatives of this sort on Jenny's part were clearly not to be tolerated. I turned and saw that Wendy was frowning her disapproval.

'I think Dean should put his bag in his room first,' said Wendy. 'And find some more suitable shoes for wearing indoors. You can show him to Ingleton, Jenny.'

'Of course,' said Jenny, wiping her hands on her apron. 'You've been to a conference here before, Dean, haven't you?'

'Nope. First creative writing course I've ever done,' he said.

'Oh . . .' she said, then shrugged. 'My mistake.'

As they headed off up the stairs, Fliss said to nobody in particular, 'Well, it seems everything is on again?'

'Sorry?' said Wendy.

'You said it was off if nobody else turned up. They have. Dean. He's here. So, it must now be going ahead.'

'I was speaking very generally,' said Wendy.

'Hmm,' said Ethelred. 'I don't think we can let him slog up here through the snow to his first ever course and then leave him playing Scrabble. I'll run my sessions anyway, if anyone wants them.'

'Me too,' said Jasper.

'Yes, why not?' said Hal, slightly reluctantly.

'I'm happy to do my bit,' I said, though his not having chocolate had clearly been a crushing disappointment. I'd check the fridge later to see if there was a little something to keep my strength up.

Fliss looked at Wendy. 'Of course, you don't have to talk to us about John Dickson Carr if you don't want to.'

'I shall certainly run my session on the history of crime fiction,' said Wendy indignantly. 'It's scheduled.'

'Looks like that's settled then,' said Fliss. 'We're good to go, folks. See you all in the sitting room in ten, eh?'

'We'll start *after* lunch,' said Wendy firmly. 'We'll eat at twelve-thirty precisely and begin the first session at half past one. On the dot, if you please – that means all of you. We have a great deal to get through.'

'There have been two slightly unexpected developments this morning,' said Ethelred, when we were alone again in the sitting room.

'Two?'

'Well, the first wasn't that big,' he said. 'It's just that, when I saw Claire and Wendy come back from their chat last night, I thought that they must have fallen out in a big way. But this morning Claire was defending Wendy at every possible opportunity.'

'So, maybe we got it wrong last night?'

'No, Wendy's expression was one of total shock and disbelief. Like Hal and Jasper.'

'But all's well now?'

'Between Claire and Wendy anyway. Somehow they seem to have made it up in a big way.'

'And the second unexpected development was Dean's arrival?' I asked.

'Yes, that was a lot bigger of course.'

'True. So, if these things are supposed to happen in threes, then we can expect a third unexpected event? Though if we expect it then it won't strictly speaking count as unexpected. So, it won't be one.'

'It might if it's big enough,' said Ethelred. 'Each iteration trumps the one before. The final wish wipes out the previous two. The third pig sees off the wolf. The third Billy Goat Gruff demolishes the troll and heads over the bridge to the grass on the other side. So, according to the theory, the final one could be massive, though I can't think what that might be, stuck here on our own.'

'Well, it certainly won't be your lecture on late fourteenth century dialogue,' I said.

CHAPTER NINE

Ethelred

Having achieved some sort of quorum, we had all decided, for reasons of duty or pleasure, to assemble in the sitting room. First Elsie and I, then the others one by one. Wendy was the last, having needed to interfere with whatever Jenny was currently doing. She knelt down and started to lay the fire, scrunching newspaper into balls. The Hall had a boiler somewhere, powered by oil, which ran a rather inefficient hot water and central heating system, but the fire was the centrepiece of the room – the thing that we were supposed to gather round. The lukewarm bedroom radiators and the blazing fire were just part of the armoury that Wendy had at her disposal to ensure that we were where she wanted us to be.

'Look,' I said to her, 'is there anything we can all do to help you and Jenny this morning? You've been running about after us – Jenny especially. I guess we've reached the mucking-in stage. Can I lay the table or something?'

Wendy paused. Delegation of any sort was obviously something she found difficult. And allowing us to lay the table was fraught with too many dangers to contemplate. 'I suppose you could get some more logs in,' she said uncertainly. 'The woodshed is round the back of the house – just follow the path and turn right. There's a bin full of kindling – we'll need some of that too.'

'Good,' I said. 'That sounds easy enough.'

'I'll give Ethelred a hand,' said Hal. 'It's freezing out there. Two of us will do it faster.'

'I'll bring some in,' said Dean. 'Looks like a job for the boys, eh?'

Eventually we agreed we would all fetch a basket of wood or two and I'd also bring in sufficient kindling for the next few days.

When I opened the back door, the cold hit me, like jumping into an unheated swimming pool without first checking the temperature. It instantly stung my face and hands. There was a small, clean drift of snow to step over and then a thickish layer of large fluffy flakes that made me glad I'd brought my walking boots. Everything crackled and sparkled in the sun. Snow draped the windowsills and powdered the rough edges of the walls. There were gleaming white heaps in the approximate shapes of watering cans, stacked flowerpots, coiled hoses and, against the wall, a garden bench that nobody would want to sit on for a while. I crossed the smooth surface of what had, the night before, been a cobbled path and round the corner to where a large shed was situated. I removed the wooden peg that had been rammed into the hasp in place of a padlock and opened the door. There was certainly no shortage of fuel. I returned with the kindling, my shoes caked with snow, before anyone else had started out, but, as we all went backwards and forwards, the drifts became more compacted and the walking easier. In the end only Claire and Elsie excused themselves completely on the grounds of unsuitable footwear. The rest of us made two or three trips each. It wasn't exactly efficient, but there was a sense of achievement, as when you complete some contrived team-building thing on the sort of management course that I used to attend years ago. We stacked the wood in an alcove in the sitting room, half hoping it wasn't enough and that we'd have to repeat the exercise at some point.

Though the fire was now lit, and most of the guests were sitting round it, Dean unexpectedly stood up, stretched and announced that he was going back to his room to finish unpacking and get his notebook and pens.

'There'll be time for that after lunch,' I said, knowing my own notes were still in the freezing room at the end of the long corridor. 'I mean, we ought to have finished eating by one.'

'May as well do it now,' he said. He glanced out into the hallway. 'Yes, I'd better go. You all stay where you are – I don't want to break up the cosy little group.'

I sat for a while admiring the fire, then decided I should do the same as Dean. My first session was scheduled for mid afternoon and I might as well reread my notes now as do anything else. But as I entered the hallway I heard low voices. Dean and Wendy were at the far end, by the stairs.

'Look,' Dean was saying, 'It will be fine. Trust me.'

'You think so?' Wendy demanded. She sounded very bitter.

'You'd probably be surprised to discover how many people already know.'

'I've been careful to avoid that.'

He shook his head. 'It wouldn't mean you had to shut the operation down or anything.'

'Well, thank you for that,' she said, though she did not sound especially grateful.

'Things would be a bit different, of course. I mean, whatever they think . . .'

His voice tailed off as he saw me standing there.

'I'm just going up to my room to get my notes,' I said. 'Did you find yours, Dean?'

'I got delayed – we were just talking about the course. Weren't we, Wendy?'

'Yes . . . there are a lot of courses like this now. Lots of competition. We may have to rethink some of it or . . . shut down . . . as Dean says. Maybe we should do that.'

'Well, I've said, that's not my view,' said Dean, slightly irritably, I thought. 'We can talk about it later.'

'Probably not,' she said. 'I don't think we need to discuss this again, Dean. And that's my final word on the matter.'

Dean was about to say something, but looked at me, turned on his heel and headed off up the stairs.

I smiled at Wendy, but I don't think she saw me as I walked past her and started in my turn to climb the treads to the next floor. Her expression was not unlike the one she'd had after her discussion with Claire the night before. The programme had not got off to a good start. When I reached the top of the stairs, I looked to see which way Dean had gone, but he had already vanished. He was clearly very anxious to unpack.

'So, that's the third unexpected thing?' asked Elsie. 'Because, if it is, I'm not very impressed.'

'I didn't say that,' I said. 'I just said it was odd. Anyway, the whole business of things happening in threes applies to fiction, not real life.'

'My grandmother used to say things happened in threes,' said Elsie. 'If she accidentally smashed a couple of things in the kitchen, she'd break a match straight away so that her best teapot didn't bite the dust later. And she was real enough.'

'Fine,' I said. 'Forget it then. It's of no interest.'

Elsie shook her head. Having made her point, whatever it was, she could now admit that she was intrigued.

'So, you caught them together, hiding away in the hall . . .'

'Not hiding exactly – just over by the stairs.'

'Talking in whispers?'

'Well, I could hear them – just about – as soon as I came out of the sitting room. But I think the discussion had started to get heated at that point. They may have been quieter earlier.'

'And he said something about everybody knowing now . . .'

'He said something like, she'd be surprised how many people knew.'

'And she said in that case they'd have to shut the whole CIA thing down?'

'She didn't say CIA. Or MI6. She just said they'd have to close down. And he said something like they might have to operate differently in future.'

'They must have meant the CIA thing – I mean, everybody does know about that, don't they? So it was news to her that people knew and she wanted to shut up shop?'

'Yes, she said she'd done her best to keep it all secret. But now she'd made up her mind and didn't want to discuss it again. I can't remember her exact words.'

'OK. He arrives out of the blue and gives her the bad news that everybody knows what she's doing. It would be like that Mansfield short story you have to do for A Level – *Miss Brill* – where she suddenly realises that her whole existence is a bit rubbish, and it's not even worth buying cake – an epiphany moment.'

'She certainly looked shocked,' I said.

'She'd be devastated. Look, this is her entire life in a way that, to be perfectly honest with you, Ethelred, you are *not* my entire life. This is what she does, twenty-four seven, fifty-two weeks of the year, plus an extra day depending on whether it's a leap year or not. With the greatest respect, this goes way beyond cake. Her devotion is total. You're not even allowed to write books unless they're set round Butterthwaite. What does that tell you?'

'The Butterthwaite murder? That was just for Claire.'

'Trust me, she'd have had you all working on a local murder before the course ended. Which is odd in itself.'

'Why?'

'Because the weird coincidence of every book published next year being set in Butterthwaite might draw people's attention to the CIA operation here.'

'Which is a good argument against there being any such thing.'

Elsie shook her head. 'My theory is that Dean is a CIA agent, sent to tell her their cover has been blown. After all, who would walk four miles through snow drifts to listen to you talking about Middle English in the age of Chaucer or whatever you're planning to give us? Nobody, that's who. But if a CIA mission was about to go critical . . .'

'Wouldn't the CIA have access to a helicopter or something?'

'If one thing was going to make people suspicious, Ethelred, it's somebody arriving by helicopter to hear you talking about the Great Vowel Shift.'

'The session is actually on dialogue generally, not just historical,' I said. 'And there's more to it than just me talking. But if Dean is a CIA agent – or MI6 or Mossad – how come he didn't recognise Wendy when he arrived? He thought *you* were Wendy, remember?'

'True . . . but you never get Wendy's face on anything, do you? I mean, the course fliers don't have it, the website doesn't have it. For somebody who is determined to control every aspect of what happens here, she goes out of her way to ensure that nobody will recognise her when they arrive.'

'You would have thought that the CIA would have at least given Dean a rough description,' I said.

'I'm much the same height as Wendy.'

'But only height.'

'What are you saying? I'm fat or something? Don't listen to what my assistant says about diets. She thinks everyone should be on a diet. I've told Tuesday – I'm as fit as I need to be. Less than two bars of chocolate a day and I'd risk becoming seriously malnourished. It's hereditary.'

'Your mother was fat?'

'No, she was very thin. Because she didn't get anything like enough chocolate. It was a terrible warning to me.'

'Anyway, I didn't say you had to be on a diet. I'm certainly not saying you have to take Tuesday's advice – you do after all employ her, not the other way round. I just meant that Claire, say, is much more Wendy's height and build. That's all. Obviously, it wouldn't hurt you to cut down a bit on chocolate. Say half a bar—'

'Good point – Claire, I mean, being the same size. And it wasn't only Dean who had shocking news, was it? Claire had something for Wendy too. And Dean and Claire know each other.'

'What, they're all in it together? But Claire clearly didn't want Dean here. So who is Claire working for? The Russians? The Chinese?'

'I don't know yet. There are lots of permutations, when you think about it. But I'll find out.'

'I doubt you'll get very far,' I said.

'You underestimate me, Ethelred. If I can keep getting you new contracts, frankly I can do anything. I'll crack it by lunchtime.'

I looked at my watch. That was unlikely. 'Well, let me know when you do find something out,' I said. 'In the meantime, I need to reread my notes on dialogue. As you say, some people have gone to a lot of effort to be here.'

CHAPTER TEN

Elsie

So, the question was: who would spill the beans on Dean? Not Wendy, in spite of what seemed to be a difference of opinion over the viability of the CIA's vital North Yorkshire operation. Not Claire, unless she was definitely from a rival set-up and unusually talkative. But Fliss might know something. I had just to run into her and then ask her, casually and naturally, a few carefully chosen questions.

I hung around in the entrance hall, as if admiring the fox-hunting pictures, to see who came past. For a while nobody did. My stomach, which takes an intelligent interest in such things, told me lunchtime was approaching. Hal and Jasper went by on their way to the dining room. I smiled and let them go. Dean ambled along. I nodded politely. Ethelred asked me if I was coming to lunch. I said in a moment. He raised his eyebrows but didn't argue. Then, just as I was giving up, Fliss appeared, floppy tapestry bag over her shoulder as usual. I knew I had to seize the moment. I might not get her alone again today – not in a totally non-suspicious way.

'Hi, Fliss,' I said.

'Hi, Elsie. I thought it might be time to get some chow? Build up our strength for the opening session?'

'Indeed, but could we have a word first?'

Fliss checked her large, plastic watch. 'Yes, why don't we just chat as we go? They'll be serving up in a couple of minutes. I'm starving, aren't you?'

'Yes, but I really need to talk to you here,' I said.

'What, by the stairs?'

'Yes.'

She looked around, slightly perplexed. The staircase was nice enough, but it was only a Victorian addition. 'OK – shoot.'

'It's about Dean,' I said.

She looked again at the stairs and back at me. Their relevance still escaped her. 'And we need to talk about him here? That's what you're saying?'

'Precisely.'

'Because . . . ?'

'Well, when did you meet him?'

'And we need to stand still for me to answer that? I can't tell you while we're moving?'

'No.'

'OK. Totally immobile then. It was at a conference last autumn. In Scotland. Are we done?'

'Obviously not. What was he doing there?'

'Same as me – it was one of the many crime-writing

94

conferences that take place all over the country every summer. This must have been one of the last of the season. We were all there to listen to panels and talk about mystery novels, then get drunk in the bar. That's how they work. Haven't you ever been to one?'

'Did he say what he did for a living?'

'Yes, probably.'

'And it was?'

'I really can't remember. It was last year and I had no idea that I'd ever see him again. What he did was of no great interest. Had I known I was going to be interrogated on him, I'd have looked him up on LinkedIn. I'm sure he's there. He's the sort of person who would be on all the networking sites. Why don't you check him out?'

I narrowed my eyes. 'No phone signal, kid. I'd have thought you'd have remembered that.'

'Fair enough. No way of verifying his occupation. *Tant pis*, eh? Shall we go eat?'

'He didn't strike you as in any way suspicious?'

Fliss looked at her watch again, though not much time had passed since she last did it. 'No, not in any way,' she said. 'I mean, he was a pain in the arse – not for me but for Claire. He trailed around after her the whole time.'

'Why?'

'He fancied her, I guess. Don't be fooled by that mouse-like exterior. Claire has plenty of men after her. Hal for one.'

'Really?'

'Oh yes. Of course, Hal's devotion bothered her less, because she also wanted something from him.'

'What?'

'Well, he's a writer and she wants her book published. So introductions to publishers and agents would be good, plus maybe something that she can put on the back of the book when it is published. And nice encouraging comments on the current draft, of course. So, Dean was a bit in the way of her cultivating Hal. She took to sitting in any part of the lecture theatre that Dean wasn't in.'

'That must have pissed Dean off?'

'I'm not sure he noticed he was being avoided. Some men are like that. He'd accost her in the bar later anyway – often when she was trying to have a quiet chat with Hal.'

'So, did Dean follow her here? Is that what you mean?'

'No . . . well, only if he managed to find out she was coming. I can't quite see how he'd do that. Look, I'm really enjoying our little chat – swapping all the goss. We must do it again soon. But it would also be great to eat something.'

'Eat? Not quite yet, I'm afraid. Since he arrived, has Dean done anything weird?'

When I said 'weird' she looked at me pointedly, but just said, 'He made a beeline for Claire in the sitting room but she brushed him off as before. So, maybe he has now got the message.'

'Men can be a bit obtuse like that.'

'You said it, Elsie.'

'Well, no, you said it earlier. I was just agreeing in order to establish rapport. I can see we're going to get on splendidly.'

'Are we? Look, rapport's great and all that, but at this moment I'd settle for lunch,' said Fliss. She looked down the corridor towards the dining room. She wasn't really paying attention as she should have been.

'All right, then. Final question, Fliss. Has Dean ever done or said anything to suggest he was a CIA agent?'

'If I say "yes" do I get to eat lunch before it's cold?'

I narrowed my eyes again, only a bit more than last time. 'I just need the truth, Fliss. The plain, simple truth. Know what I mean?'

'OK. No, Dean has never done or said anything that suggested he wasn't a trainee solicitor – sorry, I've remembered now – that's what he said he did. Trainee solicitor. There you go! He definitely never mentioned the CIA. Not to me anyway. But why don't you ask Claire? She'd know better than I do. Can we eat? Please?'

I nodded gravely. 'OK, sister, let's eat,' I said.

CHAPTER ELEVEN

Ethelred

Elsie was late for lunch, but she arrived with Fliss, so I guess they'd been gossiping and forgotten the time. But whatever they'd been talking about they'd finished, because Fliss went to the opposite end of the table from Elsie.

Lunch was a more modest affair than dinner the night before, perhaps to ensure that we kept to time. There was a large bowl of vegetable soup and plenty of crusty bread, then later a platter of fruit was placed on the table. I noticed Fliss whispering something to Claire then pointing at Elsie and Claire raising her eyebrows.

'I was asking Fliss about Dean,' Elsie hissed at me by way of explanation.

'And?'

'He's a solicitor.'

'Yes,' I said, 'he told me a few minutes ago.'

'At least,' said Elsie, 'that's his cover story.'

'Maybe it's true,' I said. 'That little discussion by the

stairs – maybe Wendy wanted some free legal advice?'

'About the course?'

'Who knows?' I said.

'He fancies Claire.'

'That seems likely – I mean, he was doing his best to be pleasant.'

'She doesn't fancy him.'

'She seems in turn to be avoiding him as much as possible, so yes, I agree.'

'She does fancy Hal.'

'He's married,' I said.

'As if that ever stopped anything.'

'I was always faithful to Geraldine,' I said. 'All the time we were together.'

'Fat lot of good that did you. Her and your best friend. And you never even noticed.'

'Not until she walked out on me,' I said. 'Then it was a bit obvious for everyone.'

I looked across the table at Claire. She was the last to be served with soup and seemed to have less than the rest of us. Whatever she'd done, Jenny hadn't yet forgiven her.

'Is there any more bread?' she asked.

'No,' said Jenny without turning. She picked up the soup tureen and put it on a sideboard, out of reach.

Lunch was in fact over quite quickly, as Wendy had clearly intended. Claire, perhaps to avoid Dean, got up before most people had even started dessert and dashed off. But the others followed shortly after. Since I now had all the paperwork I needed, I was in no hurry and, thinking back,

I'm certain I was the last to leave the table. I proceeded to the sitting room and sat by the fire. I threw a couple of logs on, hoping that they would land at the right angle to meet Wendy's approval. They started to smoulder then burst into bright yellow flame. Occasionally I heard voices outside and people passing the door, but it was ten past one by the time the next person arrived – Dean, as it happened, clutching his notebook. He looked respectable and efficient, though I suppose spies and solicitors both do that.

'I'm the first?' he said.

'Apart from me. Still twenty minutes until we start.'

'Mind if I join you? Or are you busy?'

'Please do. I'm done with reading my notes. You can read presentation notes too much. Elsie never uses them. While I'm trying to memorise the key points, which I really know already, she's probably enjoying the many facilities of her suite for another ten minutes. Did you bring some of your own dialogue to read out?'

'Me? No, I couldn't find anything I was happy with. I'm sure Claire will oblige. I think the girls must be powdering their noses at the moment. No sign of Claire anyway.'

'You looked for her?'

'Yes . . . a bit. I mean, there was something I wanted to talk to her about.'

'Ah,' I said, remembering her rapid departure. 'I suppose everyone will be here by one-thirty.'

If she knew Dean was still after her, then she might not return until the last moment. But it wasn't my business to tell him. If he wished to keep trying his luck, that was his affair.

'Jasper told me he was going to take a quick look outside,' he said. 'I think he means he's going to have a crafty smoke. Not the first one today either. And I saw Hal going back to his room. It's just that I haven't seen Claire.'

'Let's hope she hasn't got lost,' I said. If Dean and – I strongly suspected – Fliss were not planning to be particularly active participants, then Claire was all I had to prevent the session becoming a long monologue from me.

It was a good five minutes before anyone else came in. Dean looked up eagerly, but it was only Elsie. She joined us on the sofa as the clock was striking the quarter. Then Jasper arrived, saying it was freezing outside and that it looked as if we'd get some more snow soon. His slightly guilty air probably stemmed from the illicit cigarette. Hal turned up a couple of minutes later, followed by Fliss.

'Have any of you seen Claire?' asked Dean.

Fliss looked up from a search of the interior of her tapestry bag, having temporarily misplaced something other than her friend, and shook her head. 'Haven't seen her since lunch,' she said. 'She didn't come back to the room with me. I thought she would show up because she'd left her notebook there. Gone for a walk outside maybe?'

'I didn't see her at the front of the house,' said Jasper. 'Saw Wendy, coming out of the front door then hurrying off round the back. Don't think she saw me about to light up though.'

'Claire was here in the sitting room earlier,' said Hal, but since she clearly wasn't there now that didn't help much.

Finally, on the dot of half past, Wendy arrived. She still looked worried, though whether that was because of what

Dean had said earlier that day or what Claire had said the previous night or whether it was simply the responsibility of running the course, I couldn't say.

'Are we all here?' she asked, glancing round the room.

'Claire's not,' said Fliss.

Dean frowned but said nothing.

'Well, we can't wait,' said Wendy. 'We all have a lot to get through.'

'Give her five minutes,' I said. 'I'm sure she won't be long. She's thirty three per cent of the participants.'

'Was she in your room?' Wendy asked Fliss.

'No. I've just told Dean: she wasn't in the room earlier. But she left her notebook behind, so she's probably just gone back for that. She wouldn't deliberately miss the start of the course. Not for anything. She won't be long, I promise.'

We waited five minutes. Then another five. Wendy grew increasingly tense as the schedule slipped further and further.

'Look, I'll check the room,' said Fliss. 'Like I say, maybe she went back for the book and . . . well, I don't know. Lost track of the time. This really isn't like her at all.'

'I'll check the ladies' room,' said Elsie. It would, after all, have been a safe haven, inaccessible to Dean.

But both returned empty-handed.

'No sign of her,' said Fliss. 'Funny though – her black notebook's still there on the dressing table and she normally goes nowhere without that.'

'So, perhaps she went outside after all?' asked Dean. 'Just for a moment – planning to go back to the room afterwards? But then . . .' His voice tailed off. None of us could see her sitting round in the snow for longer than necessary. And certainly not this long. Even Jasper's much-needed cigarette break must have been quite brief.

'Well, I certainly didn't see her,' said Jasper. 'Not at the front of the house. Did you see her round the back, Wendy?'

'Me?' asked Wendy.

'Yes, I saw you come out of the front door and then head straight round to the back of the house in your blue padded jacket. Twenty minutes ago – maybe twenty-five.'

'I haven't been out since we collected the wood,' said Wendy. 'And my blue jacket is hanging up by the back door.'

'If you say so. But somebody who looked like you was certainly there just after lunch. Unless Claire has a blue jacket too?'

'She has a green one,' said Fliss. 'Tweed. A bit lightweight for the conditions up here. It was in the wardrobe just before I came down. I noticed it there.'

'So, this person was heading for the back of the house?' I asked.

'Yes,' said Jasper.

'I'll go and check there,' I said.

Wendy looked agitated. 'But surely she'll be along soon? Let's just get things under way . . .'

'It would be easy to slip on the path out there,' I said. 'If she's fallen and knocked herself out . . .'

'I'll come with you,' said Dean.

'Wait, I'll come too,' said Wendy. 'You don't know your way around. If it's slippery out there I could have you all laid out unconscious, if you're not careful. And I can't just phone for an ambulance if you do.'

We crossed the hall and headed for the back door.

'See, there's my coat,' said Wendy pointing to hooks by the door. 'No . . . actually it's gone.'

She looked disbelievingly, then selected a green Barbour and changed into some boots. I wondered how much searching we would need to do. My own boots and Dean's were still by the door, but my coat was in my room. Hopefully, we wouldn't have to hunt for long.

The path as far as the woodshed was well trampled from our wood-collecting session, but there was no sign of footsteps going beyond – just a fairly fresh set of prints coming round in the other direction from the front of the house, where Jasper had seen the blue-jacketed figure. Small footprints.

'Well, if those are Claire's,' I said, 'she either went into the woodshed or back into the house. With all these other prints, it's difficult to say which, but it must be one or the other. Unless she levitated.'

'Better try the woodshed,' said Dean. 'I mean, that's the most likely . . .' He looked nervous, but so did Wendy.

The door was slightly open. I pushed it gently. Dean's guess was right. Claire lay stretched out, on her face, on the floor of the shed. She was wearing a blue quilted jacket. Wound round her neck was a piece of rope.

'Claire?' said Dean.

But he already knew he wasn't going to get any response. I knelt down beside her, touched her face and took her wrist. Her face was no more than cool to the touch, but her hand was already icy cold. There was no pulse.

We looked at each other. 'Call an ambulance' was what we were all thinking, but Wendy had already reminded us of that impossibility.

'We ought to try CPR,' Dean said.

'There would be no point,' said Wendy.

'I can do it,' said Dean.

'So can I,' said Wendy. 'I've told you. It's one of the things I'm trained for. And that's why I know we would be wasting our time. She could have been like that for almost half an hour.'

'I'm willing to do it, nevertheless, if you're not.'

Wendy shook her head, but knelt by Claire and untied the rope, then started to apply pressure to the chest. Dean and I stood back, but after five minutes Wendy rose to her feet again.

'Perhaps a bit longer, using a bit more force?' said Dean. 'I know that the professionals push so hard they sometimes break ribs. Let me have a go.'

'Dean, I've said I've had proper training – it's essential, running courses up here and with no way to call medical services. I can tell you there's nothing more to be done.'

'So have you found her yet?' said a voice from outside.

We turned to see Elsie entering the shed. A detailed explanation of what had happened over the past few minutes seemed unnecessary in light of what she could already see.

'Wendy tried to save her,' I said. 'After we found her like this. But it was too late. Somebody must have been waiting for her and strangled her. From behind, judging by the way the rope was tied round her neck. But I don't know where they got the rope from.'

'It's always hanging there on a hook,' said Wendy. 'Just part of the junk that accumulates in a place like this.'

'Is that the missing coat?' I asked, indicating the blue jacket Claire was wearing.

'I suppose it must be,' said Wendy. 'That was exactly what I was looking for on the hook. I'd need to check inside the coat to be sure it's mine, but we'd better leave everything as it is, until the police can get here, and that may be some days. I'll lock things up in the meantime. We don't need to come here again for wood – not for the moment – and I certainly don't need the jacket.'

'Wait a moment,' said Elsie. 'Nobody can get in or out of Fell Hall, right? The valley's blocked? And we'd see tracks in the snow if anyone had come or gone?'

'Well, there are certainly no tracks, other than Dean's, leading away from the house and onto the fells or down the valley,' I said. 'We'd have seen them. So, it's unlikely anyone else arrived or left today. Obviously, our trips here earlier to get logs mean that there are plenty of footprints between here and the house – almost everyone's I would have said.'

'That's my point. It's got to be one of us and it could have been any one of us,' said Elsie.

'I hope you don't include me in that,' said Wendy.

'On the contrary,' said Elsie. 'Everyone is a suspect.'

'Including yourself?'

'Well, obviously I know I didn't do it,' said Elsie. 'But in all other respects, yes. In principle I suspect myself as much as I suspect you. But only in principle, because to actually suspect myself when I know I didn't do it would be a bit perverse. Unless I had amnesia.'

'Fine,' I said, before the conversation sailed away into as yet uncharted seas of speculation. 'Let's just accept we're all suspects. It's fairly irrelevant what we agree now between ourselves anyway. The police will still want to question us all when they get here.'

'But what about in the meantime?' said Elsie. 'We have an actual murderer amongst us. We can't just ignore that.'

'Logically that's true,' I said. 'But if you mean that they may strike again, that's not something you could possibly say without knowing why Claire was killed. Killers don't just kill randomly because it's what they like doing. Not in real life.'

'Exactly,' said Elsie, as if I'd just agreed with everything she'd said. 'We don't know why Claire was killed. And, that being the case, we don't know how much danger we may all be in. Since I doubt anyone will be very interested in Chaucerian dialogue—'

'Dialogue generally,' I said.

'Whatever. There's no point in going ahead with the course. So, we may as well use our time to at least narrow down who the killer might be. That way we all know who to avoid late at night. It's all right for you, Ethelred, in your tiny and remote room. Nobody will ever find you there. But in my luxury suite I'm very easy to locate.'

'You are in danger, even following the slightly dubious convention of crime novels, only if you happen to know who the killer is. And you don't.'

'I am in danger, following the well-respected convention of crime novels, only if the killer *thinks* I know who the killer is. And for all you know, that's exactly what he thinks.'

'I hope you are not considering interfering with a crime scene?' I said.

'Ethelred, it is permissible to interfere with a crime scene in order to save lives.'

'That applies to medical staff treating casualties, not to amateur detectives.'

'I'm not sure why you say "amateur detectives" in that condescending way. Your Master Thomas is an amateur detective.'

'Yes, but he lives in the fourteenth century, when there was no police force or fingerprinting or DNA testing. I also write about Sergeant Fairfax, who would have very strong views on a civilian marching through a crime scene in big boots. We should just secure the shed, as Wendy proposes, and wait for the police to arrive. The snow may have melted by tomorrow – at least enough for one of us to get down to Butterthwaite and phone them.'

'Or then again, I may have been strangled in my bed – or on my very comfy sofa or in my vast and many-functioned bath, or at my enormous desk. I'm at least going to check for clues.'

'I forbid you to touch the body,' I said.

'Wendy's already tried CPR. And quite clearly removed the rope. The body has been touched very comprehensively. A bit more touching won't make any difference. And I bet you tried for a pulse or something? Yes, I thought so. Why should I be the only one who doesn't get to touch anything? Why is your DNA so well-behaved and mine likely to screw up the entire investigation?'

'That's not the point,' I said.

She knelt down beside Claire.

'Wait!' said Wendy. 'Ethelred's right. I simply can't let you do this.'

Elsie looked up at her. 'But, since we've agreed you're a suspect, I can't allow you to interfere with my investigation.'

'Do not touch that body,' said Wendy.

'Or what? You'll call the police?' said Elsie. 'I'm just going to check the pockets. That can't do any harm, can it?'

Wendy gave a little gasp. She was not used to being contradicted like this in her own domain.

'That's *my* jacket,' she said.

'And what's in the pockets?' asked Elsie.

'Nothing,' said Wendy. 'Nothing at all. But you've no right to touch my things. In case you've forgotten, you're not actually the police. You're a literary agent. You'd only have a right to do that if I were one of your authors and you had a clause in the contract saying you could go through my stuff whenever you wished.'

Elsie looked thoughtful. She could see that sort of clause might be useful in future.

'I agree with Wendy,' said Dean unexpectedly. 'You should leave the pockets alone. They haven't been tampered with yet. The police can at least check those themselves.'

But Elsie's little hand was already drawing a piece of paper from the jacket. It was folded and seemed to have been ripped from a notepad, leaving ragged perforations along one edge. She held it aloft triumphantly.

'And you say the pockets were empty?' she asked Wendy.

'They were first thing this morning,' said Wendy rather stiffly.

'So this little piece of paper isn't yours?'

Wendy glared. Under that gaze, most people in my agent's position would have swallowed hard and apologetically returned the note to the corpse. Elsie simply unfolded the sheet of paper and read out loud. 'I need to talk to you urgently. Don't worry, I'm on your side.' Elsie paused and looked at Dean. 'And it has your signature on it, Dean. Hmm. Strange you didn't want me to check the pockets, isn't it?'

CHAPTER TWELVE

Elsie

'It's not what you think,' said Dean.

'I think it's a note from you,' I said. I held it up in front of him. 'It's definitely a note, so is this your writing, or are you saying it's a fake? We could check your notebook and see if the paper matches.'

'No, that's my writing. And my paper.'

'Then you were completely wrong there. It is exactly what I think it is. What does it mean, Dean? Why are you telling Claire not to worry?'

'I can't tell you that,' said Dean.

'Even though Claire, by the look of it, should have worried quite a lot? Not the best legal advice, was it?'

'The note has nothing at all to do with Claire's death.'

'You'll have to tell the police,' I said.

'Perhaps.'

'This will have your fingerprints on it.'

'And yours,' said Dean.

Well, fair enough. I could see now that it might have been better not to have touched it.

'But more of yours than mine,' I said.

'I admitted I wrote it. So obviously it will have my prints on it. I just said it has nothing to do with Claire's death.'

'You may as well tell me everything. Before the bad cops come. I'm the good cop, Dean.'

'You're actually not a cop at all,' said Dean.

'If I were, I would be,' I said.

Dean looked at me, puzzled. 'If you were what?'

'A cop.'

'And what would you be?'

'A good one.'

'If you say so. What are you going to do with that, now you've contaminated it?'

I really needed an evidence bag to preserve Dean's fingerprints. And mine. But there weren't any in the woodshed. Just wood and stuff. I jammed it into my most secure pocket, next to the half-bar of chocolate.

'Don't lose it,' said Dean.

'In your dreams,' I said.

'That would seem to be that, then,' he said. 'Unless you're planning to arrest me?'

'Not at present, Dean,' I said. 'But don't go anywhere.'

He looked pointedly at the snow on the ground and then up at the dark menacing clouds.

'Good point,' I said.

* * *

'We've made an excellent start,' I said, as Wendy closed the shed door behind her and pushed the wooden peg back into the hasp.

'We?' said Ethelred, watching Dean heading back towards the warmth of the sitting room. 'I wasn't aware I said I'd do anything other than wait for the police. And Wendy certainly hasn't. As for an excellent start, I assume you're referring to the fingerprints you've put on the only concrete piece of evidence we have.'

'I mean we've established Dean as the key suspect. And you've got the rope. That's evidence. I haven't touched that.'

'But you've told Dean you suspect him. I thought that you were safe as long as the murderer didn't know that?'

'All the more reason why we have to continue to act quickly.'

'All the more reason to leave it to the police.' Ethelred turned to Wendy. 'You agree, don't you, Wendy?'

Wendy looked blank for a moment, then said, 'No, Elsie's right. Until the police get here, this crime scene and the safety of the guests are my responsibility and mine alone. First, I have to stop the others getting access to the woodshed to preserve whatever evidence is still here. That means securing the door – usually I just push a stick into the catch, but I think I've got a spare padlock somewhere. At the same time, if there is a further risk to life, I have to do everything I can to reduce that too. So long as we have no idea who killed Claire, I don't know who or what I am trying to protect people against. If you think you can make any progress at all, then you should certainly ask what questions you wish and report back to me. I couldn't forgive myself if somebody else was killed and I'd done nothing to prevent it. And now, if you'll excuse me, I also need to go back to the house. I want to tell the others what has happened, before Dean does. It should come from me, not him.'

We watched her go. Now it was just the two of us and, on the other side of a still unlocked door, one dead body.

'That wasn't quite what I expected Wendy to say,' said Ethelred.

'But she's right,' I said. 'Look, the police can't get here and, even if they could, we have one big advantage over them. We're pretty well acquainted with all of the suspects by now. We've already had a first pass at finding out who might have a motive – I mean, we've talked to everyone, haven't we? We've observed their behaviour. But now we need a second pass. We need to interview them again – properly.'

'Interview them all? I thought you'd established that the murderer was Dean?'

'He's certainly the prime suspect.'

'Because of the note?'

'No, not just because of the note. It's obvious. Dean is with the CIA. Claire has found out about the operation here. So, in a way yet to be established, he discovers that she's on this course, travels up here, wading through snow for the final four miles because he's so desperate to shut her up. She sees him and is immediately suspicious but there's nothing she can do – she's trapped. He tries to break down her defences – he sends her a note saying that he's basically on her side. He invites her into the woodshed at very short notice.'

'How do you know it's short notice?'

'Because of Wendy's jacket. Claire didn't have time to fetch her own and borrowed Wendy's. Accountants don't nick stuff, Ethelred, or even borrow it without permission. Most of them never even bunked off school. It would have gone against all her instincts to take a coat without the owner's express authority. So, it's got to be short notice. And that also points to Dean because, unlike the others, he couldn't have fixed it up last night or earlier this morning.'

'OK. What next?'

'She heads off to the shed at once. As she comes through the door in Wendy's borrowed blue jacket, he grabs her. He's a strong lad, let's not forget – the strongest man here by a fair bit, with the greatest respect to Jasper and Hal. He puts his hand over her mouth and wraps the rope, which is conveniently in the shed, round her neck. He pulls it tight. She falls to the floor. He checks her pulse and smiles cruelly. Then he races back to the sitting room to establish his alibi, where he fortunately finds you waiting. When a search party is got up, he immediately volunteers because he wants to know what the reaction is when the body is found. He goes out of his way to tell Wendy to try resuscitation, even though there's no point, because it will look good for him when the police come. Then he suddenly realises to his horror that his note must still be in the pocket of the coat. He advises against searching the body, planning to come back later and retrieve the note himself.'

I paused and waited for the compliments that I knew were my due. Hell, I could churn out crime novels one after the other, if there was decent money in it.

'But Wendy said she would lock the shed,' Ethelred said. 'He knows he can't come back.'

'With a crap padlock of the sort you'd use on a woodshed? Who's going to be nicking wood up here? He'd just snap it between his finger and thumb.'

'Because he's the strongest man here by a fair bit?' asked Ethelred. 'Stronger than Jasper and Hal – those were your exact words, if I remember.'

'I'm so sorry,' I said, patting him on the arm. 'And stronger than you of course. Much, much stronger than you. My apologies for not saying so at once.'

'Apology accepted,' he said. 'If Dean did it, he must have acted pretty quickly. He was back in the sitting room by ten past.'

'You remember the time then?'

'I recall it very well,' he said. 'You came in about five minutes later, just as the clock was striking. So he had a bit over ten minutes, dining room to sitting room via the woodshed. The problem is it's all very much dependent on Claire knowing he worked for the CIA – or MI6 if you prefer that version. We've no reason to believe he is.'

'He was talking to Wendy,' I said. 'You saw him. He told her Claire knew—'

'Not Claire specifically. It was people generally who might already know something.'

'But think – if they're both with some intelligence agency—'

'Which is doubtful in the extreme.'

'But possible.'

'Possible but doubtful.'

I shrugged. That was good enough for me.

'There's no evidence that Wendy and Dean had ever spoken to each other before this week,' said Ethelred, 'let alone that they're part of some conspiracy.'

'Yes, but consider this: one unanswered question is how Dean knew Claire would be here. Wendy must have told him. She had the list of all of the participants. She'd had it for months.'

'I think,' said Ethelred, 'we can rule out any solution that involves the CIA. It's hardly likely that they would set up an operation in such a way that almost every crime writer in the country would know about it. Even if they did, Dean and Wendy are most unlikely operatives. They are both English, not American. Dean is a trainee solicitor. Unless his employers are also in on the scheme, I don't see how he gets the time off to be a spy for anybody. As for Wendy, we know nothing about her to suggest she has any links with any secret service organisation.'

'Which is what you would expect if she did have,' I said.

'Time is getting on,' said Ethelred. 'If we are to establish who the killer is before you retire to your high-tech bath again, perhaps we should focus on the facts rather than speculate on rather unlikely scenarios? If we are really going to interview everyone as you propose, I think we should begin with Jasper. He was, after all, the last one – or the last we're aware of – to see Claire alive.'

'I know Jasper,' I said. 'I think he's much more likely to let his defences down if questioned by an attractive young lady.'

'Fair enough. But where are you going to find one of

those . . . oh, you mean yourself?'

'Obviously.'

'OK,' he said. 'I'll go and talk to Dean then.'

'And Fliss,' I said.

'I agree, she ought to know something. But haven't you just talked to Fliss?'

'Yes, but it went a bit weird. It might be better if you conducted the interview.'

He didn't look as surprised as he should have done.

'Fine, I'll talk to Fliss first, then Dean. You deal with Jasper as you see fit. I'm assuming that Wendy has already told everyone what's happened – if Dean didn't get there first. They'll all be in shock and Fliss most of all. I don't know what she'll be prepared to say to either of us. I can't force her to do anything she doesn't want to do, even in my role as bad cop.'

'I never said that you were a bad cop,' I pointed out. 'Only that I was a good one. You can't just appoint yourself bad cop. It doesn't work like that.'

'I'm very happy not to be a cop at all,' said Ethelred.

I nodded. He was just a civilian helping me with my enquiries. Making coffee. Doing the filing. Addressing me as 'ma'am'. Or maybe as 'Super'. An investigation of this sort merited the presence of a senior officer.

'Well, at least we now know what our third unexpected incident is,' I said. 'Big Billy Goat Gruff has just gone right over the bridge.'

THE SECOND PASS

CHAPTER THIRTEEN

Ethelred

'It's such a shock,' said Fliss, staring out of the window at the snow. 'I can't quite take it in. I mean, she was right here in this room with me only this morning. But in a funny way, I'd expected it.'

'Really?'

'Yes. From the moment we got the train at King's Cross. She seemed to be . . . I don't know . . . plotting something. Then when we got here – it was clear that she hadn't made a mistake. She'd always intended to arrive early.'

'You actually thought she might be killed?'

'No, no – I didn't say that. I just meant that she seemed to be getting too deep into something. Something risky. But something that needed her to be here yesterday evening.'

'Concerning Dean?'

'I don't think she knew Dean would be here at all – she definitely didn't expect to see him yesterday evening. And when he did arrive, she seemed as surprised as anyone to see him, didn't she?'

'Yes,' I said. 'She certainly seemed to be. And Dean said something about her not expecting him. Did *you* know he was coming?'

'Me? Why should I?'

'Because he turned up,' I said. 'He seemed to be expecting Claire to be here. So, somebody must have told him. Other than you and Wendy, who could have done that?'

'No idea. It wasn't me. You'll have to ask Dean.'

'I shall. Elsie said she had a talk with you, by the way.'

'About Dean? Yes, that was strange – though maybe less strange in retrospect.'

'The note Dean wrote to Claire was certainly odd.'

'Note? What did it say?'

'I can't remember the precise wording, and Elsie now has the note carefully stored away – at least I hope she does. But it was something like he was a friend, in spite of what she might think, and he'd like to talk to her.'

'Then she goes to the woodshed for clarification of that and gets strangled?' said Fliss.

'Yes, while wearing Wendy's coat. Which suggested to Elsie that it must be a last-minute arrangement. Claire wouldn't have just taken a coat without permission. Not unless she was desperate.'

'True. She was a bit of a goody-goody – at least over things like that. It would have instinctively felt wrong. But she might have done if she needed a coat urgently and didn't have time to come back and fetch her own.'

'I suppose you didn't see when Claire received the note?' I said.

Fliss shook her head. 'No, I'd have said straight away. I was with her most of the time and I really can't think when he could have passed it to her. Claire was avoiding him as much as she could. But, like I told you all before, I didn't see her after lunch – so maybe then?'

'Here's another odd thing, though. The note said Dean needed to speak to her but it didn't say where or when. There was nothing to tell her to go to the woodshed. And they didn't go there together because Jasper saw Claire alone, leaving the front door then heading round to the back – he thought it was Wendy at the time, of course. And there was only one set of footprints from the front. So how did Claire know where to go?'

'Maybe Dean told her where to meet when he passed her the note?'

'So, if he spoke to her, why write the note in the first place? And if he didn't think he'd get a chance to speak, why not mention the woodshed in the note? The note, as it stands, simply doesn't work.'

'More good questions for Dean, don't you think?' said Fliss.

'And Claire doesn't seem the sort of person to just wander into danger,' I said. 'Accountants don't – even forensic accountants.'

'I said to Elsie there was a lot more to Claire than met the eye. She might look at first sight as if she wouldn't say boo to a goose, but she was a complex character. She may have been fending Dean off, but she was doing her best to reel Hal in. And while at first sight you'd think her the silent type, she could gossip till the cows came home, that one.'

124

'I see,' I said. Claire had certainly told me a great deal about Fliss's love life without any provocation at all.

'It wasn't safe to tell her anything,' said Fliss, as if reading my mind. 'Like a lot of basically quite shy people, she discovered that others found her more interesting if she had something juicy to regale them with. I don't think she did it deliberately. I don't think she even knew she'd done it half the time. She once told me in no uncertain terms that she could keep a secret in a way that I couldn't. As if! In a way, it's why we drifted apart. I mean, with your close friends, you need to be sure that what you tell them won't be repeated all round town, don't you?'

'Yes,' I said. 'You certainly do.'

'Hang on,' said Fliss. 'I bet she's already told you masses about me, hasn't she?'

'A little,' I said. 'She implied you were having problems at home.'

'Implied? Claire rarely leaves it at implying.'

'She said you were having an affair with James but wanted to stay with Ollie. That was the gist of it.'

'Thanks, Claire,' said Fliss. 'Thanks a bunch. Loyal and discreet to the very end.'

'Was that the only reason you drifted apart?'

'I suppose a lot changed. I married Ollie. We were a couple. We did things with other couples. Sometimes I thought of inviting Claire to something, but she didn't fit in any more. It wasn't just that there was only one of her – she simply wasn't into joint mortgages and babies and keeping-in-touch days during your maternity leave.'

None of that struck me as terribly interesting either, but

then, like Claire, I can't claim to be a couple. I used to be, but I'm not one any more.

'And you in turn lost interest in writing,' I said. 'It can become a bit of a bore to listen to all that stuff from somebody who is still into it – the triumph of writing five thousand words in a day, the despair when you then have to delete four and half thousand of them . . .'

'True,' said Fliss, with more feeling than I had expected.

'You weren't jealous of her?' I asked her.

'What are you implying? That I'd bump her off because I was resentful of her talent?'

'I didn't say that.'

'But you're thinking it,' said Fliss. 'You actually think I might have killed her, don't you? Hell, she hadn't even really made it. Just the first half of a potentially brilliant debut. It would have been a success of course, if there was any fairness. But she still had a long way to go. I'd have probably waited for the *Sunday Times* review before deciding one way or the other about murdering her.'

'Well, somebody thought there was good reason to do it now. Look, Fliss, I'm just trying to get a picture of how things were. For example, I don't understand why, if you'd ceased to be friends and you didn't want to write, you carried on coming to conferences.'

'Not to lure her into a woodshed and then strangle her. I mean there must be other ways of stopping writers writing.'

'Not in my experience,' I said. 'As Elsie has observed in the past, only kindly death releases us. So, why did you come?'

'Well, my family originally lived round here – don't be

fooled by my Birmingham accent – we moved down that way when I was a toddler. Before that the Verity family had lived in Yorkshire since the times you write about in your Master Thomas books. You don't stop being Yorkshire just because you live in the West Midlands and sound like a Brummie.'

'You could have had a family holiday up here.'

'I suppose that's sort of the point. I couldn't. Things are a bit tense at home, if you see what I mean. Sometimes I need to get away. This is better than having to think about whether I really want James or Ollie. Or it was until just after lunch. Then it wasn't quite so much.'

'Claire said you should stick with Ollie, if that helps at all.'

'I wonder how many people Claire has told. Do you think any of my friends don't know yet?'

'Hard to say. If you have a lot of friends, maybe not all of them.'

Fliss shook her head. 'Well, I doubt if anything she said here will get back to Ollie. But if I had a big secret – I mean a really big one – then Claire is the last person I'd want to know all about it.'

'Me too,' I said.

CHAPTER FOURTEEN

Elsie

I knocked on Jasper's door. He opened it and his dark-jowled face peered round.

'Oh, it's you,' he said.

'Hoping for somebody else?' I asked.

He blinked. 'Not really. What can I do for you, Elsie?'

'Well, could I come in?'

'Yes, I suppose so,' he said.

It wasn't the warmest of welcomes, but I had yet to establish that I was a bona fide *femme fatale*, like a Raymond Chandler blonde bombshell but with immense influence in the London book trade.

'What a lovely room,' I said.

'It's OK,' he said.

'And that looks a very comfortable bed. Very comfortable indeed.'

He looked at it.

'Yes,' he said. 'It's OK.'

'But – oh dear – I shouldn't be saying things like that, should I? Not to you.'

'I can't see why not. You're quite right. It is very comfortable.'

'I mean, I might give you the wrong idea.'

'In what way?'

I sighed. Chandler's characters were so much quicker on the uptake than this guy.

'I mean that you might think I was trying to seduce you.'

'No. That hadn't occurred to me at all. Were you?'

I had been about to drape myself all over him in a sultry manner, but I decided that, on second thoughts, I couldn't be arsed. He wasn't remotely worth the effort.

'Just sit on the bloody bed,' I said. 'I'll sit in a chair over here and ask you about the murder.'

'It's not that comfortable for sitting on – a bit too soft.'

'Sit, Jasper, or I'll come over there and seduce you properly. OK?'

He sat.

'Now,' I said, 'you were the last person to see Claire alive.'

'I suppose I was,' he said. 'I thought it was Wendy at the time, of course. I mean the blue coat.'

'And how did she strike you? Worried? Tense?'

'I didn't see her face. But she was certainly in a hurry.'

'Heading for the back of the house?'

'That's right. It seemed odd.'

'How?'

'Well, there was a lot of snow around. If you wanted to go to the back of the house, why not go out of the back door

129

rather than the front? Less wading through drifts in the cold.'

Yes, that did seem odd.

'But,' he continued, 'it would have been much odder if it had been Wendy. Once I knew it was Claire . . . well, perhaps she was a bit lost – didn't know the quickest way to wherever she was going.'

'To the woodshed?'

'Oh no. I don't think that's where she was going.'

'But she was strangled in the woodshed shortly after. So, based on that fact, my guess is that's what she did.'

'Yes, later she went there. But not straight away.'

'How do you know that?'

'Because I heard her voice about five minutes later.'

'So that would be about one-fifteen?'

'I think so – yes. I saw Wendy, as I thought, and, knowing she didn't approve of smoking anywhere, I wandered off in the other direction to find somewhere more peaceful to light up. I must have selected a spot just outside the kitchen. There was a bit of banging – I guess Jenny was washing up and the window was open. Kitchens can get steamy, can't they? There was some conversation I couldn't quite make out, then I heard Claire say something like "And I'll have a cup of coffee if you don't mind, Jenny."'

'In the middle of washing up? What did Jenny say?'

'I don't know. I was trying to have a quiet fag, not eavesdropping. Having realised I was outside the kitchen, I didn't want my smoke drifting in and giving the game away. So I went a bit further and found a nice sunny corner to enjoy my ciggie. I chucked the butt into a convenient snow drift and came back inside.'

'It didn't seem odd that Claire had gone round to the back door and then, from there, to the kitchen?'

'Not at the time – as I keep saying, I thought I'd seen Wendy, not Claire at all. There was no reason why, then or a few minutes later, Claire should not have been in the kitchen or anywhere else. But later, yes, it did strike me that Claire had taken a very long way round to the woodshed in that blue coat.'

'You didn't say that before.'

'I'd assumed we were all going to give our evidence to the police, not each other. To be perfectly honest, it's as important that we don't influence each other's evidence as it is that we don't interfere with the crime scene. Once one witness says something publicly, there's a danger that the others think they remember the same thing. It's a big problem when taking evidence from a group like this who've had a chance to compare notes. But I'm happy to talk to you – just so long as you don't tell everyone else.'

'You're certain the voice was Claire's?'

'One hundred per cent. Her voice was quite distinctive. very middle class but also clearly a young person's voice. It's not like yours or Wendy's.'

'Thanks,' I said.

'And not like Fliss's – she's from Birmingham, I think. Even less like Jenny's Yorkshire accent. Oh, and it certainly wasn't a man's voice. No, that was Claire's voice. Couldn't have been anyone else's. I'll swear to that.'

'So, Claire was killed after one-fifteen?'

'Must have been if she was ordering a coffee then and

131

thought she'd live long enough to drink it.'

'And you say you stayed outside, not far from the kitchen?' I asked.

'No further away than I needed to be. The snow wasn't good for a long walk.'

'Any proof of that?'

'The cigarette butt may still be in the drift.'

'I'm sure there is a butt in a drift. There's no proof of when you put it there.'

'And my footprints,' he said.

We looked out of the window. Snow was starting to fall again. He would do well not to rely too much on the footprints to prove his innocence. I pointed this out him.

'I'm not sure I'll need any proof,' he added. 'I mean, why on earth would I have wanted to kill Claire? The police are hardly going to suspect me.'

'You looked pretty sick after your conversation with her, last night.'

'Did I?'

'It looked as if she'd given you a hard time.'

He swallowed hard. 'She just wanted a chat.'

'That's all?'

'Absolutely.'

'So, what did she want to talk to you about, Jasper?'

He paused for quite a long time.

'Getting published,' he said experimentally. 'She wanted my help.'

'Are you sure? It seems to me that you could have just said no, if it was in any way inconvenient. I'd have said she'd given you some very bad news indeed. There's no point in lying. We all saw your face.'

'Yes, I suppose you did. This is slightly awkward . . . Elsie, can I be completely honest with you?'

'Of course,' I said with my very sweetest smile. 'You can trust me.'

'No, I mean really,' he said.

'Just tell me,' I said.

'OK, it's like this. I don't need to explain to you that things have changed a bit – what you can say and what you can't.'

'I guess.'

'Well, back in the infancy of social media I may have said one or two things on Twitter that would now be regarded as a bit . . . well, unacceptable. Sexist, if you can imagine that.'

'I *can* imagine that,' I said, soothingly. 'Tell me more, Jasper.'

'I mean, you're not the sort of person who takes offence easily, are you?'

I did a quick estimate of Jasper's value as a prospective client of my agency. I'm good at calculating fifteen per cent of most things.

'I never take offence at anything one of my own writers says,' I replied.

'I mean, a bit of banter . . . that's all it was. I didn't mean I'd really *done* any of the stuff I tweeted about. The tweets do not in any way represent my views now.'

'I am not here to judge you,' I said. 'Think of me as a priest.'

'I'm an atheist.'

'OK, think of me as a very good friend who hasn't been to church lately.'

133

'Thank you. What I said wasn't illegal. Hell, people have said worse on camera. Not knowingly on camera, but still they said it.'

'I don't doubt you.'

'But even so if it all came out, just as the television series was getting under way . . .'

'The film company might not welcome the bad publicity.'

'The actors might walk off the set – well, the women might. The men probably wouldn't be bothered, though they might have to pretend they were.'

'Can you make the series just with men?'

'No. My protagonist is a female forensic accountant. Take her out of the plot and not much happens. It would just be shots of ledgers and spreadsheets.'

'A forensic accountant like Claire?'

'Yes, but blonde and with short skirts.'

'How short?'

'Very.'

'You're absolutely sure those tweets don't represent your views now?'

'Not a bit.'

'And the story is all based on your own experience as an accountant?'

'I wasn't an accountant. I trained as an accountant. I was a banker. Harefoot International.'

'And Claire was going to reveal what you tweeted?'

'I *think* that's what she was saying.'

'What did she say exactly?'

'I can't remember *exactly*. She talked a bit about wanting my help and I was a bit evasive, I admit. Then she said she'd always enjoyed my tweets. I said, really? She said, yes, especially the ones I'd done a few years back. Very amusing, she said. Of course, she added, you probably couldn't say things like that now. Not with all this political correctness. Professional suicide. I offered that, with the benefit of hindsight, maybe I shouldn't have said what I did. I apologised if they had given any offence. You know the sort of stuff you have to say if you want to sound sincere? She laughed and said she wasn't planning to retweet them. She probably wouldn't have time, not since she was writing her book. Especially if it got published and she had lots of editing to do and a sequel to write.'

'Anything else?'

'Maybe some other stuff – it's not that important now, is it? I mean, I didn't take notes. The threat was clear enough.'

'And what she said worried you?'

'Of course it did. If I didn't help her, she'd retweet this stuff from years ago and my name would be mud and the TV series would be cancelled.'

'But she didn't say that specifically?'

'Blackmailers don't,' he said.

It was one of those things that sounds quite convincing coming from somebody like Jasper, who must have done masses over the years that he could be blackmailed about. Later it seemed to me that a really efficient blackmailer would say precisely what they knew and how many Bitcoins they wanted. But I had bigger fish to fry.

'So, you decided to kill her . . .' I said.

'What?' he asked incredulously.

'You knew she could destroy your career. So, when you

135

saw her after lunch, heading for the back of the house, you followed her. You caught her somewhere near the back door and asked if you could continue the previous evening's discussion in the woodshed. You had an offer that might interest her very much. She smiled and followed you. Once there, you took the rope and strangled her. Then you went off for a cigarette to calm your nerves. While you were smoking, you made a decision – you'd say that you saw her outside, then later heard her voice, thus moving the likely time of her death to one when you couldn't have done it.'

Jasper shook his head. 'Of course not. Yes, her threats shook me up. But I thought about it overnight. First, I don't need the money from the TV series. Second, half the writers I know actually hate the screen adaptation of their books – having a total stranger appointed as scriptwriter with plenipotentiary powers to change the carefully constructed plot, wreck the subtle characterisation, screw up the dialogue and write whole episodes that are merely loosely based on your series at best. The loss of control. The loss of readers, who see it on telly and think your books must be equally crap. Did I really want that? As for my general reputation, there's plenty worse out there, tweeted by people who still have jobs. I'd lose a few readers but I'd gain others. It was inconvenient. I'd rather she didn't. But it wasn't the end of the world. So, as far as I was concerned, let her do her worst.'

'Why tell me about it?'

'Because you very cleverly spotted that I was a little distressed. And I suspect it may now come out. Claire was hardly the most discreet person. She's probably already told Fliss. Maybe others. I'd just like you to promise, if you hear this stuff from anyone else, you'll take what I've said into account, not start looking back on Twitter. It isn't relevant in any way at all.'

'I can't look back on anything. I love a bit of boys' banter, especially career-ending banter, but there's no signal here.'

'I mean later. Look, Elsie, none of you has to say anything to the police. It doesn't need to come up in court. The coroner doesn't need to know. It doesn't need to be reported in the press as part of the evidence given by Claire's closest friend. You can just ignore it all. It's not why Claire died. I didn't kill her.'

'So, who did?' I asked.

'Well, Dean did surely?'

'Because of the CIA thing?'

'That's unlikely,' said Jasper.

'I thought you said it was quite possible this was a safe house – you told Ethelred you had lots of inside information on the world of espionage or was that just random bullshit?'

He shook his head impatiently. 'I only mean there's a much simpler explanation. Dean followed her here. He wrote her that note. He was clearly smitten. She wasn't. He invited her to the woodshed to declare his love, or whatever his plan was. She rejected him with a finality born of irritation with his constant unwanted attentions. To ensure that he would finally get the message, she laid it on as thick as she could. She left no stone unturned. He was left feeling like something that had just crawled out from underneath one of the stones in question. He wouldn't be the first to kill somebody under those circumstances. Can I get off the bed now? I'm getting backache.'

'Yes,' I said. 'We're done, Jasper. We're done.'

CHAPTER FIFTEEN

Ethelred

'I was expecting the good cop,' said Dean.

'Busy elsewhere,' I said.

'What can I do for you?'

'Just a chat.'

'Fire away then.'

'I was just wondering what made you come on this course,' I said.

'Much the same as everyone else. I talked to Claire in Scotland and liked the sound of it. I hadn't thought of writing fiction until then, but I decided to give it a go. Lawyers do write crime fiction: Jeffery Deaver, Chris Ewan, Martin Edwards, M. R. Hall, Cyril Hare. So, I looked up the course on the internet and registered just before Christmas.'

'Claire told you she was coming here?'

'Yes, I think she'd already booked at that stage.'

So that explained very simply what had appeared to be a puzzle that was inexplicable – for some people – without reference to the CIA. Claire had informed Dean herself that she would be here. There was no need at all to invoke anyone's secret service. It was a helpful reminder that you can overcomplicate things if you're not careful.

'And you said you're currently a solicitor?'

'I've just qualified.'

'Congratulations.'

'Thank you. But my newly acquired legal brain tells me that you're not here for a casual chat about my literary ambitions. That and the fact that Elsie has already accused me of the murder. I don't think you want to know how I'm going to have time to be a hotshot lawyer and write novels. I mean, you're not interviewing me for *Mystery People*.'

'Not at the moment.'

'Obviously I'm not asking to be accompanied by a legal representative. I've done plenty of criminal law during my training. I'm just telling you, for the record, that any refusal on my part to answer any or all of your questions should be viewed in the context of your having no right to ask them. Or do you think that you have some authority to do this?'

'Wendy has agreed that it would be a good idea to find out as much as we can as quickly as we can. For our own safety. But you're quite right that you don't have to cooperate in any way whatsoever. Of course you're going to have to explain that note to somebody. Eventually.'

'If Elsie doesn't lose it. But I don't need to explain it now to you. It has nothing to do with Claire's death.'

'It was all just a coincidence then? You pursued her here. You wrote her a note. Then she died. No connection between any of those things?'

'None at all, Ethelred. I didn't pursue Claire here. I've told you how I knew she'd be here, but that's not why I came.'

'So, when did you last see Claire?'

'At lunch. She was sitting on the far side of the table.'

'Deliberately away from you?'

'I think she may have misinterpreted my being friendly for something else. It didn't bother me in any way. I had no plans to be more than friendly. It was pretty clear in Scotland that she was after Hal.'

'Was it?'

'I'd say so. I think it was probably obvious to everyone else as well.'

'So you left them to it?'

'No. It didn't strike me as a good idea at all. Hal is married with a young kid. Happily married, I'd have said. And Claire was frankly being a bit obvious. People noticed. It was only going to end in tears. I didn't want that for either of them.'

'So, what did you do?'

'Not much really. It's not as if either was a close friend and I could take them to one side and have a chat about their personal life. But sometimes Claire would hint that I should leave them alone and I deliberately ignored the hint.'

'That was very moral and upright of you.'

He gave me a crooked and unlawyerly smile.

'Just out of interest,' I said, 'have you ever heard a rumour that Fell Hall was run by MI6 or somebody?'

He looked genuinely perplexed. 'Really? Why on earth would they want to do that?'

141

'One theory is that it's used as a safe house.'

He drew a deep breath. 'Yes, I can see that. It would be easy to smuggle people in. Then there are whole months when nobody comes up here. And there's only one proper road – you'd be able to spot somebody heading this way, long before they got here – but loads of footpaths leading away up into the fells. Nobody would know whether that story is true except Wendy – oh, and Jenny, I suppose. I doubt if Jenny misses much at all. It would be difficult to keep something like that from her, for all that Wendy treats her as a lowly minion. But is there any proof of the MI6 thing?'

'Merely rumour. Plus a slightly more common rumour about the CIA. And Mossad. And the KGB.'

'And the French? Couldn't it be their safe house?' said Dean flippantly. 'What's their secret service called?'

'They used to have a thing called the Deuxième Bureau until 1940,' I said. 'Quiet a catchy name. You'd have to be very keen on spy novels to know what it's called now. I certainly don't.'

'And you're saying that Wendy is running the operation for whoever it is?'

'You tell me. What exactly was your discussion with Wendy about, by the stairs the other day?'

'You're saying our conversation was espionage-linked?'

'Again, you tell me. You were in on the whole conversation. I just overheard part of it.'

'Which is all you needed to hear,' he said. 'I don't have to tell you everything or explain why I won't tell you something or expand on something you had no business to hear in the first place. The conversation had no relevance to Claire's death – or none that I know of.'

'Wendy said it was about the course.'

'Fine. You have your answer.'

'And you have the expertise to advise Wendy on running courses?'

'She might have asked what I thought, as a first-time attender. How the place was advertised. Why I'd chosen this course rather than others. Whether being out here in the wilds, with no contact with the outside world, was a plus or a minus – for normal course participants, not spies. I might have given her my advice. That's the lawyer's job. We get involved in other people's business. People tell us stuff they wouldn't entrust to their priest. They have to.'

'Yes, you'd have to be good at keeping secrets,' I said.

'We are. I enjoy your books by the way – especially *All on a Summer's Day*. Very well told – not a wasted word.'

'Thank you,' I said. The compliment was not unwelcome but, in a strange way, made me trust him slightly less than I had before.

I got up. It was time to go and find Elsie. Like Dean, I was doubtful about her ability to keep the note safe and was far from convinced that it was irrelevant.

CHAPTER SIXTEEN

Elsie

'That's interesting about Jasper hearing Claire's voice,' said Ethelred. 'If he did hear her at one-fifteen, then it lets Dean off the hook completely. He was with me by ten past, and I didn't lose sight of him until we went off to search for her.'

'Jasper could be lying,' I said.

'Why?'

'To cover up that he did it.'

'In which case it still wasn't Dean,' said Ethelred. 'It was Jasper. So, Dean's off the hook either way.'

'But he wrote the note,' I said. 'He admits it.'

'I hope you still have it,' said Ethelred.

'How often have I lost a piece of evidence that was vital to a conviction?' I asked. 'Don't count on your fingers like that. It really isn't that often.' I checked my chocolate pocket. The paper was still there, though sadly the chocolate had now gone.

Ethelred looked round my sitting room again. The

contrast with his own accommodation was, he had informed me, quite remarkable. My bathroom alone was bigger than his entire quarters. It was also much warmer, being nearer the boiler and having windows that fitted very well. A vase of flowers, a nice touch, sat on the coffee table. I wondered just for a moment whether to offer to swap with him, so that he could have the pleasure of saying, no, I deserved every square inch of deep-pile carpet. But there was always a small chance he'd say yes, which would have been awkward. Right now, this wasn't so much a luxury suite as the operations centre of a murder investigation. I needed the largest bathroom and the fluffiest towels I could get, or somebody else might die horribly. I didn't want that on my conscience for the rest of my life.

'I still don't quite trust Dean, though,' said Ethelred. 'He seems decent enough. I believe him when he says Claire told him she'd be here. I believe that he does have an interest in being a writer. I believe that he hadn't heard that Fell Hall might be a safe house. But he does like to poke his nose into things. I mean the advice he was giving Wendy. I'm sure that, like most courses, there's a questionnaire at the end – didn't Wendy actually say somebody had commented favourably on the cosy fire? Wendy wouldn't have asked for Dean's feedback on day one, before he'd even had a chance to enjoy the amenities. At the very least, he just decided to approach her and give her his views. Just like when he realised Hal and Claire might be having a bit of a fling together in Scotland. He did his best to break it up, on the grounds that it was inappropriate. I'm sure he was right that it would all end

145

in tears, but that wasn't any of his business either.'

'Sometimes,' I said, 'if a very good friend of yours – one of the clients at your agency, say – was getting involved with a totally unsuitable woman, then it can be right to intervene on humanitarian grounds. Don't look at me like that, Ethelred, she was simply trying to manipulate you. You can see that now, can't you? It was for your own good.'

He asked which occasion I was referring to because – according to his recollection – I'd screwed up more than one promising relationship of his. I said I didn't keep count – it was all part of the service.

'Dean liked *All on a Summer's Day,*' Ethelred added proudly. It's always been his own personal favourite.

'But most people don't,' I said. 'Far too short. Scarcely more than a novella. And Sergeant Fairfax isn't the most sympathetic of characters – old, morose, an alcoholic and with few interests apart from Norman churches.'

'And baroque music,' he said.

'Oh yes, you put all of that stuff about *La Folía* in the last one,' I said. 'I mean, who cares if a zillion dead composers have used it? And most people will have no idea how it sounds because nobody listens to that sort of thing these days.'

'What sort of thing?'

'The sort of thing you listen to.'

'I thought it was interesting.'

'You thought Norman churches were interesting.'

'Fine,' he said. 'We still need to speak to Hal. Shall I do that?'

We tossed for it. My coin. Ethelred won but I didn't tell him he had.

'I'll let you know what Hal says,' I told him.

'I saw him in the sitting room, as I was on my way to talk to Dean,' said Ethelred. He felt that the coin-tossing hadn't been quite as transparent as he would have liked but, as the only senior officer available, I needed to take responsibility for things personally.

I felt for Dean's note again. I was pleased to discover I still hadn't lost it. How wrong Ethelred was to doubt me.

'Perfect,' I said.

Hal was alone in the sitting room. Logs were smouldering away in the grate, sending out more than enough heat and a pleasant smell of woodsmoke. The electric lights were on because little daylight was available. Windblown snow plastered the lower half of the windows. The upper half showed dark grey clouds and swirling flakes. Outside, Jasper's vital footprint evidence would have long since vanished. Gone too would be the mass of prints leading from the back door to the woodshed.

Hal was warming his hands in front of the fire. He did not look well – almost as if he'd seen a ghost and, at the same time, felt slightly guilty for having done so.

'Did you want me or Wendy?' he asked. 'Wendy was here a moment ago.'

'I'd like a word with you,' I said.

He nodded doubtfully. Seeing another ghost would be preferable. 'Wendy said you might.'

'Any objection?'

'No, Elsie, not if it helps clear things up. I mean, once the snow melts I'd like to be away from here as soon as I can. I've had enough of this place. I can't see how Wendy manages up here twelve months of the year.'

'A bit of a change from publishing.'

'Is that really what she did? I've heard various things.'

'Of course,' I said, 'if she had been put here by the CIA, then that would explain why there's no record of a past career anywhere.'

'On the contrary. If she'd been put here by the CIA I'm sure they would have invented a complete backstory for her, including made-up Twitter and Facebook accounts going back years.'

'Or maybe, knowing we'd think that, they wouldn't.'

'Well, I've only written one spy novel,' he said. 'Perhaps you should consult Mick Herron on that.'

I nodded. 'I loved *The Spy Before Yesterday*, of course,' I said, remembering that he might be detachable from his current agent. 'Did I say that before?'

'You didn't say it when I first sent you the manuscript,' he said. 'You said you hoped some other agent would like it better than you did.'

'Did I really?' I asked.

'You know perfectly well you rejected it.'

'No, I mean was I really that polite?'

'Yes.'

'I didn't say it was a pile of crap?'

'No.'

'There you are, then. I obviously loved it. It was only your previous sales figures that put me off. They were a pile of crap.'

'Well, Francis and Nowak took it. They saw its potential.'

'It's uniqueness,' I said.

'People have said that already, but thank you.'

'It was a big change of direction for you.'

'But it worked,' he said. He shook his head and turned back to the fire. He seemed to feel that he'd given me a shot at it and I'd missed my chance. Not necessarily, of course.

'So, how are things for you there? At Francis and Nowak?'

'Great.'

'You're not considering a move yet?'

'After a year?' He looked at me incredulously.

'To a really dynamic agency, run by somebody totally respected in the book trade for her uncanny instinct for what sells?'

'Move? When they supported me and got me a brilliant deal?'

'Yes.'

He shook his head again. 'So, do you want to know my movements over the past twelve hours or something?'

'OK, if you insist. Where did you go after lunch?'

'I went back to my room, picked up my notes and came back down again.'

'You were one of the last to arrive in the sitting room,' I said.

'And one of the first to leave the dining room, I think. I didn't rush back. There was no need to.'

'Did you see Claire?'

'After lunch? No. Oh, wait a minute – yes, very briefly. I think I said earlier: I looked into the sitting room as I was on my way to pick up the notes. Claire was in here, hunting for something.'

'Did she say what?'

'I didn't ask her. I just saw her. And she was so intent on what she was doing, I didn't like to disturb her. I was more concerned about finding my own notes for the afternoon session anyway.'

'And that would be at what time?'

'I don't know. Like I say, immediately after lunch. Probably just before one?'

I thought about it. If Claire was alive at one-fifteen, then the fact that she was also alive at five to one was not breaking news.

'You hadn't arranged to see her after lunch?' I asked.

'Why should I?'

'You must have been the first two to leave the dining room. You could have been meeting up.'

'Yes, we could, but she went to the sitting room, I went to my bedroom.'

'So you claim. Did anyone see you on the way to your room?'

'No, everyone else was still in the dining room.'

'You were quite pally with Claire in Scotland?'

'I suppose so. A bit.'

'Legend has it that it was quite a lot of a bit.'

'Were we being that obvious?'

'So I'm told.'

'By whom?'

'My lips are sealed.'

'So, that's Fliss or Dean then.'

I smiled in a sphinx-like way, because the answer was

both. But he'd never hear that from me.

'Nothing would get me to reveal the names of my informants,' I said.

'Informants? So it was both of them?' he said.

'Whatever,' I said.

'Claire and I – we didn't go to bed together.'

'No?'

'I knew what she wanted. She wanted me to take a look at her manuscript. She wanted introductions. That's all.'

'And in return?'

'Nothing. I was flattered she thought I had that sort of influence. *The Spy Before Yesterday* hadn't come out then. I was a fairly obscure writer of traditional humorous mysteries. Dean was a pain, but we managed to lose him. We had a few drinks together in my room. Talked about literature. Talked about her book. She was very complimentary about my work, very complimentary indeed. I was happy to listen to that for a bit.'

'No harm done then. If that really was all.'

'That was all. The only problem was that, as she was leaving, who should come past but Fliss, slightly pissed and on her way back to her own room.'

'Awkward.'

'As you say. Fliss raised her eyebrows and staggered on. I have to admit I was a bit worried about what she would say to people.'

'And what did she say?'

'Nothing that ever got back to me. Maybe she doesn't gossip like Claire. Maybe she was so drunk she didn't notice. I couldn't be sure. Later Claire sent me a brief email saying that she'd enjoyed our lengthy chat and would let me have the manuscript when it was ready. It didn't really seem to need a reply from me.'

'You deleted the email in case your wife saw it?'

'Obviously.'

'And then?'

'And then I more or less forgot about it all until I got here.'

'When Claire asked you to take a walk outside?'

'Yes.'

'And she said that she was about to inform the world?'

Hal swallowed. 'It was really just a chat about her writing.'

'I don't think so. Everyone saw your face when you came back into the room, Hal. Nobody is going to believe that's all it was. You may as well come clean.'

There was a long pause. 'Elsie, can I trust you?'

'Of course, Hal.'

'No, I really mean it.'

I wondered whether to try the priest analogy again, but he didn't seem any more religious than Jasper.

'Just tell me,' I said. 'I know plenty about you already. I can probably guess if you don't want to spell it out.'

'OK. I just wouldn't want this stuff becoming public knowledge. Claire said that she'd really enjoyed meeting me in Scotland. *In my room.* I said, yes it had been a great chat. She said not to worry that Fliss had seen her leaving. She'd explained to Fliss. Fliss wouldn't cause any trouble, though it was good it had just been Fliss. Others might have thought there was something going on. I said, OK. She said it was great that I'd promised to do whatever I could for her writing career. I said that I'd do as much as I was able to do. Anything within reason. She said excellent. That's what she was hoping for. She asked how my wife and son were. I said, good. Really fine. She said she'd love to meet my wife one day. And chat. She said she felt they had so much in common. I said, well, a bit in common maybe, but not much – hardly worth trying to find a window in their respective diaries. She said it would be fun – they could compare notes on me. I said, I'd never helped my wife with her manuscript. She laughed and said that wasn't what she meant. She'd like to tell my wife how grateful she was to me. How much I'd gone out of my way to help a young woman on her own. Chatting until the early hours in my bedroom. Fliss would back her up on that. I said that would be great – really, really kind of her to think of it – but actually quite unnecessary. I wouldn't want to put her to the trouble. She said, well, it was up to me, wasn't it? Whether that happened or not. That was my choice.'

'Anything else?'

'Isn't that enough?' he asked.

'She'd at least promised to keep quiet,' I said.

'I'm not sure she was capable of keeping quiet, Elsie. During our little chat – the one in my room – she'd dished the dirt on more people than I could count. She couldn't stop herself.'

'So, Claire having reminded you of your promises and so on and so on, you both returned to the sitting room?'

'Yes.'

'With you looking like death?'

'I didn't check in the mirror. Was that what I looked like?'

'Slightly worse, to be absolutely fair on death. You then thought about things overnight?'

'Little else.'

'And, at breakfast, you worked out you would have to kill her to keep her quiet.'

'What . . . ?' he said.

'Fine, over lunch then,' I said, charitably. 'Because that's the only way to deal with a blackmailer.'

'On the contrary. I'd decided to go along with it and give her whatever she wanted. You see, a regular blackmailer will take the money then come back a few months later for more. But this was different. If she became a successful author, she was off my back. Successful authors rarely blackmail people. Or, if she flopped, then she'd probably see that there was nothing more I could do. Either way, this was a one-off. Kill her? Why, when I just had to say nice things about the manuscript then write a blurb for the back of her book? And, as a crime writer, I am well aware how inadvisable it is to kill somebody when snowed in at a house in the middle of nowhere with no escape route. John Dickson Carr could have pulled it off, but not me.'

'Fine. Just don't try to leave,' I said. 'As you say, you're not John Dickson Carr. Not in real life.'

We looked at the windows. Only a tiny area of glass at the top of each pane was now clear of snow. The wind was howling across the moor. The sun would soon be setting.

'More of a Gladys Mitchell,' he said. 'I wasn't planning to go out tonight anyway.'

CHAPTER SEVENTEEN

Ethelred

Elsie departed, leaving me sitting on her sofa. She was right. It was very comfortable. Outside, the snow was still falling, in the way you wish it would at Christmas, but it almost never does. There was a hypnotic quality to it – flake following flake following flake following flake. Slow, silent, mysterious, wrapping the world in a white cocoon, from which we would eventually emerge, somehow purified and with a list of New Year's resolutions.

I mentally went through the roll call of suspects we had already spoken to: Fliss, Dean, Jasper and now Hal. That left Wendy and Jenny. Only Agatha Christie believed that staff were never the murderer. I decided that I might as well wander down and see if Jenny was in the kitchen.

The kitchen was, in its way, quite magnificent, designed to provide for a Victorian household. Though the owner of High End Hall – as it would then have been – disliked guests, he had apparently kept the usual quantity of staff, and the kitchen had had to cater for them and provide them with somewhere to assemble during the long, dark evenings. But, even allowing for that, it had been constructed on an impressive scale. The flickering light of the oil lamps would scarcely have reached its high, vaulted ceiling. At one end was a tall, gothic window with elaborate tracery and stained glass showing selected aspects of medieval food production. As with many things at the Hall, it was difficult to decide what was genuinely old and what was Victorian. The glass was clearly a romanticised view of Merrie England, heavy on hay-making, feasting and dancing, and light on the Black Death and the feudal obligations of the fourteenth century peasant. The colours were bright, and it was certainly no earlier than the middle of the nineteenth century. The fine stone tracery, on the other hand, looked original. I wondered if this was part of the earlier medieval farmhouse – the monk's kitchen or even refectory. Things are often not quite what they seem.

Jenny was almost lost in its vastness, sitting at the long, scrubbed kitchen table, which would almost have taken all of the tutors and students of a typical course, if Wendy had wanted to serve food there.

'Yes?' she said, as I came in.

'I wondered if I could give you a hand with anything,' I said.

'That's kind of you, Ethelred. I was about to start doing dinner. I've received no instructions to the contrary from her ladyship, so I'm assuming that the menu is unchanged. One place setting less, of course. It's going to be a miserable meal, whatever I cook.'

She sighed, then went over to the larder and came back with a sack of potatoes.

'Can you maybe give me a hand peeling a few spuds?' she asked.

For a while we sat side by side, getting into a steady rhythm of selecting a potato from the sack, running a peeler over it and throwing it into a large pan of water.

'You live round here?' I said.

'Yes, just outside town – not far from the railway station you arrived at the other day. I still live with my mum and dad. Property's not cheap round this way. Nice scenery. Nice houses. Nice prices.'

'Have you worked here from the beginning? I mean when they started to run courses?'

'No, not quite. Wendy recruited me after it had been going a year or so. She tried to manage on her own but couldn't. It's not full-time, even now – not like Wendy's job. Honestly, she prefers it when there's nobody else here. There are sometimes quite long gaps between courses, especially in the winter. So, when Wendy doesn't need me, I help on Dad's farm. It's not much more than a smallholding really, so he does it all himself mostly, but at lambing and harvest time he needs an extra hand or two. And I help Mum with the farm shop. Between the three things, I keep busy enough.'

'And you've always lived there?'

'I have. The family had a farm higher up the valley once. But it's bleak. You've no idea unless you've actually lived there. I'm not sorry we're where we are – even if that means a thirty-minute drive into work on my days here.

Actually the drive is a piece of cake. When I was younger, my brother and I would cycle up here sometimes. Long slog up but very easy going home again. In those days this house was still a ruin – a dangerous ruin, my mother would have said. We were warned to go nowhere near it. So, we had to lie when we got home. Eventually I knew every inch of it. Sometimes I look at it now and I remember how it was. It's sort of like having X-ray vision and being able to see behind the new tiling and plasterwork. I'm surprised neither of us got killed, the state it was in, but we had some good times here – in the house and up on the fells beyond. I've walked all the trails round here at some time.'

'It's a great part of the country to live in,' I said.

'It's all right,' she said. 'Growing up somewhere with a bit of life in it might have been better – London, say. Or Harrogate. I'd have liked that. Somewhere you can go out of your front door without everyone knowing your business.'

For a while we peeled potatoes silently. The saucepan gradually filled up.

'So, are you going to ask me if I killed Claire?' she said eventually. 'I assume that's what you're really here for, though I'm grateful for the help with the veg and all that.'

'I'm not sure what reason you'd have to kill her,' I said.

'Well, I didn't much like her,' said Jenny. 'I suppose you'd noticed that?'

'A bit,' I said.

'I don't want to speak ill of the dead, but she really was a snotty cow.'

'High maintenance?'

'Never-ending stream of demands, from first thing this morning.'

'You mean the coffee?'

'And never a thank you.'

'Sometimes,' I said, 'people who are shy can come across as a bit abrupt.'

'I guess. So, it was a bit obvious that I was pissed off with her?'

'You gave her less soup than anyone else at lunch.'

'So I did. Oh my God! And that was her last meal ever.'

'If we could see into the future, we'd do all sorts of things differently.'

'True. But still . . . what a bitch I was, eh? Another ladleful wouldn't have hurt me, would it?'

'Was lunch the last time you saw her though? Did she come into the kitchen afterwards?'

I was still not completely sure about Jasper's evidence. It seemed worth trying to confirm the exact time of Claire's visit.

'After lunch? Well, this sounds terrible too, but I can't remember.' She paused, frowned at the almost full saucepan and put the potato she was holding back into the sack, where it sat on top of the others, briefly reprieved. 'She was always in and out, but I was that busy with clearing away and putting things in the dishwasher. The Duchess of Sussex could have dropped by and I wouldn't have noticed.'

'So, you wouldn't remember exactly when or what she said?'

'No . . . not for certain. Hal came in – I'm sure of that. So did Wendy. Yes, and I'm pretty sure Claire did, now you mention it. At least, I think so. Sorry – does it matter?'

There wasn't any point in pressing her. If I said that Jasper remembered it was one-fifteen and Claire had requested coffee, then by the time the police came she'd be absolutely certain that is what had happened. I'd try not to trample over the crime scene any more than I had to. At least she hadn't contradicted Jasper. For what it was worth, Dean was still in the clear.

'Have you heard the rumour that Fell Hall is a CIA safe house?'

She laughed. 'I think Wendy started that one herself.'

'Really?'

'Well, there are plenty of other courses out there. Lots of competition. A rumour or two like that does us no harm. Not if you're trying to attract crime writers.'

'No truth in it?'

'Oh, come on, Ethelred, surely you don't believe it?'

'I assume, if it was true, you'd know?'

'I'd hope I'd know too. Strange Americans coming and going in the early hours of the morning. Demanding pancakes with bacon and maple syrup. Eggs over easy. Peanut butter and jelly sandwiches. Trust me, if there was anything like that, I'd have noticed.'

'What did Wendy do before she took up this job?'

'Publishing, I think.'

'Doing what exactly?'

'No idea. Bossing people around? Is that a job in publishing? That's what she's good at anyway.'

'She didn't say which publisher she bossed people around at?'

'Probably. It wouldn't have meant much to me. I'm sure she'd tell you. We don't chat much, Wendy and me – not small talk.'

'You don't get on with her?'

'We get on OK. She just doesn't encourage chat when there's work to be done. But that's what we're all supposed to be like up here, isn't it? Tight-lipped? "'Ear all, see all, say nowt." A nod and a grunt counts as conversation.'

'She seems a hard taskmaster.'

'Look, Ethelred, what exactly are you trying to get me to say? That I hate her guts? Yes, she expects you to share her total loyalty to the Trust. It's her life. I can see that. I mean, I'm sorry for her, really. I don't share her enthusiasm, but I do understand it. And working for her pays quite well – better than the farm or the shop. Better than most jobs round here for somebody with two GCSEs. Mum will understand why I had to stay last night. She'll have plenty more birthdays, God willing. If I didn't like it I'd have quit long since. OK?'

I shrugged. She'd been close to tears when Wendy had reprimanded her for dropping the bread. If she now said it didn't matter then I guessed it didn't matter. That seemed to be that.

'Can I help with anything else?' I asked. 'I'm ace at carrots.'

'Already done and in the fridge.'

'Brussels?'

'Never do them. Too many people don't like them. You'd be surprised how few things you can risk serving at an event like this. Fish. Chicken. Lamb and beef just about.

Not pork. Definitely no sprouts, except around Christmas, when people suddenly decide they like them after all. Right, I need to parboil the spuds, then get them in the oven.'

'Fine,' I said.

I stood up. I didn't have much to report back to Elsie.

'There's just one other thing before you go,' she said.

'Yes?' I said.

'Dean,' she said.

'What – him and Claire?'

'No. It's just that it's not the first time he's been here.'

'I thought he said it was his first creative writing event?'

'He did. When he arrived, I thought, there's a face I know – I asked him, if you remember, whether he'd been on one of the courses before.'

'Yes, I do remember that. But he said he hadn't.'

'He'd come here before though. It was only afterwards – after I'd taken him to his room – that I remembered when and why. It was back last summer. You have to understand that not many people come up the valley road unless they are coming here for a course. There are good hiking trails in the fells beyond the Hall, but it's a boring slog up that road. Long, steady climb by bike or on foot. Not a lot to see. There's a much better path, for the walkers anyway, along the ridge, with views halfway across the county, and that's the way most of them go. The ones that do get here are usually lost. You see them standing there looking at their maps and, if I don't have more important things to do, I sometimes go out and tell them which path to take. That's how I met Dean.'

'He was consulting his map?'

'No, he actually knocked at the door and asked for

directions. That doesn't happen very often at all – unless it's bucketing down and people need to shelter for a bit. So, I told him which way to go. Then he said, is this where they run the courses? Because there's no sign outside saying that's what we do, just one saying Fell Hall. If you're on a course here, you get joining instructions and the taxi drivers all know us. But if you just walk up the path, there's nothing to tell you this is anything other than a big private house. So, it wasn't surprising that he didn't know. I said, yes, we ran the courses. Then he said, are you the course director? I said no, she was out. Her ladyship *was* out actually, spending the day walking, don't remember where exactly, so it was true. But there was something about the way he asked that I didn't like. I'd have probably said she was out anyway. Shame, he said. He'd hoped to talk to somebody about coming on a course here. Obviously he didn't think I was good enough, with a dustpan and brush in my hand. I told him he should email, and to take the right-hand path, like I'd said. I don't know why, but I watched him to see he did take that path and kept watching until he was safely out of sight. Well, now he's back, exactly as promised. But you'd have thought he would have mentioned his previous visit, wouldn't you? At least to say thank you for the nice directions I gave him?'

'Yes,' I said. 'You'd have thought he would have mentioned it.'

CHAPTER EIGHTEEN

Ethelred

'So, did you get anything out of Hal?' I asked.

'He's determined to stay with Francis and Nowak,' said Elsie. 'But I'll work on him. I don't give up that easily.'

'I mean about Claire's death,' I said.

'Obviously I was coming to that. Hal had a long and rather inadvisable chat with Claire in his bedroom at the hotel in Scotland. Well, he claims that's all that happened. Believe it or not as you choose. Fliss saw Claire emerging in the early hours of the morning. She can probably be trusted to stay quiet, but Claire would have told everyone anyway, as a matter of course. He'd done a deal with Claire – he helps with getting the book published and she doesn't tell his wife how wonderful he is. Claire could have caused him minor problems at home but he had a way out of it – just do what the lady told him – something you do far too often, Ethelred, so there's no point in looking like that. No, I think we can rule Hal out as a murderer. What did you find out from Jenny?'

'Jenny doesn't dispute that Jasper could have heard Claire in the kitchen at one-fifteen – though she doesn't absolutely confirm it either. I'm still inclined to believe Jasper heard her voice then.'

'So that's Dean with no opportunity,' said Elsie. 'Though Jasper reckons Dean might have killed her, if he'd been able to, because Claire rejected him. It seems unlikely. I mean, Dean doesn't strike me as somebody who does things on the spur of the moment, any more than Wendy does. Hal conversely had slightly more opportunity than Dean, leaving the dining room early and coming back late, but really no motive at all.'

'I agree about Hal,' I said, 'but there's something about Dean that still worries me, in spite of his alibi. Jenny claims he showed up here last summer, nominally as a lost hiker, but asking to talk to Wendy. She thought it suspicious. So do I.'

'He hasn't mentioned a previous visit here,' said Elsie. 'Not to me.'

'Nor to me. And now he's here, he collared Wendy at the first opportunity,' I said. 'Also he told us that he heard of the course when speaking with Claire in Scotland. But he seems to have made up his mind to come here well before that. So, what's he playing at?'

'You're going to be rude about any suggestion that he might be a spy?'

'Yes.'

'No idea in that case, but he's being less than honest,' said Elsie. 'According to Fliss, he constantly pursued Claire in Glasgow. But you say his version is that he wasn't interested in her at all – he just wanted to stop her making a fool of herself with Hal.'

'It looks like it was Hal who was made a fool of,' I said. 'But I really think he and Dean are both in the clear as far as the murder is concerned.'

'Could Jenny have killed Claire? She clearly didn't like her,' asked Elsie.

'She said that, actually, it didn't bother her that much. She's guilty she didn't give Claire more soup, but there's not much that can be done about that now. But another odd thing: I thought Jenny was daggers drawn with Wendy, but she says not. She has no hard feelings and needs the work.'

'She doesn't resent being treated like a fourteenth century peasant?' asked Elsie.

'Her terms are slightly better than that. She can after all leave at any time, unlike the peasants. Of course, the problems of late fourteenth century peasants are somewhat exaggerated. Though they would have had to pay heriot and merchet, feudal obligations were being progressively converted to rent payments and daily wages rose significantly in the wake of—'

Elsie held up her hand. 'I'm happy to take your word for it,' she said. 'As for leaving, none of us can do that. More to the point, there's a killer amongst us, who may strike again at any minute. And we've got no phone signal. Now that's a problem the average medieval peasant never had to worry about.'

We looked out of the window. The snow was still

falling. It definitely wasn't the Middle Ages, but it was still getting dark. Very dark indeed.

'Thank you for updating me so thoroughly,' said Wendy.

Elsie had not wanted to update her at all, pointing out that she was most certainly a suspect and probably a spy. The less we told her the better. But I had said that our authority, such as it was, derived entirely from the fact that Wendy was responsible for the crime scene until the police could be contacted. So, we had tracked her down in her quarters at the back of the house and given her a summary of what we had discovered.

The rooms that she occupied had once been the housekeeper's – a spacious, low-ceilinged sitting room with a small and slightly bleak bedroom attached. The sitting room had doors that opened straight onto the fells, perhaps more useful in summer than now. What had been a store for the housekeeper's tools of the trade had been converted into a shower room. An oil lamp was burning on a side table in the main room, though it must have had electricity the same as the rest of the house.

'We have a dozen or so in case of power failures,' she said. 'It's a bit of a waste of our reserve supplies of oil to light them at other times, but I like it. Sometimes you want a softer focus to things. Particularly when you look in the mirror. Where do the years go?'

The sitting room was comfortably furnished but showed little of the occupant's personality. There were no pictures – just a framed map of the surrounding area. There were no books, though I suppose she had permanent access to the many bookshelves in the rest of the house. There were no family photos. There were no tongue-in-cheek souvenirs of foreign travel. The walls of both the sitting room and bedroom were plain white. The floor was stone throughout, with a large, soft, stone-coloured rug in the main room and a smaller but very necessary one by the bed. It was as if she had started the job yesterday and had not yet had a chance to unpack her own things.

'You were in publishing before you came here?' I said.

'Freelance,' she replied. 'Then I was away for a bit.'

'Out of the country?'

'Here and there. When you've no permanent base of your own, you dream of somewhere you can settle. I'm here now for as long as the Trust wants me.'

I looked round the room again.

'I've never needed much stuff,' she said. 'They provided me with all I asked for.'

'Jenny said the Trust was a generous employer.'

'Did she? She's always telling me she's due a pay rise. Personally, I've no complaints. I'm left to get on with things – select the wine and whisky I want to serve. Sometimes you find yourself, through no fault of your own, in places where you simply can't get decent malt. It's nice to drink it when you can.'

'Do you have a lot of contact with the founder of the Trust?'

'Hiram? No, not really. I send him a report every now and then. He has a lot of other interests. Fingers in many pies. He doesn't like to be bothered too much.'

'But you've met him?'

'Once. Otherwise, I've never needed to. He'd already been over, purchased the site and appointed builders before he advertised my post. I moved in as soon as my own quarters were ready and started to develop the courses. Most of the construction work had been done by then. I just let Hiram know that everything had been completed to a satisfactory standard. Initially there were payments from him made into the Trust bank account here, but now we're largely self-supporting.'

'Tricky to sign off building work you haven't commissioned.'

'I knew generally what he wanted – and what we were permitted to do with a listed building. Make it comfortable but keep as much of the original fabric as possible. Board over old features if necessary, but demolish nothing unless it was essential to do so. Preserve anything that future generations might value. I think they did a good job.'

'And he's an industrialist?'

'He's a fund manager. Deals with a very select group of clients. You need to be approached by him. You can't just ask him to invest for you.'

'He doesn't advertise?'

'He keeps as low a profile as he can. That's why it isn't the Shuttleworth Trust. There are a number of centres like this – all with a slightly different remit, but all running courses. There's one in South Africa, one in Israel, one in Thailand, one in Brazil.'

'And one in Butterthwaite,' said Elsie. 'Are the others in equally obscure places?'

'Sometimes,' said Wendy. 'But they all have a slightly

different remit. They're wherever they need to be.'

'So, you have no financial problems?' I asked.

'No, as I say, we make just about enough money. Hiram doesn't worry about turning a profit. Like I say, I'm free to select whatever wine I want to serve.'

'Very nice,' I said.

'Thank you.'

'But, in that case, why was Dean worried about competition?'

'I'm not sure he really is. He just thought I could do things differently. But I'm happy with things the way they are.'

'It seemed a very intense discussion,' I said.

'Well, it wasn't,' said Wendy. 'And frankly it's none of your business. Or his.'

'Jenny said that Dean turned up here last summer,' I said.

'Did he?' Wendy seemed genuinely surprised. 'Then that might explain . . .' She frowned.

'Might explain what?' asked Elsie.

'Nothing,' said Wendy. 'Nothing important. Only why he chose to come on this course now. Well, I'm grateful to you both, but we seem no closer to knowing who killed Claire. Isn't that what you're saying?'

I nodded and was about to stand when, to my dismay, I heard Elsie say: 'Unless you did, Wendy.'

Wendy nodded, unperturbed. 'You said we're all suspects. Of course, I know exactly where I was every minute after lunch, so I have no need to speculate as you do. I grant you that, unlike Dean, I have no cast-iron alibi.'

'So, what did you do?' asked Elsie.

'I helped Jenny take some things to the kitchen. Later, I came back here for a few minutes – there were some papers that I had mislaid, but I did eventually find them. Then, once I'd sorted everything out, I went straight to the sitting room. I'm sure I looked a bit flustered when I arrived. It was a bit of a rush.'

'You were the last to get there,' said Elsie.

'So you are saying that I potentially had more time than anyone to kill Claire? But what on earth would my motive have been?'

'You certainly didn't like her much,' said Elsie.

'She arrived early, that's all.'

'But it disrupted the preparation for the course.'

'That's the best you can do by way of a reason?'

'When she took you outside for a chat, you came back looking distinctly worried.'

'Yes, I suppose I did.'

'Because she knew about the CIA operation?'

Wendy finally permitted herself a smile. 'That wasn't mentioned. We talked about her book and my suggestion. Afterwards I was worried that I shouldn't have pressed the Butterthwaite murder on her the way I did.'

'Why?'

'Has nobody you spoke to explained that it would have been inconvenient for them, if she had gone ahead?'

'No,' I said.

'Then perhaps I should say nothing further and make it worse than I already have. As it turns out, Claire cannot now write either the book that she was considering or the

Butterthwaite book – or the financial book based on her experience as a forensic accountant, for that matter. I think that there may be more than one person sleeping easier in their beds tonight.'

'So, are you saying that stopping her writing the Butterthwaite book could have been a reason for killing her?' I said.

'All I said was that it should have been clear to me the Butterthwaite book wasn't a good idea. I have nothing more to say on the matter.'

'Who should we speak to then?' I asked. 'About Butterthwaite?'

'Nobody,' said Wendy. 'Forget that I even mentioned it. I think you've done as much as you can and I'm very grateful for that. In a day or so I may be able to get down the valley. Then we can call the police. In the meantime, do you feel up to delivering your talk on dialogue and language tomorrow or even tonight? It's one of the more abstract and academic topics. I think it would help everyone if we had something like that to concentrate on rather than the murder.'

'If you wish,' I said.

'Good,' she said. 'Let's discuss it all further over dinner and see what people think.'

Outside the snow continued to fall. We might have drawn the curtains to shut it out, but the succession of snowflakes continued to demand our attention. They floated in the yellow light that spilt from the window out into the bleak world beyond. Each flake seemed to push back, by a few minutes or seconds, the time when we would finally be released. We were being buried alive.

Elsie sat on her large sofa in her large sitting room, frowning. 'So, nobody killed Claire, then,' she said. 'It should, by rights, have been Dean . . .'

'There's no doubt that he's acted suspiciously,' I said. 'What was his earlier visit last summer all about? What was he really talking to Wendy about by the stairs? The explanations given by him and by her simply don't add up. Why does he seem to be following Claire around? Why are his story and Fliss's version so different? And yet he has the closest thing to a cast-iron alibi you can get. Claire was killed after one-fifteen and from ten past one he was with me.'

'So, whatever he's up to, it can't be him,' said Elsie. 'Hal . . .'

'Hal had the opportunity – bags of time. But all he had as a motive was that Claire could have told his wife about their night together.'

'As he said, all he had to do was give her a bit of help with the book and Claire was off his back. The risk was small compared with the risk of being arrested for murder. And he'd just had his breakthrough with the new book. Why throw that away?'

'Exactly,' I said. 'His luck had finally turned.'

'Jasper . . .' said Elsie experimentally. I got the impression he had gone down in her estimation for some reason.

'A bit of a creep,' I said, 'but that doesn't make him a killer. Claire seemed to be threatening him with that social media thing from years ago. But again, the price she was demanding for her silence – if that's what she was doing – doesn't seem to have been high. I believe him about the TV series too – if it had fallen through, there were compensations. Why on earth would he have risked killing her in a place from which he couldn't escape?'

'Jasper's a bit of a fake, when you think about it,' said Elsie. 'A total bullshitter. A lot of moustache twirling, but he'd run a mile if some attractive woman actually took him up on his nudges and winks.'

'Why do you say that?' I asked.

'No reason. It's just obvious. To me anyway.'

'How about Wendy . . . ?'

'There's the CIA business.'

'No, there isn't,' I said.

'All right, but she didn't much like Claire – she messed up her nice tidy world. The business of the Butterthwaite murder was odd, though. I mean why suggest Claire writes about it if she knows that it will really annoy somebody if she does? And, if she cares little enough about that person to suggest it anyway, why get so upset when Claire appears to be agreeing to go along with it?'

'Who is the upset person?' asked Elsie.

'Somebody with the same plot idea?' I said. 'But how would Wendy know what Hal or Jasper had planned. Or Dean?'

'Dean said he'd thought of writing crime fiction,' said Elsie. 'So, maybe that was going to be his first book? Maybe that's what his trip here last summer was about?'

'Dean hadn't even arrived when Wendy suggested it last night. She didn't know him – let alone what he might be planning to write about.'

'Unless he's with the CIA . . . OK, OK, not him then.'

'As for Hal and Jasper,' I said, 'they were both encouraging Claire to write it – or at least they wanted Wendy to tell them the story. And do authors kill over plot ideas? We've already said most books are just reworkings of the same plots anyway. There's Jenny of course. She's local. And don't forget she dropped the basket of bread just as Wendy mentioned the case. But surely that was just a coincidence? It would have all happened way before she was even born.'

'Still, we mustn't forget Jenny – could she have killed Claire for any other reason?'

'We can't rule her out,' I said. 'She's been in the background a bit, hasn't she? Nobody notices where she is half the time. We do at least know she was in the kitchen at one-fifteen when Claire spoke to her – and Wendy was also with her just after lunch. But we don't know what she was doing the rest of the time. She must know her way round the house and the local area better even than Wendy, though I can't see that would have helped her much here. Still, she had the opportunity if she could get away from the washing-up for long enough. She was even less fond of Claire than Wendy was. But, like the others, not enough to kill her. Not remotely enough.'

'Fliss?' said Elsie.

'Claire certainly knew a few of her secrets. But Claire seems to have told everyone she knew already. A bit late to stop her tongue. Hang on . . . Fliss did say she was local too, in a way. Her family used to live round here.'

'What, you mean she might somehow have been involved

in the Butterthwaite murder? She's a bit older than Jenny, but she'd have still been very young.'

'And almost certainly in Birmingham by then. OK, maybe not that,' I said.

'So, we're back to nobody having killed Claire,' said Elsie. 'Even though Claire seems to have had something on almost everyone here.'

'But nothing worth killing for,' I said.

'Unless there is something we still haven't been told,' said Elsie. 'Something Claire knew – or the person concerned thought she knew. So another round of questioning?'

'Yes,' I said, 'but let's hold off for the moment. We won't get anywhere just plunging in. There will just be the same evasion, unless we have some idea what we're looking for.'

'Where will we get that?'

'Claire's notebook,' I said. 'Fliss said it never left her side. I bet she's written stuff down in it.'

'And Fliss has it now?' said Elsie.

'I think so. Let's ask for it anyway – preferably in front of everyone else. People's response to that prospect may be quite revealing in itself.'

'Good, I'll ask and see what happens.'

But I hadn't expected things to happen quite as quickly as they did.

THREE UNEXPLAINED DISAPPEARANCES

CHAPTER NINETEEN

Elsie

Dinner after a murder has been committed is rarely the most cheerful of meals and, in that respect, this one was average.

We assembled, one by one, in the dining room. Greetings were brief. It wasn't just that one of our number was dead. One of the others was a murderer who might strike again. When you think about it, that's a bummer for any dinner party, though it might make for good reality TV.

Jenny had already come and gone. Or, at least, somebody had delivered the starters before any of us had arrived – rough country pâté, which was sitting on the table in front of us on rustic plates, with equally rustic bread in baskets. But nobody dared touch anything until Wendy gave us her permission.

Wendy was, on this occasion too, the last to arrive and slightly late. She came through the door just as Dean was asking me, 'So, how are your investigations going?'

'We've spoken to everyone we need to speak to,' I said tersely. Cops don't usually brief suspects on the progress of their case. It was time however to see what the reaction was when we took possession of the notebook. 'Of course,' I added, 'we haven't looked at Claire's notebook yet. That could be revealing. Could we have it, please, Fliss? You said that Claire had left it in the room.'

I looked round the table. Hal had more or less stopped breathing. Jasper's knuckles showed white where he was gripping his knife. Wendy froze halfway to her seat. Only Dean seemed relatively relaxed.

'Haven't you got it?' Fliss asked.

'No,' I said.

'Oh – it's just that it's gone. I thought Ethelred must have taken it when he came to see me. I mean, it's fine. He's welcome to it.'

I looked at Ethelred. He had definitely not been expecting this.

'But it doesn't matter, does it?' asked Fliss.

'If somebody has gone to the trouble of stealing it,' said Ethelred, 'that suggests that it may matter a great deal.'

Somewhere in the background we could hear the clock in the hallway ticking slowly and confidently, as if it knew something we didn't.

'Then it must be one of you who took it,' said Fliss. 'I mean, there's nobody else, is there? Which of you was it?'

We all looked at her. Then we all looked at each other. None of us wanted to say 'not me' because it was exactly what the real thief would have said. None of us was keen to be labelled the real thief. It was only one step away from being labelled the real murderer.

'What notebook?' asked Dean, which was almost as bad. One or two people may have edged away from him slightly.

'Her writer's notebook,' said Fliss. 'Black. A4. The one she keeps all of her plot ideas and her research and her to-do lists and everything in. Normally it never leaves her side. I was surprised when I saw it in the room when she vanished at lunchtime. It was right on top of some novel she was reading. Later I noticed it had gone but I thought Ethelred had picked it up. Except he didn't.'

'Which novel?' asked Hal.

It was one of those questions that seems reasonable at first glance, then an annoying irrelevance.

'Does that really matter?' asked Fliss. 'I don't know. A crime novel. One with a skull on the cover.'

The dismissive way she said 'skull' pretty much summed it up in terms of her future commitment to the genre.

'Ah,' said Hal, perhaps disappointed it wasn't one of his own. Writers are a bit like that, even ones with blonde, boyish hair.

'You've been out of the room this afternoon?' Ethelred asked Fliss.

'Yes. Some of the time,' said Fliss.

'And the room was of course locked?' he said.

'I think so – I usually would,' said Fliss. 'Look, here's the key.' She took it out of her bag with a flourish, an impressive trick in view of the size of the bag and the smallness of the key. Perhaps she had fewer chocolate wrappers in hers than I have in mine. And receipts. We all nodded encouragingly.

We hadn't been planning to dispute she had a key. We weren't even planning to point out that the fact that she had the key now didn't mean she'd locked the door then. But Wendy was frowning.

'And the other keys?' asked Wendy. 'Claire's keys?'

'Keys?' said Fliss.

'Claire had a key to the room you shared and a front door key. That anyone would need to let themselves in after hours is, admittedly, slight at the moment, but each room always has one front door key. In the case of your room, I gave that key to Claire.'

'As the one who looked more responsible?' asked Fliss.

'Possibly,' said Wendy.

'Then she would have had the keys with her when she . . .'

'Very well,' said Wendy. 'That must be where they still are. I cannot enlighten you as to where Claire's notebook is, but I think it would be good if we recovered Claire's keys.'

'But the shed itself is locked,' said Ethelred. 'So they should be safe enough.'

'Oh dear, I meant to . . .' said Wendy. 'If you'll excuse me for a moment. As for the food . . .'

She disappeared without clarifying whether the last remark meant that she intended us to eat or not. Conversation became even less lively than before. Hal said it looked as if we'd get more snow. Jasper agreed. Hal asked Fliss if she was sure she'd locked the door after leaving the room this time, a question which always creates doubt in the most confident of people. She frowned and fell completely silent.

I grabbed some bread, now that Wendy was no longer

watching us, and one or two others followed suit, but the pâté sat in front of each of us, untouched. Though Wendy might suspect, she could never know for certain who'd taken the bread. But we were all individually responsible for our own pâté. We'd have been mad to take that sort of risk.

'So, she's gone to check the shed?' asked Hal, looking at his watch. 'On her own.'

We all shuddered inwardly but pretended we hadn't.

'I guess,' said Jasper. He was carefully using his index finger to clear incriminating crumbs from his side plate.

'Ought to take five minutes, max?' I said.

'Six, maybe,' said Jasper. He licked his finger and examined it briefly. 'It will be dark out there, of course. No light at all. She'll have needed a torch. To go in that shed. She wouldn't want to trip over . . . anything.'

'Maybe we shouldn't have let her go alone,' said Hal.

'The murderer's probably here in this room,' said Jasper. 'In which case she's in no danger. I mean, Claire's not likely to get up suddenly and attack her, is she?'

We gave another collective shudder. We'd all seen films where exactly that had happened. Especially when a member of the group went off alone into the cold, dark night. It was not a good plan.

'Well, I wouldn't have gone until tomorrow morning – not on my own anyway,' said Hal, finally conceding that crime writers are nothing like as tough as you might think. 'I mean, who would take the keys anyway?'

A full fifteen minutes had passed by the time Wendy returned, still clutching a large torch. Nothing especially bad seemed to have happened to her, though often it's not until later in the film that you discover that the person who went off is now possessed by the vindictive spirits of the dead. 'There were no keys,' Wendy reported. 'I searched thoroughly – in the coat pockets and anywhere in the shed she might have dropped them. But somebody had been in there. So, somebody may well have Claire's key.'

'But I thought the shed door was now locked?' Ethelred repeated. He wasn't letting Wendy – or the demon that was now occupying her body – get away with that one.

'I meant to,' said Wendy. 'I was going to look out a padlock, but it slipped my mind. I've been busy . . .'

We all glanced at each other. It was worse than we thought if things had started to slip Wendy's mind.

'But how can you be certain anyone had been in there?' asked Hal. He seemed nervous.

'The stick – the one in the hasp – I always put it back the same way. It was upside down.'

So, sometimes OCD can be quite useful.

'Were there footprints?' asked Ethelred.

'Just fresh snow,' said Wendy. 'It's coming down quite hard again.'

It could still be any of us then. Except me. And probably Ethelred, though he'd been out of my sight for long enough during the afternoon.

'So, has anyone been outside since Claire was found?' asked Ethelred.

Nobody volunteered that they had. I'm not quite sure what other response Ethelred was expecting.

'Somebody must have done,' said Wendy. 'One of us

here . . . or Jenny . . . or . . .'

There was another shudder in the room, and this time not just from Hal. We'd also seen films where an unknown killer enters then hides in a large old house, bumping off one character after another. It rarely ended well. Especially if the intruder had somehow got hold of a set of keys. We'd all seen *The Sound of Music* too of course, but somehow that wasn't the classic movie that any of us was thinking of. The fact that the murderer might be one of the group round the table no longer seemed like our biggest problem.

'Perhaps I'd better go and check that Jenny is all right,' Ethelred said. 'I can tell her we may be another few minutes with the first course, since we've only just started it.'

'She has the ghost of Father Speedwell to protect her,' said Jasper.

Some of us looked at him blankly, though the name should have rung a bell with everybody.

'The priest who was arrested here years ago and tried at York,' he said. 'I thought he haunted the kitchen, doesn't he?'

Strangely this didn't make us feel any better. Writers tend to have quite vivid imaginations and this was not a good time or place to suggest semi-proven supernatural issues in addition to psychopathic intruders with access to all areas. The wind chose that moment to rattle the windows.

'Perhaps I should get Jenny to join us for the rest of the meal?' said Ethelred. 'I mean, it can't be any fun alone like that.'

'Oh, very well,' said Wendy. 'If she really wants to. Though I doubt she's any more frightened of ghosts tonight than she was yesterday.'

Ethelred was back within two minutes. He didn't look as if he'd seen a ghost – more that he'd mislaid something. 'She's not there,' he said. His expression was not unlike the one he'd had on his face when he first saw my suite: mild surprise combined with a conviction that something underhand had just happened. 'The stew was simmering in the stove and there were roast potatoes, slightly overcooked, in the oven. But there was no sign of Jenny at all. I checked both of the storerooms and called out a couple of times, but there was no response.'

'She can't have gone far,' said Wendy. 'Not in the middle of cooking dinner. I mean she can't possibly have left the house. Not at night. Not in this weather. Not without my permission.'

'I don't want to be alarmist,' said Jasper, 'but I think we should start looking for her. And I think we should search in pairs, not alone.'

I wondered whether to suggest that we ate something first – we could have pudding, say, quite quickly and maybe a couple of After Eight mints to follow, if there were any – but I knew, deep down, I would be the only one voting for this course of action. That gust of wind had taken things up a notch.

In a fight to the death between a crime writer and a recently qualified solicitor, I'd back the crime writer to win, three out of five times. Four out of five if the crime writer was M. W. Craven. Tonight, however, I decided I'd rather be with Dean (undoubtedly a solicitor but fit, muscular and with a watertight alibi) than Ethelred (likely to mull over all of his options for longer than he actually had to live), Jasper (poor taste in women) or Hal (whose stated reluctance to go out in the dark counted against him as a credible bodyguard). After a bit of jockeying for position we ended up in the following teams:

1 Me and Dean, deployed as searchers of the lower floors of the house, including the priest-haunted kitchen and the ancient cellars

2 Ethelred and Jasper, ordered to search the dark and spooky exterior, as far as was safe and practicable, using heavy duty torches

3 Fliss and Hal, who had volunteered to search the extensive but well-lit and ghost-free upper floors of the house

4 Wendy alone, who would remain in the dining room in case Jenny returned there – either living or hand in hand with Father Speedwell – and in order that the rest of us should have a place to report back to if we discovered anything untoward

Once again it seemed to me that Hal was avoiding going anywhere dark. At least he had Fliss to look after him.

I was pleased to find, now that I had him to myself, Dean was quite an imposing presence – tall and heavily built – muscles doubtless toned by lifting heavy legal books all day.

'Law keeps you fit?' I asked as we headed along the corridor.

'I try to work out every evening,' he said. 'Weights.

Treadmill. That sort of thing.'

'Do you think if I joined your gym I'd get as fit as you?'

'You'd have to actually go there – not just join.'

'OK, maybe not worth the money then,' I said. 'Ah, here's the kitchen. Why don't we start there?'

I switched the lights on as we entered, revealing a vast room with vaulting that rose a couple of normal storeys up to the ceiling. Giant, well-worn flagstones made up the floor – attractive but unforgiving if you happen to drop a plate.

'This bit goes back to the fifteenth century,' said Dean.

'How do you know that?'

'I looked it up online. It's a listed building. When they did it up, they were instructed to preserve as much of the original fabric as they could, so they had to use this room as something. They might have made it a lecture hall, but they clearly decided it was better suited to mass catering. Perhaps they thought that heating it as a lecture theatre would be pricy.'

Dean obviously did his research.

'Maybe they didn't want the ghost of Father Speedwell messing with the PowerPoint presentations?' I said.

'It's what I'd do if I were a ghost,' said Dean.

The lights gave a little flicker – scarcely noticeable when you are at home in your cosy little Hampstead flat but more memorable in a shadowy fifteenth century kitchen.

'And this is definitely the bit he haunts?' I said, hoping Dean's research would indicate otherwise.

Dean smiled. 'Are you worried we'll bump into him?'

'I just like to be prepared. I was briefly a Girl Guide. Old habits die hard.'

'Well, Wendy says it's the kitchen, but I'm not so sure.' Dean took a deep breath, preparatory to explaining a bit more scary stuff. 'Speedwell had been sent over from France to serve families loyal to the old faith in the North. Unluckily for him, the authorities had stepped up their persecution of Catholics and his presence in England was quickly betrayed. He was apparently safe in this remote spot, but a badly treated servant sent word to York. The people who owned the house did their best to conceal him, but the soldiers searched and found him, and carried him off to a rather nasty death at the stake. What happened at the execution was—'

I held up my hand. 'If you're short of time, I don't need all the details at the moment,' I said. 'The headlines are fine.'

Dean grinned. 'Fair enough. But the story is that he haunts wherever it was that they arrested him – and this is probably the only bit of the house that is still more or less as it was in his time, so it makes for a plausible tale. But he might not have been arrested in the house at all – if I'd been him, I'd have made a run for it while I could. You'd have seen the soldiers coming up the road, with their halberds and arquebuses. Of course, it would have depended a bit on the weather. I mean, if they'd had snow like this, he'd have had to wait here – it would have been a question as to whether the snow would let him get away over the fells before it allowed the troops to get up the valley.'

'You sound as if you've thought it through?' I said. 'The snow. The authorities closing in. How you get away before anyone can arrest you?'

Dean smiled. 'I'm probably not the only one. Even as we

speak, the imminent possibility of arrest must be weighing on somebody's mind, don't you think? But I don't reckon I'd make a break for it yet, not unless I knew the countryside round here very well indeed. I'd wait for the thaw – easier going and no prints left in the snow. Of course there's always the option of staying on and brazening it out, if you think you can get away with it or shift the blame elsewhere. So, where shall we check first? I'll try those storerooms over there, I think.'

I decided to examine the fridge for evidence. It contained two rows of chocolate mousses in small glass pots. I'd only eaten three when Dean yelled that there was nobody in either of the storerooms.

'All clear here too,' I mumbled, closing the fridge door.

Dean looked at me as he re-entered the main kitchen, his steps echoing on the flagstones. 'Is that chocolate round your mouth?' he asked.

'It's the ghosts,' I said. 'They play tricks like that when they can't get into PowerPoint. Never a dull moment with a poltergeist. It was a good call not making this a lecture theatre, wasn't it?'

'I'll give the stew a stir,' he said. 'And turn the heat right down in the oven. Some of us may be hungry later.'

We toured the corridors as far as the back door, checking cupboards en route, then returned to the sitting room, which had fewer nooks and crannies than the kitchen, though Hal did take a look up the chimney.

'You can't see far. We should have claimed one of the torches,' he said. 'But I don't think you'd get a fully grown person up there.'

'Not somebody with a decent appetite,' I said. 'Anyway, why would a killer stuff a body up a chimney?'

'You're assuming she's dead,' he said. 'She could be tied up somewhere. She could be the murderer herself and have done a runner. She may or may not want to be found. This might be a game of hide-and-seek.'

'I don't think she's the murderer,' I said. 'She had no reason to kill Claire.'

'What if she didn't mean to kill Claire?' said Dean. 'Claire was wearing Wendy's coat. Jasper thought he'd seen Wendy coming out of the house. Jenny might have thought the same thing. She had plenty of reasons to kill Wendy.'

'But Jenny said she was grateful for the job. There were no ill feelings at all.'

'Well, she would, wouldn't she? Especially if she'd just accidentally strangled Claire. If I'd done that, I'd certainly start saying how much I liked Wendy.'

'So, Jenny ran into Claire near the woodshed and strangled her by mistake?' I asked.

'It could be. I mean, Jenny spent a lot of time in the kitchen on her own. None of us knows where she was half the time – it wouldn't have occurred to most of us to even ask what she was up to. You and Ethelred ask questions. The net tightens. Then Jenny vanishes. What do you think?'

'If you're right, then at least we don't need to worry about a murderer amongst us,' I said. 'Not any more.'

'Exactly,' said Dean. 'We can all relax. Now, Elsie, why don't we take a little trip down to the cellar?'

CHAPTER TWENTY

Ethelred

'We'd better take a torch each?' I said.

Jasper nodded and pulled his tweed hat firmly onto his head. We were both warmly wrapped for our expedition into the unknown, but I had not brought headgear with me. I passed Jasper one of the two heavy, rubber-coated torches hanging by the back door. They felt substantial enough to use as weapons if we had to.

I turned the key in the lock and we stepped out into the cold air. It had stopped snowing and we could see stars above us – the usual ones and the mass of lesser stars that you become aware of only in the depths of the country. Below the stars was the blank outline of the high fells, stretching away into the dark night.

'That's the Milky Way over there?' asked Jasper.

'I'd say so,' I said.

'And that would be Venus?'

'Possibly.'

We stood for a moment looking up at the sky, but we were only putting off what we knew was our first task. Jasper took out a packet of cigarettes but I shook my head. Not where we were going.

'OK, I suppose not,' he said. 'There's a lot of flammable material in the woodshed. I guess we do have to check it, even though Wendy's done it recently?'

'I'm afraid so,' I said. 'The whole point is that we check everywhere more or less at the same time.'

We crunched through the deep, fluffy snow until we reached the shed. I flashed my torch at the hasp. As Wendy had said, it was still secured only with a short stick, stuffed into the staple where the padlock should have been.

'Wouldn't keep a ghost out,' said Jasper. 'Or in. I wonder which of us came here earlier and put that stick in the wrong way up?' He was still in no hurry to enter, but we were just getting cold hanging around.

'Let's get it over with,' I said.

I opened the door cautiously and let the torch beam throw its light round the interior. There was at least nobody lying in wait. The rows of piled logs were still in place. The kindling was in its bin. And Claire's body still lay stretched out on the ground, waiting for the police to come. I allowed the light to rest on Claire's face for a moment.

'Yes,' said Jasper. 'I'd been thinking the same thing. That maybe we'd find Jenny's body in place of Claire's. It's what comes of writing too many crime novels. Your imagination runs away with you.'

I walked carefully round Claire and shone the torch as well as I could into the stacks of wood. But there seemed to be no way of hiding anything as big as a second body there.

'Are we looking for a corpse or a living person, though?' asked Jasper.

'Could be either.'

Jasper shivered. 'OK, Ethelred. Are we all done here? Wendy's already checked the whole shed looking for the keys – so she said. I'm sorry but this place gives me the creeps.'

'Yes, we're done. It's funny isn't it?' I said. 'We write about death all the time, but it still hits you when you actually see it.'

'I'd have been happy to miss out on that.'

'Think of it as research,' I said.

I studied Claire's face for a moment – grey in the torchlight and stiff – simultaneously so like her and so unlike her. Would it be in bad taste to use any of this in a future book? A good writer wastes nothing. But Jasper was already looking towards the door. There were bright stars out there and a long, clean streak in the snow from some electric light that had been turned on in the house. They both beckoned to us.

'Where next?' he asked, as I refastened the door with the stick.

'Let's work our way round the building and see if there are any footprints leading away from it.'

There were none, but there were still other buildings to check. We entered the unlocked garage, which housed Wendy's Land Rover plus the usual collection of engine oil, screenwash and tyre chains. A small outhouse, also unlocked, contained a variety of gardening equipment. A greenhouse with a few pots of dead plants on wooden racks completed our tour. There was no sign of Jenny. Eventually we fetched up at the back door again.

'So, no sign of footprints,' said Jasper. 'But maybe there were some earlier and the snow has covered them?'

'Dinner was still cooking on the stove. Jenny can't have left more than an hour ago. The snow had started to ease off by then. I think we'd still see something.'

'So you reckon she's on the premises somewhere?' he said.

I looked at the snow. How much did you need to cover old tracks? Maybe very little.

'OK, she could have gone down the valley,' I said. 'Or even up into the fells. But it would be risky. My best guess is she's still here. Hopefully one of the other search parties has already found her somewhere indoors.'

'Well, I hope she's OK, wherever she is. But one of the others could have killed her, couldn't they? I mean if she'd found out who killed Claire?'

'I don't know,' I said. 'A second murder would be a crazy thing to do.'

'I agree. Of course, an intruder could have got into the house without our knowing. Somebody who actually is crazy.'

'Yes, I think that idea has occurred to most of us. But when?' I said.

'Yesterday? When we all came up here. They could have got a taxi up here – we wouldn't know. There was yours. Mine. Hal's. The girls'. Even Wendy might not have noticed an additional one dropping somebody off, just inside the gate. Or this person could have come on foot. There wasn't much snow until quite late. And Dean made it through even this morning, so it could have been any time during the night.'

'Where have they hidden since then?' I asked.

'The garage? It's unlocked.'

'Too chilly,' I said, though I doubted it would have been much colder than my bedroom.

'Not if they were well-equipped – like Dean. Good down jacket. They could even have a sleeping bag. You can be crazy *and* well-prepared.'

'I suppose so.'

'And now,' said Jasper, 'they could have Claire's keys. The crazy person could be anywhere in the house.'

'Then one of the search parties will find them,' I said.

'If they don't find the searchers first. But everyone should be fine if they stick to their pairs. Do you mind if I have a quick fag now? Before we go back in? You don't have to wait here, of course.'

'I think we should stay together. I don't want to be part of a search party looking for your body next.'

'That's decent of you.' He located the packet again, shook out a cigarette and lit up. He breathed in the nutritious smoke that I had deprived him of earlier. 'I hope Jenny's all right. Nice girl. A lot more to her than meets the eye. You see her at first and think she's just Wendy's downtrodden servant. But she has a sense of humour. And she's a great mimic. I've heard her imitate Wendy – that's a scream. And you, Ethelred. She's got your tone of voice to perfection. So funny.'

'Well, I've heard her do Wendy,' I said. 'She was very good. I hadn't realised that she took in all of us.'

'Not everyone. Wendy mainly and you a bit. She could be on the stage – or one of those radio programmes.'

'And she could do anyone? Claire, say?'

'Oh yes, I've heard her do Claire too . . .' He looked at me thoughtfully. 'Sorry, I see what you mean.'

'So, yesterday, when you heard Claire's voice coming from the kitchen?' I said.

'Yes, of course. It could have been Jenny. I mean, the voice came from the kitchen after all. That's where Jenny is a lot of the time. It's much more likely when you think about it that that's what I heard. Jenny talking to somebody and giving them an imitation of Claire. Well, no harm done. I'll have to remember to say to the police that it only might have been Jenny's voice. That would affect the possible time of death.'

'It blows a hole in Dean's alibi,' I said.

'Does it?'

Some ash dropped unnoticed from Jasper's cigarette onto the snow.

'He was with me from ten past,' I said. 'If Claire could have been killed earlier . . .'

'Dean might have done it? I suppose. Where is Dean by the way?'

'He was searching the ground floor with Elsie,' I said. 'And the cellar. Wendy also asked them to go down into the cellar.'

CHAPTER TWENTY-ONE

Elsie

Dean led me to a spot in the hall where the pattern of oak panelling was broken by a doorway. The door itself was old – it had survived two restorations of the house and as much neglect in between as the fells could throw at it. It was gnarled and knotted and rough to the touch. It was a door that could look after itself. It was not a door to mess with if you knew what was good for you. There was a small keyhole, almost unnoticeable at first sight, but no key. Dean reached out and pushed the door open. It swung silently on well-oiled hinges.

'After you,' he said.

'You knew it was unlocked?' I asked.

'I happened to try it earlier,' he said.

'Ah,' I said. I peered into the darkness that dropped away before us. 'Perhaps we should have brought a torch, as you said.'

'There weren't any by the back door – I checked when

we were over that way. Ethelred and Jasper must have taken them all. It's not a problem. We won't need one.'

Dean reached out again and pressed a switch that I hadn't noticed. Electric light flooded the staircase – worn stone steps that descended in a straight line towards the shadowy depths. Above the stairs sloped a long, vaulted ceiling, a scaled-down version of that in the kitchen. The cellars lost no opportunity to remind you that they were old. They'd seen it all. Nothing we could do on this visit could shock them.

'There's another switch at the bottom,' said Dean. 'For the lights in the cellar itself.'

'That's good to know.' And I started down the stairs. The regular tap of Dean's footsteps sounded behind me. His tread was pretty confident, bearing in mind how uneven the steps were. He'd obviously had a sneaky look round earlier. Every step had worn in a slightly different way. Too many monks had used them to pick up a flagon or two of ale.

'A handrail would be good,' I said. 'You could fall quite a long way if you missed your step.'

'There's a rope on the wall on your left,' said Dean.

'So there is,' I said. 'Well-spotted.'

We found ourselves on a stone floor. When Dean had switched the second light on, I could see that we were in a substantial undercroft with brick pillars supporting an arched brick ceiling. It smelt earthy but was dry and almost warm. And it was very quiet. You couldn't even hear the clock, far above us in the hallway.

'Good for storing wine,' said Dean. 'The temperature down here probably doesn't vary by more than a degree or two all year. Chilly in the summer, I grant you, but it may have been the warmest place in the house in the depths of winter.'

There were, in fact, several dozen bottles of wine in racks along the wall and some boxes of apples and potatoes.

Dean went round the walls, inspecting them closely.

'Secret passage?' I asked.

'This is where you'd expect to have one. But it could only take you out onto the fells via some inconspicuous external door. There's nowhere else for it to go. But I don't see any sign of an exit. Jenny didn't come this way. Of course, she only had to walk out of the back door and onto the fells.'

'So, you think that Jenny might have escaped, having killed Claire?'

'You have to admit it's a possibility. I certainly think she knows the country round here well enough. And if I were the murderer I'd want to get away as fast as I could before the police came. Being stranded here in the snow is a curse in that sense, but a blessing in that the police can't get here to make an arrest.'

'But it could still be one of the others?'

'Yes, of course. In which case Jenny has vanished for totally different reasons. She might know who the murderer is.'

'The murderer wouldn't risk killing a second person, though, would they?' I said.

'I might if that person knew I was the killer and was about to expose me. It might be my only chance.'

I looked at him. His face was partly in shadow and I couldn't tell whether this was a serious proposition. He seemed to be smiling. That was good, wasn't it?

'Well, at least I know it's not you,' I said. 'I'd be quite nervous down here otherwise.'

'How do you know it wasn't me?'

Yes, of course – we hadn't told anyone any more than we needed to. Dean wouldn't necessarily know how we'd ruled him out.

'You were with Ethelred when the murder took place,' I said.

'Which was when?'

'One-fifteen at the earliest.'

'Based on what?'

'On Jasper having heard Claire's voice from the kitchen.'

'From the kitchen?'

'Yes.'

'And did anyone actually see her in the kitchen?'

'No.'

'Did Jenny say she'd seen her there?'

'She couldn't remember exactly. But she didn't contradict Jasper. It's as well you have that alibi.'

'Is it?'

'Well, yes – bearing in mind that you showed up out of the blue like that, having pursued Claire in Glasgow.'

'Excellent. I have an alibi then. Of course, if it wasn't Jenny who killed Claire it leaves plenty of other suspects, don't you think?'

'Who?'

'Well, I wasn't going to say anything, but it was a bit of a coincidence Jasper showing up here, wasn't it?'

'Why?'

'He and Claire both used to work for the same company. Didn't you know that?'

'Harefoot International?'

'Yes, she told me in Glasgow that that's who she was with. It's funny Claire didn't mention it this time, isn't it? You might like to ask Jasper how well he knew her – if you get to question him again.'

'You're quite keen that I think it's Jasper, aren't you?' I said.

'I'm just telling you what I know.'

'But how do you know all this?'

'I said, I spoke to Claire in Glasgow.'

'Not just that. How did you know where all the light switches were coming down to the cellar?'

'I just like to check things. I like to do my research. Then nothing's a surprise.'

'Is that why you showed up here last summer on a walking trip?'

'Who told you about that?'

'Jenny,' I said.

Of course, the fact that he didn't murder Claire didn't mean that he hadn't killed Jenny. She might know something that had nothing to do with Claire at all – something odd she'd spotted in her time at the Hall. So, it didn't mean that he wouldn't kill me, if I had just revealed that I knew something too. I was trying to remember exactly what I'd said when I heard a welcome voice.

'Elsie?'

I turned to see Ethelred coming down the stairs, stooping slightly to accommodate the low ceiling.

'Hi!' I said.

'Are you OK?' he asked. 'The rest of us are already back in the dining room.'

'I'm absolutely fine. We were just about to come back upstairs. Time to eat. There's chocolate mousse for pudding, but we may be one or two short.'

Our second attempt at dinner was no more cheerful than the first, having now lost a second member of the party, but we did at least have something to talk about. Over very well-cooked stew and slightly burnt potatoes, we all reported back on the results of our search.

Hal and Fliss said that the upper floors were clear – all bedrooms, occupied and unoccupied, storerooms and cupboards had been thoroughly searched. Fliss at least seemed a little embarrassed that they'd had an easy time of it.

Ethelred and Jasper, their faces still red with the nighttime cold, reported that it was possible Jenny had got away over the snow but that it had been such hard-going, even just round the house, that it was doubtful if she could have got far.

'Of course, she'd have needed a torch and, thinking about it, we'd have seen the light,' said Ethelred, who appeared to have thought a lot about it. 'Even if she'd just flashed it on for a moment.'

'There's a bit of a moon,' said Dean. 'You'd be surprised what you can do in these conditions, with some moonlight. Did the two of you take all three torches from the hook by the back door, by the way?'

'No, just the two,' said Jasper.

'Well, they'd all gone when I got there,' said Dean. 'So who took the third one? Unless I miscounted before?'

Wendy confirmed that there had certainly been three.

'So, does Jenny have the third, or are there more of us in the building than we think?' I said.

'Don't,' said Fliss. 'You're giving me the creeps. The other key to my room is missing, in case you've forgotten.'

'Well, if a stranger was hiding here, we ought to have found him or her,' said Ethelred confidently. 'We've done a fairly thorough search.'

'Look,' said Dean, 'if it helps, my own view is that Jenny has done a runner, probably with the torch. I mean, we can't find her, can we? And the torch has gone. Maybe she left earlier than we think – while the snow was still coming down – and it covered her tracks. She knows the country round here better than any of us. Don't you think so, Wendy?'

'I agree,' said Wendy. 'She's clearly not here. She must have gone. As you say, she's quite capable of it.'

'No, wait,' said Ethelred. 'You mentioned a priest hole somewhere. We haven't checked that, have we?'

'I think that's very unlikely,' said Wendy. 'It's cramped and uncomfortable. I can't believe that even the most desperate priest would really have used it. I suspect that's why Speedwell was caught.'

'We ought to check it,' said Ethelred.

Wendy shook her head. 'I feel claustrophobic just thinking about it. It's the last place Jenny would have thought of hiding.'

'Where is it?' asked Ethelred.

'Just outside in the hallway,' said Wendy. 'Oh, very well, if it would satisfy your curiosity.'

Wendy took us all to a door in the panelling and opened it. Inside there were shelves with various cleaning materials on them.

'We need to clear this stuff first,' she said, starting to pass cans and bottles and clean yellow dusters to whoever was nearest.

Once the shelves were empty she said: 'OK, now I'll need one of you to take the other side of the bottom shelf. Thanks, Ethelred. Now lift as I do.'

The shelves rose, pivoting on a hidden hinge, to reveal a small space behind. As Wendy had said, it was narrow and claustrophobic. It was also empty.

'Father Speedwell is supposed to have hidden there?' I asked. 'I think you're right. I'd have tried to run for it instead.'

'That seems likely, doesn't it?' said Wendy. 'I couldn't have stood it in there for more than a few minutes. It would be like a coffin. But maybe if the alternative was being burned to death . . .'

'Quite easy to find too,' said Ethelred, 'if you knew what you were looking for.'

'He was found,' said Wendy.

'So, maybe arrested as he tried to run for it, or found all too easily there?' said Dean.

'He had few if any good choices,' said Wendy. 'Obviously, I could tell Jenny wasn't going to be there now.

I mean, she'd have had no way of stacking the shelves again once she was inside – not unless she had an accomplice. It's pretty much impossible to get into and out of unaided. Once inside, you'd be trapped until somebody got you out again.'

Wendy and Ethelred lowered the shelves and we all helped to put the cleaning materials back in place.

'Right,' I said, 'back to the dining room?'

Wendy shook her head. 'I think I've eaten all I can manage. It's getting late anyway. We should simply retire to the sitting room.'

The others nodded.

'Or perhaps we would all feel a little stronger after pudding?' I suggested.

But everyone seemed to think that they were as strong as they were likely to get.

'If you want a pudding, Elsie, I assume you know where they are,' said Wendy.

'Fine,' I said. 'Can I get one for anyone else? It's chocolate mousse – apparently.'

There was still no enthusiasm for yummy chocolate.

'I'll come with you,' said Ethelred. 'I think we should still not wander round the house alone.'

'So,' I said, as we sat at the kitchen table with several empty pots in front of us, 'you reckon Dean's alibi is a busted flush? And he does seem keen to push the blame onto Jenny all of a sudden. Or onto Jasper. Are you sure you wouldn't like one of these? I probably can't eat sixteen.'

'No, thank you. They are all yours. As for Dean's alibi,

I don't know why I didn't consider that it might not have been Claire's voice. Jenny has treated me to her mimicry already. It should have occurred to me that, coming from the kitchen, it was as likely to be Jenny imitating Claire as Claire herself. It was never really believable that Claire would put on a coat, go out of the front door, go round at the back door, then to the kitchen, then return to the back door and thence to the woodshed. Why she should leave by the front door to go to the back of the house is still not quite clear, but it makes more sense if she went direct from where Jasper saw her to the shed. Dean is back in the frame as the murderer. And we have to come back to the fact that Claire borrowed the coat for a last-minute appointment. That's so much more likely to be Dean who invited her than somebody who had been around since the previous evening.'

'Then there's Jasper,' I said. 'It's not just that we now know there was a connection between him and Claire through Harefoot International, which Jasper has failed to mention. It's also the way he keeps saying that his days in finance were boring and he doesn't want to talk about it. He's hiding something.'

'Finance actually isn't that interesting,' said Ethelred.

'It usually is to people who've been in finance.'

'Maybe. And we mustn't forget Jenny as a suspect.'

'Yes, I thought it was a coincidence that she dropped the bread on the floor just as Wendy was talking about the Butterthwaite case – I mean, what connection could she have with it? She's too young. But now that she's disappeared like this, I'm beginning to wonder. One way or another, it's a game changer.'

'Exactly. Jenny might have wanted to stop Claire writing about it. But would she actually resort to murder?' Ethelred frowned.

'It depends exactly how she was mixed up in it. There was some girl involved, wasn't there? Somebody who did a lot of fell walking?'

'But we've said, she's much too young. She's only just about old enough to be the Other Woman now. It was over twenty years ago, wasn't it?'

'I'll look it up on the internet . . . oh no, I can't, can I? You really do take the world wide web for granted these days. Not having all the facts at your fingertips instantly feels distinctly weird. Perhaps Wendy would tell us.'

'Yes, perhaps. The more I think about it, the less I can see how Wendy manages without access to the outside world.'

'She likes it,' I said. 'She really enjoys not having mobile reception – just as you would. Come on, Ethelred, you'd like nothing better than to leave the twentieth century behind.'

'Twenty-first century,' he said.

'Ethelred, you have to pass the leaving exams for the twentieth century before you're allowed into the twenty-first. Maybe you're not even quite ready for the twentieth century yet. I see you as an early Victorian at heart. Your parents were quite prescient naming you Ethelred, when you think about it. What's your middle name, again?'

'Hengist,' he said.

'There you are then,' I said. 'They could tell.'

'I still wouldn't live here,' he said.

'Jenny's departure is odd,' I said, 'but there have been

some other unexplained disappearances that we need to consider.'

'Such as?' he said.

'Well, the third torch to begin with.'

'Well, Jenny must have taken it.'

'Or was it the person who broke into the woodshed?' I said. 'The one who put the stick back the wrong way.'

'It's pretty dark in there. A torch would have been good. What were they after in there? Was it really Claire's keys?'

'If not, what did they want?' I asked.

'What about Claire's notebook? They might have thought she had that with her. Fliss said it was unusual for her not to. What if it was somebody who'd seen her at another conference and knew that was what she did?'

'Hal? Dean?' I suggested.

'Or Jasper. Or Jenny. Or anyone. It didn't need to be at another conference, actually. It's not difficult to guess that's what she would do.'

'So the book goes missing. Then the torch. Then Jenny does,' I said. 'That's *three* things that have gone missing,' I said. 'And the biggest disappearance is the final one.'

'True, though we don't know for certain that's the order,' said Ethelred. 'The torch could have been the last thing to go. In which case the last object wasn't actually that valuable and has probably just been mislaid. And you're forgetting the keys have gone missing too – unless you think that's a red herring. Anyway, that rule only applies to fiction. Not real life. The missing book doesn't necessarily prove anything about Claire's death – or Jenny's absence. Shall we join the others in the sitting room before this discussion becomes too far-fetched? Or is there still another chocolate mousse to eat?'

I counted the empty pots on the table. 'One still left in the fridge,' I said. 'But I'm done for the moment. They were a bit too rich for my taste.'

CHAPTER TWENTY-TWO

Ethelred

'No sign of any intruders out there?' asked Hal as we entered the sitting room.

'No sign of anyone,' I said. 'It's as quiet as the grave out there.'

If I'd been hoping for a laugh, I would have been disappointed. But it didn't look as if anyone had been telling jokes. The atmosphere was if anything gloomier than it had been in the dining room. The only cheerful note was the blazing log fire.

'You were a long time,' said Fliss. 'Were you washing up?'

'No,' I said.

'Leave the washing-up for the morning,' said Wendy. 'We'll do it then. We've all had enough excitement for one day.'

This, coming from Wendy, was a surprise. It went against her sense of order, her tidiness, her routines. But when I looked at her I saw exhaustion on her face. She was responsible for Fell Hall and it was falling apart in front of her eyes. A participant had been murdered. Her only staff member had apparently fled. We all wanted to get away from here. Yet even when the police had finally got here and finished their investigations, she had nowhere else to go but the ruins of her old life.

'I'll move you to another room, Fliss,' Wendy added. 'You're not safe with Claire's keys missing.'

'There's a pretty solid bolt on the door,' said Fliss. 'I'm too tired to contemplate moving now. Maybe tomorrow.'

That Wendy made no objection to the rejection of her plan showed how bad things had got.

'I wish we knew when the snow would stop,' said Jasper, echoing everyone's thoughts.

'When I know anything about that, I'll tell you,' said Wendy, wearily. She rubbed her eyes, burying her face in her hands. 'It won't be for much longer.'

'Your own private weather forecasting service?' asked Fliss.

Wendy looked up and blinked several times. 'I've sat out more storms like this than I can remember. You get a feel for when a thaw is coming. Something in the air . . .' Wendy's voice tailed off again. She stared into the fire.

'It's only when you're away from the internet that you realise how much you depend on it for everything,' said Jasper. 'Once this is what it would have been like for everyone – no clue as to the next day's weather or when the plague was coming or which army was over the hill, plundering the neighbouring villages. You had to sit and wait for the plume of smoke.'

'They were very different times,' I said. 'If you went into the next county, nobody would have had the first idea who you were. Over the border was pretty much a foreign country. The people there would have scarcely understood a word you said, and they would never have heard of your own village. And if, as a peasant, you could flee to a town and stay there unrecognised for a year and a day, you were a free man. We've lost a lot of privacy but have admittedly gained better weather forecasts and pictures of cats who look like Hitler.'

'Very different times . . .' said Wendy.

'But that would have suited you?' said Hal. 'I mean, you choose to be here, not in Harrogate or York?'

'It depends,' said Wendy. 'A medieval peasant would probably have opted for York every time, if he could get there and find work. People have always reinvented themselves if it suited them.'

'You've reinvented yourself, haven't you, Hal?' said Fliss. She had a whisky glass in her hand and, with or without Wendy's consent, had contrived to fill it. Her combative tone suggested that it wasn't the first glass.

Hal looked at her cautiously, uncertain where this was leading.

'As a writer of thrillers? I suppose so, though I haven't been one for a year and a day yet, so the comic crime writers could still demand my return in chains.' He gave us all a weak smile. It wasn't the evening for anything more than that.

'And you, Jasper?' she said.

214

'I've always written thrillers,' he replied stiffly.

'I mean from being a banker to being a writer.'

'Yes, I suppose so.'

'In your case, it's been much more than a year and a day. You're a free man, aren't you? Absolutely safe. Glad you escaped the bank?'

'I've said I find anything to do with finance very dull indeed. I never think about banking unless I can help it.'

'You got away with it, though, didn't you?'

Jasper looked daggers at her. 'You could say that.'

'Oh, I do, Jasper, I do.'

Elsie looked at me. I shrugged. While we were out of the room, Fliss had had more than enough to drink. Her apparent scepticism over Hal's reinvention of himself had been unexpected, but Fliss had never exactly liked Jasper. Still, I wasn't quite sure why she was doing this now.

'And are you trying to escape the law, Dean?' Fliss asked, suddenly turning her fire in his direction.

'Escape the law?' he said. 'Oh, I see what you mean. No, I'm very happy doing what I do.'

'Wills and house purchases?'

'A bit. You have to do most things as a trainee. I thought I explained in Glasgow what I was planning to specialise in.'

'Did you?'

'Yes.'

'I've forgotten.'

'I do civil liberties.'

'Human rights?'

'That sort of area, yes. I work for Pentangle.'

215

'Ah,' I said.

'Oh,' said Jasper.

'Really?' said Hal. 'Pentangle? *That* Pentangle?'

I think we'd all heard of Pentangle. As human rights lawyers they had a very high profile indeed. Their name was in the newspapers and on television most weeks. Accidents. Appeals against deportation. Miscarriages of justice. High profile sackings. Half the time, media reports ended with a note that the litigants were represented by Pentangle. They had an uncanny instinct for finding cases.

'It's a chance to make the world a better place,' said Dean.

'A better place? Yes, I do sort of remember you saying that,' said Fliss.

'Obviously some people are a bit cynical about us—'

'Cynical? You don't say? No win, no fee, is it?'

'Sometimes. Sometimes it's the only way that people can get access to justice.'

'And what percentage do you take?' Fliss asked.

'It varies.'

'I bet it does.'

Elsie caught my eye again. I nodded. Fliss had clearly reached the stage in the evening when she wanted a fight with somebody. This wasn't helping. Perhaps it was time to wrap things up before the evening got unpleasant.

'Maybe I should tidy a few things away,' said Wendy. 'You can all go to bed.'

'No,' I said. 'You go to bed too. You look done in. And I don't think any of us should be wandering the corridors alone – or no more than we have to.'

We all said our goodnights. Fliss left straight away, then Jasper. Hal seemed in no hurry, but eventually ambled off. I agreed to see Elsie back to her room on my way to my own. Wendy stayed, fiddling with the fire.

'Fliss was running out of people to attack,' said Elsie, once we were out of earshot of the rest.

'She's angry,' I said. 'Her best friend is dead, and somebody here may have killed her. The whole death thing is only just coming home to her. She blames herself for not watching over Claire better.'

'Watching over Claire wasn't her job.'

'We can see that, but she can't. Not yet. She'll be better for a night's sleep – not right exactly, but better. We'll all be washing up together tomorrow like one big happy family.'

'That sounds overly optimistic,' said Elsie.

'Yes,' I said. 'It is. But from here things can only start to improve.'

It was not until I got to my room that I remembered that I had intended to borrow a book from the shelves in the sitting room. Cursing mildly, I set off on the long trek back to the other end of the house. The sitting room was dark, but the fire was still glowing, casting an eerie red half-light over everything. I pressed the light switch and crossed the room towards the bookcases. Then I noticed something odd on the fire. Smouldering gently was a black book. I quickly retrieved it with the fire tongs. It was not in fact that badly burnt. The back cover crumbled as I took the book in my fingers, but the front was clear enough. Strangely it was not Claire's notebook as I had suspected it might be. This was no attempt to destroy evidence. It was a crime novel that somebody had decided to throw on the fire and allow to chargrill slowly overnight. I've had bad reviews myself, but nobody had yet told me that they'd disliked the book enough to condemn it, like Father Speedwell, to the flames.

The cover design was simple – a grinning white skull on a black background, with the title and the name of the author below. It looked a bit like the one that I'd seen Claire with and that Fliss had mentioned as having been left in the bedroom. But I did not recognise the author Charles Straw. Nor did the book's title, *In Search of Forgotten Death*, ring any bells. It certainly wasn't a book I had ever read or could recall seeing reviewed. The publisher too was unfamiliar. It had been issued some twenty years before. The library at Fell Hall was mainly classics – majoring on the 1920s, '30s and '40s. There were some more modern books – P. D. James and Ruth Rendell for example – and one or two contemporary writers, such as Sarah Vaughan and Ruth Ware, that must have been personal favourites of Wendy's. But there was nothing else like this – a long out of print book by a completely unknown author. It wasn't just unclear why it was on the fire – it wasn't obvious what it was doing there at all.

For a while I sat on the sofa, the fire in the hearth still smouldering, the book cooling to room temperature. I carefully located the opening chapter, trying not to damage the now brittle pages and spine. I read.

And I read.

And I read.

The fire burnt down until it was just glowing embers. I read on. I heard the radiators starting to click and knock as the central heating system shut down for the night. It grew colder.

But I continued to read.

CHAPTER TWENTY-THREE

Elsie

'This had better be good,' I said to Ethelred. 'You've just woken me up – and probably half the other people in the house. Couldn't it have waited until the morning? It's – past midnight. Way past midnight. Everyone else went off to bed before ten. And locked their doors in case you were wrong about things getting better.'

'I've been reading this book,' he said.

He showed me what appeared to be a self-published crime novel with a poorly designed cover.

'And you have dropped in to give me a reading recommendation? That's so sweet of you. Well, thank you. I can see that couldn't wait until the morning when I was able to open my eyes and read. It was much better that I should know about it now when I was asleep.'

'You don't understand,' he said.

I looked again at the black cover with its crude skull. '*In Search of Forgotten Death* by Charles Straw,' I said.

'Wait . . . that wouldn't be the Charles Straw that nobody has ever heard of and who never wrote anything worth reading? And published by . . . some publisher that I haven't tried even with one of your manuscripts. So, you thought of me here – me who never has to read any total crap – and decided, why don't I wake Elsie up and show her the worst book that's been published in . . . how long?'

'It was published a bit over twenty years ago. But—'

'Hold on! Now I see the condition of the cover I understand what you were trying to do. You reckoned that in this state it was so collectable that, no matter how shit the story was, I'd just have to have it because of what was left of the superb binding? A bit's just dropped off by the way. What a shame! It must have reduced its value by twenty per cent – that's about one penny, if you round it up to the nearest penny.'

'Have you finished?' asked Ethelred.

I thought about it. Had I? 'Not quite. Where the hell did you find that heap of rubbish?'

'On the fire,' he said. 'I thought it was Claire's notebook at first.'

'And having seen it wasn't, it didn't occur to you to throw it back?'

'Read it,' he said. 'Just the opening paragraph, if you wish.'

I sighed and took the book from him. I read the opening paragraph. 'Holy bloody shit,' I said.

'Exactly,' said Ethelred.

I read the second paragraph. 'This is . . . unbelievable. It's Hal's book. It's *The Spy Before Yesterday*. But it's also

221

by Charles Straw. And it's also called *In Search of Forgotten Death*. Is it the same word for word?'

'The opening is, pretty much. Later it's more the plot and the general feel of the thing. And character names and locations aren't the same. Also Hal's version is jokier and there are references to modern technology that Charles Straw could not have predicted twenty years ago. And, due to the attempt to burn it, *In Search of Forgotten Death* is missing its back cover and the last half dozen pages, so I can't be sure it's the same ending. But it's basically the same book. Same style. Same amazing twist halfway through. Maybe the same ending before it went on the fire.'

'And it somehow found its way here? Wendy purchased it to add to the library?'

'Or somebody brought it here with them this time,' said Ethelred. 'Claire had a book a bit like this with her this morning.'

'So who put it on the fire?' I asked.

'I don't know. But Hal's book – his totally original book, like nothing that had gone before – is plagiarised from beginning to very close to the end.'

'Every major paper has reviewed *The Spy Before Yesterday*. Nobody, but nobody, suggested that it resembled another book.'

'I doubt many people have read this,' said Ethelred. 'I've never heard of the publisher. It may not have been in many bookshops.'

'But the author – Charles Straw – must have realised his ideas had been stolen. Hal's book has had masses of publicity.'

'Yes. If Straw is still writing. If he's still reading crime novels. If he's still reading book reviews. Otherwise, no.'

'Hal couldn't have taken the risk,' I said. 'Somebody would have tipped Straw off. Hal must know that Straw is dead or something.'

'Claire said to Hal that his book reminded her of something.'

'So, she'd made the connection?' I asked.

'My guess is Claire had picked this up in a second-hand bookshop somewhere, by chance, and realised what had happened.'

'She then brought it here with the aim of blackmailing Hal?'

'I think so,' said Ethelred. 'Hal's little world was about to come tumbling down. They'd have had to withdraw his book and pulp any remaining stock. He'd have been thrown out of the Crime Writers' Association, if they ever do throw anyone out. If he'd stayed a comic crime writer he would at least have had some respect.'

'Not much,' I said.

'True. But more than if he'd been exposed as a fraud by Claire. Which she was clearly about to do. I'd have said that was a pretty good motive for murder, wouldn't you?'

'I think it's time to haul Hal in for questioning again,' I said.

'Haul him in where exactly?' asked Ethelred in the pedantic manner he usually reserves for telling me about comparative mortality rates in Middlesex and Surrey during the Black Death.

'We'll talk to him in his room,' I said. 'I'll be the bad

cop this time. You're better suited to good cop, now I think about it.'

'I think we should approach this round of questioning in an altogether more circumspect manner,' said Ethelred. 'Before we expose anyone to either the good cop or the bad one, let's check this really was the book that Claire had. Maybe let's talk to Fliss about it. Then, by all means, you can be the bad cop, if that's what you want to be.'

'Let's do it,' I said.

'As you say, it's past midnight,' said Ethelred. 'Right, I'm going to bed. We'll catch Fliss tomorrow, before breakfast. She's not going to be able to escape overnight. And I don't think Hal will risk going far either – not now it's dark out there.'

THE THIRD PASS

CHAPTER TWENTY-FOUR

Elsie

Fliss sat in her pyjamas with the duvet wrapped round her. Somewhere, outside, daylight was creeping reluctantly across the fells.

'Yes, that was Claire's,' she said, turning the fire-damaged goods over in her hands. 'She brought it up from London with her. How did it get like this?'

'Somebody decided to torch it,' I said. 'But they didn't do so good a job, hence my assistant here was able to retrieve a vital piece of evidence.'

'Evidence?'

'Well, somebody thought it was worth stealing from Claire and trying to destroy it. It's a piece of the jigsaw.'

'Somebody must have taken it from the room yesterday evening – it was there before dinner. I noticed it when I realised Claire's black notebook was missing. And I locked the room when I went down to dinner. I really did.'

'But the woodshed was broken into and Claire's key is missing.'

'Shit,' she said. 'Of course. So, locking the door was pretty much irrelevant. Well, at least I did remember to bolt it last night – in spite of having had maybe one drink too many.'

'What do you know about the book, Fliss?'

She looked at it disdainfully.

'Nothing. I mean, it's just an old paperback, isn't it? Why would anyone want to steal it?'

'You tell us, sister,' I said.

'If I was able to tell you, I wouldn't have just asked you that question.'

Behind me, the good cop sighed.

'Did she ever talk about the book, Fliss?' he said. 'I mean, did she say why she was bringing it with her?'

'No,' said Fliss. 'She doesn't have to justify to me everything that's in her suitcase. I don't recognise the author's name, but then there are so many crime writers around.'

'Far more than anyone could possibly have a use for,' I said. 'She didn't happen to say that it was like Hal's latest book, I suppose?'

'Is it?' She pulled a face. 'I thought Hal's book was unique . . . no, Claire did say it reminded her of something, didn't she?'

'Exactly,' I said. 'But this isn't just a bit like it. It *is* Hal's book, only written by somebody else about twenty years ago.'

'So, Hal just copied it? That's what you're saying?'

'Not quite copied,' said Ethelred. Good cops, it seemed, were scrupulously fair. 'But nobody reading the two books could doubt that Hal's book was based on this one.'

'Claire never mentioned that to you?' I said.

'No,' said Fliss. 'And there was me saying that she couldn't keep a secret. She kept that one all right. So was she going to—?'

'Shake him down?' said Elsie. 'It would look very much like it.'

'I thought she was getting too deep into something. I just didn't think it was this. Not for a moment. So, she tried to put the squeeze on Hal and he killed her?'

'That's the word on the street, kid.'

'What street?'

'I mean, that's what my assistant and I think.'

'Your assistant?'

'Ethelred.'

'OK. Just so we're more or less clear what we're talking about.'

'Anyway,' said my assistant, 'do you think that Hal could have taken the book when you were searching up here for Jenny?'

'We came into the room together – we were doing all the rooms. I checked the wardrobe and stuff while he just waited. Yes, he could have easily taken it then. I wouldn't have noticed or cared. Actually he had only to have asked. But, as you say, Claire's key is missing, so somebody else could have come here last night, while we were eating or in the sitting room. There was a lot of coming and going. Anyone could break in, thinking about it. Maybe I'd better take up Wendy's offer to let me switch rooms.'

I nodded. 'Thank you, madam. That concludes the interview.'

'If it was Hal . . . who killed Claire . . . what are you going to do with him until the police come? I mean, you're *not* the police yourself.'

My assistant coughed.

'OK, I concede we are not the actual police,' I said. 'Not totally anyway. Good idea about changing rooms. I'd do that if I were you.'

Ethelred declined to go outside and cut off Hal's exit through the bedroom window, pointing out that there was a considerable drop to the ground and that it was extremely unlikely, based on everything we knew about Hal, that he'd want to jump that far, especially since it wasn't quite light yet. Accordingly we both just knocked on the door of his room and, when Hal said 'come in', I turned the handle and entered. As police raids go, it was fairly routine.

Hal looked up from his computer. 'I'm just trying to finish this chapter before breakfast,' he said. 'While I can still remember the idea I had overnight. The second book in a series is always very tricky.'

'Didn't Charles Straw write a sequel for you, then?' I asked.

Hal paused slightly too long, then said, 'Who?'

'Charles Straw. Author of *In Search of Forgotten Death* – maybe you've read it?'

I held up Charles Straw's masterpiece. Another page fell off the back and fluttered gently to the floor.

'Where . . . ?' said Hal.

'Where did I find it? I found it where you left it to burn. It's called destroying evidence, in the trade.'

'The trade? The book trade, you mean? You know you're not a policeman, don't you?'

'Don't try and change the subject, Hal. Did you or did you not throw this on the fire? I warn you, I've read it cover to cover, or Ethelred has, which is much the same thing when you think about it. And I, or at least Ethelred, know that this book is pretty much identical to your own recent publication. This was Claire's copy, as verified by Fliss. You were in their room when you were looking for Jenny. You took the book while Fliss's back was turned. Claire was onto you, wasn't she, Hal? And she let you know that first evening, didn't she? What did she want in exchange for her silence? Something you couldn't deliver on? Do you realise how much trouble you're in, Hal, or do I need to draw you a picture?'

'Are you now claiming to be an artist as well as a policeman?'

'I'm claiming to be a leading literary agent, which means I'm pretty good at spotting plagiarism. That's when one writer copies another, in case you didn't know.'

'The books aren't exactly the same,' said Hal.

'True,' said Ethelred. 'You've changed some names and added a few jokes – old habits die hard, I guess. But the basic plot structure is the same. The *feel* of the book is the same. I mean, I can see why you did it. You have my sympathies.'

I frowned at him. I'd hoped for something a bit grittier,

even from the good cop, but Hal now had his head in his hands anyway. It was confession time.

'You know what it's like, Ethelred. You write book after book and the royalties are rubbish.'

Ethelred nodded.

'And your agent's commission,' I said. 'That's rubbish too.'

'Some of my books have sold reasonably well,' said Ethelred.

'No, they haven't,' I said.

'Anyway,' said Hal, 'about two years ago, I came across that book in an Oxfam shop. I'd never heard of the author, but I opened it at the first page out of curiosity. Hell, I was hooked straight away. I bought it along with a couple of others I fancied and took it home. When I finished it, I thought, well, Straw's written a masterpiece, poor bastard, and he's had no more recognition than I have – less, actually, because a lot of people have at least heard of me, and I'd never come across Straw before. I thought I'd at least email him and say how much I'd enjoyed it. So I searched on the internet for his website, to get a contact address or something. But there was nothing. No website. I checked Amazon and it seemed this was the only book he'd ever written. There was just one copy of it available second-hand. It took a while, but I eventually pieced the story together. Straw had self-published the book twenty years ago. Only a handful of copies had ever been printed. There had been no reviews. Just a brief piece in his local paper saying that he'd published a book called *In Search of Death* – they hadn't even bothered to get the title right – and that it would be the beginning of a glorious literary career. Then about a year after that there was another short piece on Straw: cyclist killed in accident with lorry, it said. No mention that the cyclist had ever written a book, just that he was aged twenty-seven, unmarried and he'd worked as a civil servant. So, that was that. Straw's glorious literary career was over before it had begun.

'But I kept thinking what a brilliant book it was. That twist in the plot . . . it should have been a bestseller for him . . .'

'So, you thought it would be a bestseller for you?' I asked.

'Well, it might as well be a bestseller for somebody.'

'Good point. I mean, *really* good point. Didn't you think somebody would spot it though?'

'He didn't seem to have any surviving family. I systematically bought up, and destroyed, every copy of the book that I could find for sale. They cost me fifty pence each on average. Say around eight pounds in total. And I didn't copy it word for word – just the ideas. There's no copyright on ideas.'

'But if somebody had chosen to point out the similarities it would have been awkward?'

'A bit.'

'Then Claire picked up a copy somewhere . . .'

'She must have done, mustn't she? She had it with her that evening when she suggested we had a quick chat. She told me how much she'd loved my latest book, then sort of waggled Straw's in front of me.'

'How much did she want?'

'She didn't say. But it was clear what she meant.'

'You said before that she'd merely threatened to tell

234

your wife that you'd shared a cosy chat?'

'Well, I had to say something to you. You could scarcely have missed that I was a bit shocked when I returned. And I knew that Fliss would corroborate the cosy chat thing. So it was as good a story as any. A bit of truth is always good in an alibi, isn't it?'

'And so that's why you killed her,' I said.

'Killed her? No, of course not. I've no idea who did that. I was a bit relieved, I admit it. Even if she hadn't planned to blackmail me, you could never be sure what she'd say to anyone. She had the loosest tongue I've ever come across. Then of course I realised that the damned book must still be around somewhere. I couldn't afford to leave it wherever it was, with the police swarming all over it, bagging up every little piece of evidence, presenting it at somebody's trial. I had to get it and destroy it. Hell, I'd destroyed every other copy I could find – why not that one too? Fliss might notice it had gone, but nobody could ever prove I took it. I'd have done pretty much anything to get it back. My first thought was that Claire would have kept it with her. So, I went to the woodshed. That was creepy, I can tell you – even in the middle of the day. I don't know how Wendy did it at night. I went through Claire's pockets, but found nothing. I didn't realise there was a right way and wrong way to put that wooden peg back.'

'With Wendy, there's always a wrong way to do something. And you took the key to Claire's room?'

'No. If the keys were there, I missed them. I didn't even think of that, to be honest. So, when I went up to see if the book was in the room, I just found it locked.'

'But later, you and Fliss were searching the top floor . . .'

'Exactly. I volunteered to do the top floor. We did all of the rooms, including hers – I insisted we should, just for completeness. She thought I was being a bit pedantic but humoured me. I grabbed the book when she wasn't looking. Then I waited until you'd all gone to bed and lobbed it on the fire.'

'From where Ethelred retrieved it,' I said. 'Another five minutes and it would have gone – or at least been unreadable.'

'Thanks a bunch, Ethelred,' he said.

'My pleasure,' said the good cop. He didn't have many lines, but this was mainly bad cop territory.

'So what now?' Hal asked. 'I mean what do you intend to do with that thing in your hands?'

'It's evidence,' I said. 'Like you say. I'll bag it up, if I can find a bag anywhere. I'll put it with the note Dean wrote to Claire, wherever that is.'

'But you don't need to give it to the police. I mean, it's not as if I was really a suspect.'

'But you are, Hal,' I said. 'As things stand, you're really the only person here with a half-decent motive.'

'Me? What about Fliss?'

'What about her?'

'I bet she told you to come and question me?'

'That is a confidential matter.'

'So, she did then. I thought as much. Haven't you noticed how she's been trying to deflect the blame from herself? Her accusations against Dean for pursuing Claire, when Dean says he did nothing of the sort?'

I nodded. That was true.

'But why?'

'Because maybe Fliss killed Claire.'

'And her motive was . . . ?'

'They go back a long way. They know a lot about each other. Haven't you asked yourselves what Fliss is doing here anyway? Why did she come with Claire to a place in the middle of nowhere?'

'Her family came from round here,' said Ethelred. 'Also she says things were getting a bit tense at home.'

'That last is an understatement,' said Hal.

'OK, kid, spill the beans,' I said.

'You know her child isn't her husband's?'

'No?'

'No.'

'Does her husband . . . ?'

'Not yet, he doesn't.'

'And the child's father is . . .'

'James of course.'

'You're certain about all this?'

'It was one of many things that Claire told me during our literary discussion in Glasgow. In between Thomas Hardy's early unpublished novel and Anthony Berkeley's run-in with the traffic cops.'

'Your discussions on the book world were wide-ranging.'

'You don't know the half of it.'

'I would if you told me the rest.'

'But you don't need to know.'

'Fair enough – though we've got plenty of time if you'd like to tell me. I mean, I'm a good listener. So, what's it to

Claire who the father is? She's Fliss's mate after all, not Ollie's.'

'Ollie was previously Claire's boyfriend. She forgave Fliss for stealing him but resented her cavalier treatment of him thereafter.'

'Did Claire have any plan of action?' I asked. 'Was talking to Ollie any part of it? I mean, she seems to have told you most things.'

'Not when we were in Glasgow. She may have formed one subsequently. The point is Fliss had as much to lose as I did if Claire's tongue wasn't stopped.'

'That's not a bad motive, as these things go. Actually that's the best so far. But you're not off the hook by a long way. You're still a suspect,' I said.

'We're all still suspects,' Hal replied.

CHAPTER TWENTY-FIVE

Ethelred

We paused outside Fliss's room. It was very close to breakfast time but Elsie had insisted we act straight away.

'Let's get one or two things straight,' I said. 'First, you are not a policeman. Second, even if you were, you are not from Bay City. You don't have to address anyone as "madam", still less as "sister". Third, even if you were from Bay City, you would be after evidence, not gossip. Fourth, don't fire off random accusations that you may later have to retract. And fifth, keep it short.'

'I'll do,' she said, 'whatever I need to do to crack the case. Bay City's a swamp, and we need to drain it. Cover me, partner. We're going in.'

I knocked on the door. A rather resigned voice told us to enter. We did.

'So, you've talked to Hal?' asked Fliss. There was a cautious note in what she said. We were back too soon.

239

'Here's how it looks to us, sister,' said Elsie. 'You're very keen to shoot off accusations about other people. But you didn't tell us that James was the father of your kid.'

'Hal told you?'

'Why do you think that?' asked Elsie.

'Because you've just come back from talking to Hal and you haven't really had a chance to talk to anyone else about me.'

'So, is that true?' Elsie asked.

'Is which bit true?'

'About the baby. That it's James's.'

'I don't know . . . I mean, yes . . . probably. I haven't actually done any DNA tests. It would look pretty suspicious if I did, don't you think? Ollie doesn't know anything. Nobody knows except . . . hang on – did Claire tell Hal that?'

'I haven't said we got it from Hal. Maybe we did, maybe we didn't.'

'Elsie, this is a difficult conversation at the best of times. I can't run the whole thing in the conditional tense. Can you just admit you got it from Hal?'

'OK, we got it from Hal.'

'And he got it from Claire in Glasgow? Again, it would make life simpler if you told me.'

'Fine, I've now told you. Hal also said that Claire used to go out with Ollie. Is that true?'

'Sort of. I mean it wasn't that serious.'

'For Ollie or for Claire?'

'It may have meant more to Claire than Ollie. That's the way these things go.' Fliss shrugged.

240

'And if you and Ollie split, then she and Ollie would get back together again?' said Elsie.

'I doubt that very much. Some people move on with their lives.'

'But she might have thought they would?'

'I suppose so. Yes, actually that is how her mind works. Worked.'

'So, you killed Claire to stop her telling Ollie,' said Elsie.

'That really doesn't follow,' said Fliss.

'That's true,' I said. 'It's somewhat tenuous.'

Elsie gave me a look. Whether I was bad cop or good cop at this point, my comments were not required.

'Claire knew too much,' said Elsie.

'Well, that's true anyway,' said Fliss. 'Claire seems to have had something on almost everyone here.'

'And it was recorded in her black book?' Elsie asked. 'Victim by victim.'

'How would I know that?'

'Because you have seen the black book yourself.'

Fliss considered this. Would we believe she hadn't taken even a tiny peek? 'Is Hal accusing me of killing my friend?' she said.

It was Elsie's turn to mull over the various answers to this question and, of course, the need to protect her sources of information.

'Yes,' she said. 'He is.'

'And you believe him?'

'I don't trust anyone, sister. You ought to know that by now.'

'I've seen the book, of course,' said Fliss. 'As for being

241

arranged victim by victim, it was really organised as you would expect – a series of notes on plot ideas and on books she'd read. I suppose in some cases you might have been able to tell who she was talking about, if you were the person concerned. But most of it appeared quite innocuous at first glance. Only the person referred to might understand what it all meant. I hadn't picked up the stuff about Hal, for example.'

'But you had picked up the stuff about somebody else?'

'Possibly.'

'Who exactly would that be?'

From far away, the breakfast gong sounded. Fliss picked up her tapestry bag, as if ready to leave.

'You almost made me miss lunch yesterday,' she said. 'I'm not missing breakfast. I'll tell you what I know later.'

'Will it take long?' said Elsie.

'It depends on how many stupid questions you have to ask.'

'Let's get breakfast,' I said.

Jasper had helped Wendy prepare the meal. It seemed that he too had been up early. Nobody claimed to have slept well.

We were served bacon, egg and mushrooms – just mushrooms for Fliss. Then toast made from home-baked bread and chunky marmalade. Seeing what could be done under the circumstances, I was sorry that I was not experiencing the centre as it usually ran itself. The cooking under Wendy's supervision was excellent and everything continued in spite of Jenny's absence.

'Whenever we go into the kitchen, I expect to see Jenny there,' said Fliss, as we gathered the dirty plates. 'But I guess she's gone.'

'It wouldn't be easy to get away down the valley,' said Hal. 'Still less to make your way up and over the ridge.'

'Well, we've searched the house and grounds,' said Jasper. 'Including the priest hole. She can't be here – kitchen or anywhere else. Dean's right – she's long gone.'

'I didn't say she had. Merely that it's possible,' said Dean.

'Maybe she's gone, but not far. Is there anywhere else nearby?' I asked. 'A shepherd's hut or anything?'

'There's a ruined shepherd's hut a little higher up the fells,' said Wendy. 'But you wouldn't want to hide out there – you'd freeze to death in this weather. And nobody actually saw any tracks going in that direction.'

'Maybe we should check it anyway?' said Hal. 'If it's not too far.'

'Even if Jenny has been that stupid, I can't allow the rest of you to be. If you vanish too, it isn't possible to call a rescue helicopter to find you. We just have to wait for a thaw. Jenny knows the area better than anyone. Maybe she did make it down as far as Butterthwaite.'

'I agree,' said Dean. 'Wherever she is, there's no point in going after her.'

We looked out of the window. It was a bright sunny morning. There had been no more snow overnight, but the cover seemed as thick and even as ever.

'If she did try to leave during the storm,' said Jasper, 'she could be lying somewhere under that lot and we'd never know. Actually she might have been killed and her body just left out there for the snow to bury it. It could be just a few feet from the house.'

We shuddered silently. I suppose we'd all been thinking that, but Jasper was the first to voice it. Though any of us might have said much the same, the remark, coming from him, seemed in some indefinable way to be a bit tacky. Perhaps it was the use of the word 'it' rather than 'her'. Perhaps it was the suggestion that the body was only feet away, rather than yards – almost touchable. Perhaps it was just that Jasper had said it. He stroked his stubbly chin and turned back to a silent contemplation of the vast white landscape and all that it might be hiding.

'What would be the point?' asked Hal. 'Killing her and leaving her outside like that?'

'It depends on how much time the killer wanted to buy,' said Jasper, without looking at us. 'It would all be absolutely fine if he only needed until the snow melted.'

Again, I was left with the feeling that this was insensitively phrased.

'So she's fled the killer or been killed by him – or she's the killer herself,' said Hal.

'We'd know better if we had the black notebook,' I said.

'Perhaps we should search for it,' said Elsie.

'Somebody would have found it when we were looking for Jenny,' said Fliss. 'I mean, if it was somewhere obvious.'

'But we were looking for something big – not an A5 notebook,' said Elsie.

Nobody ventured an opinion. I suppose we all had a pretty good idea by now of what the book might contain – some much better than others of course – and none of us wanted to be the one who suspiciously suggested that it wasn't worth doing.

'Oh, very well,' said Wendy. 'Dean and I can clear all this away. I'll get the spare keys one more time for you to check everywhere. Including the keys to my rooms – I have nothing to hide. Divide yourselves up again and hunt for it, if that's what you want to do with the morning.'

I was with Jasper again – pairs were still considered safer, though logically it left one of us alone with the killer while the others dispersed to the far corners of the house.

We searched mainly in silence. We went first to the woodshed. Wendy had finally found a padlock and secured the door, but we had the key. Claire's body now lay under a sheet – another early morning task for Wendy, it seemed. But we tacitly agreed that the body had already been searched as many times as it needed to be – by Elsie, Wendy and whoever had taken the keys. So, we checked as well as we could with a torch behind the stacks of logs. We emptied the bin of kindling. We breathed a sigh of relief as we finally closed the door and locked it again.

'What about just under the snow?' asked Jasper.

'Because, for a book, it would be only a temporary hiding place and, once the snow melted, it would be able to testify, unlike a dead body,' I said. 'If it hasn't been destroyed it will be somewhere inside, carefully stashed away. Where would you hide a book?'

'Amongst other books.'

'Good point. Let's check the sitting room.'

We searched all of the shelves and behind the shelves. We looked under armchairs and sofas. I examined the ashes in the still-cold fireplace. Jasper went out to the hallway and opened the door in the grandfather clock to see if it was sitting inside the case.

I slumped onto the sofa and waited for him to return. Then, down the side of the cushion I was sitting on, I felt something small and metallic. I pulled it out and held it up for Jasper to see as he re-entered the room. It was a room key with a front door key attached.

'But maybe don't tell anyone else for the moment,' I said.

He nodded. 'Whatever you think best,' he said. 'I've had enough of playing detective to be honest.'

I stuffed the keys in my pocket.

Elsie and Fliss crossed our paths, reporting that there was nothing to be found in the bedrooms. Hal had checked the cellar, though with no great enthusiasm. He'd also searched Wendy's sitting room and bedroom.

'Well,' I said, when we were all finally back in the sitting room and Wendy had made up the fire, 'we must have checked everywhere that it could reasonably be.'

'Then it looks as if Jenny took it,' said Hal.

'Perhaps she was planning a new career in blackmail?' said Dean.

I looked round the room. Nobody for some reason seemed very keen on that possibility. When you've seen off one blackmailer, the last thing you want is that they should pass the baton to a younger, keener successor.

* * *

'We've searched the whole place twice,' said Elsie. 'We haven't found Jenny. We haven't found the black book. And remember we haven't found Claire's keys either.'

We were now back in her suite. While we had been searching, the sun had continued to shine down on the world outside. There was a warmth in the air. I wondered how long it would take to begin to melt the snow. A day? Two days? The white surface seemed somehow shinier as if covered with a thin layer of water. And there was a steady drip from the roof that formed icy little hollows in the surface below. Wendy claimed she'd know when the thaw had started properly, but she hadn't confirmed it yet.

I held up the two keys I had found.

'These were down the side of the big sofa by the fire.'

'Who knows they were?' asked Elsie.

'Just you, me and Jasper at the moment.'

'Why not tell everyone?'

'Because I'm still trying to work out what it means,' I said. 'If they're Claire's and she dropped them there, then that explains why they weren't in her pockets. Hal said he saw her desperately looking for something in the sitting room, just before she was killed. Maybe she was going to go back to her room for her coat before she made her rendezvous at the woodshed. She couldn't find the keys in her pocket or in the sitting room. She ended up not going back to the bedroom, leaving her own coat and notebook there and having to make a run for the woodshed in Wendy's coat, in order not to miss the appointment.'

'So our assumption that she took the coat because it was a last-minute arrangement may not be right. She could have got her own coat if only she'd had the key to her room. And she didn't want to borrow Fliss's key and let her know what she was doing. Claire might have been planning the meeting all day – or even since the previous evening.'

'So, it's a bit less likely it's Dean and a bit more likely it's one of the others.'

'But don't forget Dean wrote her a note,' said Elsie.

'Which didn't say to go to the woodshed. And which Dean says has nothing to do with Claire's death. The note may be a complete red herring.'

Elsie looked strangely relieved.

'You have still got the note, haven't you?'

'Absolutely. Wherever it is, it's totally safe.'

There was a knock on the door.

'I thought I'd come and see you here,' said Fliss. 'I don't want you to get the impression that I talk only when cornered. And it's a lot more comfortable here than in my own room – well done on the booking technique, Elsie. Nice one.'

'It pays to plan in advance,' said Elsie. 'It avoids all sorts of problems.'

'I'm sure it does. Anyway, I just wanted to finish telling you what I knew about the missing notebook. Like I say, I didn't see all of it or even most of it, but I did catch more than a glance at one bit. You know that Claire and Jasper worked for the same organisation?'

'Yes,' I said. 'Dean told us. Jasper didn't seem keen to talk about it. He's been going out of his way not to discuss finance in any form, and Harefoot in particular.'

'From what I read, that's not surprising. You know he

was asked very politely to leave?'

'Was he?'

'I don't know all of the details, and Claire never talked about it, which was odd in itself. But from what I read in her notebook Jasper was suspected of some sort of fraud. Claire was part of the investigating team.'

'And Jasper was sacked?'

'No, that's not how it works at Jasper's level. Sacking senior staff for misconduct of that sort worries investors and that affects the share price. Much better to present the culprit with the proof and suggest they do the decent thing.'

'They get a pistol and large glass of whisky?' asked Elsie.

'They get a non-disclosure agreement and a very large cheque. Everyone signs the agreement and swears never to mention the matter again. Jasper literally laughs all the way to the bank. Of course, the agreement is probably unenforceable and there's a danger that it will all leak out anyway – at least within the inner circle that runs the finance sector. Jasper has a reference saying that he's honest, hard-working and sober, but that won't necessarily get him another job. So, he decides to write a crime novel. Hell, he knows about crime, so why not?'

'His first book was about fraud,' I said. 'It was his depth of knowledge on the subject that made it such a hit.'

'Write what you know,' said Elsie. 'It's just that his imagination didn't stretch to anything else afterwards.'

'But Claire had the evidence that Jasper was guilty?' I said.

'I would imagine so,' said Fliss. 'The black book didn't say – or not the bits I read. If Claire kept some papers from the investigation, she could still have sent them to the police. The board may not have wanted to press charges, but they weren't judge and jury – in fact, their actions merely made them accomplices to the crime.'

'Jasper said that Claire could blackmail him about some tweet he sent years ago,' I said.

'I doubt if that's the first lie he's told,' said Fliss. 'I mean, you only have to look at Jasper to know that he must have made some dodgy posts in the past, so it's really plausible. But I think that Claire probably just told him she knew all about the non-disclosure agreement.'

'Hal might have been inconvenienced by Claire's revelations,' said Elsie. 'His reputation might have sunk to zero. He might have even had to go back to writing comic crime. But Jasper could actually go to jail.'

'Claire had struck lucky,' I said. 'I mean, both the writers she had something on turn up at the same course.'

'I'm not suggesting that she had stuff just on those two. She was a forensic accountant. She was good at prying into private matters. She may have known awkward facts about dozens of people.'

'So when you said she was getting too deep into something, that was Jasper? Or Hal?' I said.

'I didn't know. At first, I thought it was Hal – because of the Glasgow thing. Now I think it was Jasper. But honestly it could have been anyone. Anyone at all.'

She looked at me in an uncomfortable way.

'I don't think I was in her book,' I said.

'No?' said Fliss. 'Everyone has some secret they wouldn't want people to know. Something deeply embarrassing.'

'Sadly his sales figures are readily available,' said Elsie. 'So blackmail would be pointless.'

'What did she know about Dean, I wonder?' I said.

'Or Wendy,' said Fliss. 'Or Jenny.'

'Well, it looks as if Jenny now has the book,' said Elsie. 'And some pretty hot stuff on Jasper.'

'Or on herself,' I said.

'But what did Claire know about Jenny?' asked Fliss.

'I'm not sure,' I said. 'But I have an idea that I'd like to check.'

'Without the internet?' asked Elsie.

'Without the internet,' I said.

CHAPTER TWENTY-SIX

Elsie

I left Ethelred to follow up his non-electronic sources. I wasn't at all convinced about Jenny's guilt, but we did have something good on Jasper, in addition to his stubbly chin and flaky reputation. He was clearly now the prime suspect. It was time to get him back on the comfy bed and fire a few questions at him.

In the end, he wasn't in his room, but Hal said he'd seen him heading for the kitchen. I thought that might be a good place to go anyway, since I could also check the fridge and see if that last chocolate mousse was still there.

Jasper was finishing the washing-up, doubtless wanting to score brownie points with Wendy, which he might need when she reported back to the police.

'Washing up, eh?' I said, in a low-key way that would lull him into a totally false sense of security.

He looked at me suspiciously. 'Yes, obviously that's what I'm doing. Here's water and here are some pans. The plates are in the dishwasher. I thought we should all give Wendy a hand in any way we can. Have you come to help too?'

'Washing up? I think not. It's a bit too much like exercise for my taste. Are you going to help with cooking lunch too?'

'Yes, I told Wendy I would. Recent events have distracted people a bit. Nobody seems to be suggesting we carry on with the course. So, I can do a bit of cooking.'

'You're good at cooking?'

'Reasonably.'

'So what do you like cooking, Jasper?'

'Stews and curries mainly, I suppose.'

'Not books then?'

'Sorry?'

'Apparently you've plenty of experience in that field. Cooking the books.'

I narrowed my eyes. I really needed a match to chew but couldn't see one around. That's the problem these days – almost everyone's given up cigarettes and gas rings light themselves at the press of a button. Where does a detective get a match when she needs one? Jasper smoked, of course, but asking him if I could please have a match to chew menacingly might spoil the whole tough-guy thing. So I just narrowed my eyes a bit more.

'Is the sun bothering you?' he asked. 'You seem to be squinting.'

'The only thing that's bothering me, Jasper,' I said, 'is the way you've hidden your past misdeeds. And, far from the sunshine being a problem, you actually left Harefoot International under a bit of a cloud, didn't you?'

'Who have you been talking to?'

'That's my business.'

'Well, not really. You're accusing me of something, so it's obviously my business too.'

'Maybe a little bird told me.'

'That's rather unlikely up here, don't you think?'

'It could have been a snow bunting.'

'No, it couldn't. You don't get them in Yorkshire.'

'Fine, it was Fliss then. She said you and Claire both worked for Harefoot. That's something you were keen we didn't discuss. Claire was part of the team that investigated you for fraud. You were sacked for criminal activity. Claire knew a lot about your past. In fact, she knew too much, didn't she? Too much to live, eh?'

'How does Fliss know all that?'

'She read it in Claire's black book.'

'When? I would have thought Claire would have kept that pretty close to her, and it vanished shortly after she was killed. Fliss didn't lose much time before she started to go through it. Claire's body can have scarcely been cold.'

'And you, Jasper?'

'What do you mean, me?'

'What did you think of the book?'

'How would I have a chance to think anything?'

'Because you took the book.'

'And how would I have got hold of it?'

'With the key you removed from Claire's body.'

'I've never had the book. Or the key. Ask Ethelred. I was actually with him when he found the key down the side of the sofa.'

'Precisely.'

'Precisely?'

'It was convenient you were there at that moment.'

'Meaning what exactly?'

'Meaning you'd just dropped it there for Ethelred to find. So he'd think it had always been there.'

'That's nonsense.'

'Which bit?'

'All of it, but especially the snow bunting.'

'So, what did happen?' I asked.

'You're right up to a point – there was illegal activity at the bank. One of my team was trading on his own account, using the bank's money. The usual story – he was clever and would have got away with it if he'd made a profit, but he made a loss and then tried riskier and riskier trades to get the money back. He was ten million down by the time they caught him. You might say we got off very lightly. Other firms have lost billions. Claire was part of the team that was sent in to find out what happened.'

'You knew when you saw her?'

'No, she was a very junior member of the team. I'd had no direct contact with her. Later she told me who she was of course. I mean, I know now.'

'Her team did a good job?'

'You could say that. He got four and half years.'

'But you were sacked as well?'

'As I said, he was a member of my department. I should have spotted what he was doing. Somebody in senior management had to take the rap. It was decided that should be me. I'd had enough of finance anyway. I really did find it very dull. I was very happy to do a deal. I left as I'd intended but with a pocketful of cash. No regrets at all.'

'None of that is on the back cover of your books.'

'The publisher thought the *Times* review would read better. But if we had access to the internet now, you'd find it was all there for anyone who wants to know. I'm only a footnote in the story, but I'm mentioned quite clearly as having had to resign. And in fact, I do refer to the case briefly in the notes at the back of my first book – the one you've read and enjoyed so much. The one you loved the plot of. That one.'

'Great book,' I said.

'Thank you.'

'Really had me gripped.'

'You're very kind.'

'And that stuff with Julia was masterful. Brilliant red herring.'

'Juliet.'

'Her too.'

'So, in summary, Fliss told you that Claire was about to blackmail me and that I had murdered Claire?'

'Not precisely that.'

'Oh, come on, Elsie, she's been throwing accusations around non-stop. Hal told me that she'd also accused him of Claire's murder. Is there anyone she hasn't blamed?'

I thought about that. 'Ethelred,' I said. 'But he obviously didn't do it.'

'Of course not. Judging by his books, he has no idea what a real murder is like. His victims die instantly with a neat bullet hole through their forehead or by some painless and quick-acting poison. You could mop up the blood from his entire Fairfax series with a small tissue and it would still be dry enough to blow your nose on.'

'On the contrary,' I said, 'he researches those Fairfax books meticulously. He would have been quite capable of strangling Claire.'

'But he's scarcely fit enough to have run back from the woodshed as quickly as he would need to have done.'

'I beg to differ,' I said. 'He keeps himself pretty fit for a writer. Fitter than you are, Jasper. At least he's not puffing away the whole time on a ciggie.'

'Then, he's much more likely to have killed Claire than I am. So he should be high up your list, shouldn't he? Higher than me anyway.'

It was a valid point of course. To the extent that you can learn murder from wikiHow, Ethelred was well-equipped to kill small- to medium-sized victims. But statistically it's very unlikely that the murder is committed by the good cop.

'What you said about Fliss is interesting,' I said.

'Really?'

'Yes, I mean, why would she have accused so many others here if it wasn't to cover up what she had done herself? It's quite possible when you take everything into account.'

'Sorry, taking what things into account? What have you found out about her?'

'Nothing,' I said.

'But you have, haven't you?'

'Do *you* think it was Fliss?' I said, neatly sidestepping.

'I think it's more likely to be Jenny.'

'Because she hated Claire?'

'No.'

'Because she did a runner?'

'No.'

'Then why?'

'Because Claire was about to write about the Butterthwaite murder. You may have missed it, but when Wendy suggested that Claire switched to that one, Jenny dropped the bread basket.'

'No, obviously I did notice that. I just didn't know why.'

'Nor did I at the time,' said Jasper. 'I couldn't see the connection. But I'll tell you now. It's all in a book in the sitting room.'

'Do you mind if I get the last chocolate mousse out of the fridge while I listen?' I asked.

But when I opened the fridge door, there was no chocolate mousse left.

'Do you want to hear what happened,' asked Jasper, 'or are you going to stand there all day staring into the fridge in case some chocolate miraculously appears?'

It was a tricky one to call, because I was definitely hoping Father Speedwell might be able to deliver a chocolate miracle, but eventually I said: 'OK, tell me the story then.'

CHAPTER TWENTY-SEVEN

Ethelred

It was only a hunch, but I couldn't believe that somewhere on the bookshelves there wouldn't be something on the Butterthwaite murder. It took a while, but eventually I located a book entitled *North Yorkshire Murders*. It was self-published and had a badly designed cover; Wendy would have allowed it into the Fell Hall collection for only one reason. The Butterthwaite murder was chapter thirty of thirty-two.

It was all much as Wendy had described to us on the first evening. The philandering husband, the murdered wife, the disappearance of the husband, the hill-walking Other Woman, who might have used her pastime as a cover for keeping her lover supplied with necessities. But the author of the book had one additional insight to offer. He was a hill-walker as well as a crime enthusiast. He claimed to have identified a ruined shepherd's hut, in a secluded spot above High End Hall, as it still was then, where the husband had holed up until . . . until what? Had the murderer stayed until the fuss had died down and then rejoined the world under another name? Or had he died there, perhaps trapped by the winter snows? The author, who, judging from other chapters, liked to draw some morally uplifting lesson whenever he could, seemed to hope it was the latter. But a dead body in a shepherd's hut, however remote, would have been noticed eventually. The story, when you looked at it objectively, consisted of a great deal of speculation and a few well-known facts. One of those facts however leapt out at me: the surname of the Other Woman had been Cosham. The same as Jenny's.

It was at that point that Elsie burst into the sitting room.

'I've been talking to Jasper,' she said. 'And you'll never guess what he's told me about Jenny. It's all in a book called . . .'

I held up *North Yorkshire Murders*.

'OK,' she said. 'Maybe you will guess then.'

'We couldn't work out how Jenny was involved because she must have been a baby when it all took place. But she's clearly the daughter of Avril Cosham, who was the other woman in the case.'

'And also the daughter in all likelihood of the murderer?' said Elsie. 'That's Jasper's theory anyway. If so, I'd have dropped the bread basket too.'

'She's pretty close to her mother,' I said. 'I'm sure the family hoped that, after twenty-odd years, they'd finally be allowed to forget things. Jenny might do quite a lot to prevent the whole business being dug up again, this time in fiction. Yes, I can see that she might have been inconvenienced, as Wendy put it.'

'It's more than that,' said Elsie. 'Your book there might not risk saying it, but Jasper had followed the case when it happened all those years ago and reading up on it reminded him of one or two things he'd forgotten. There was apparently talk at the time that Avril Cosham was actually the murderer and that the husband vanished to ensure that the finger of blame was pointed elsewhere. It would explain Avril's continuing devotion to him. Jenny certainly wouldn't have wanted any re-examination of the facts by a forensic accountant, keen to get to the truth. Not if it led to her mother's conviction years after the murder took place. Wendy might think it was just a bit inconvenient if the truth got out, but it could be a lot more than that.'

'Then Claire is murdered and, soon after, Jenny vanishes,' I said.

'And makes a run for it to the same hideout her father had used?'

'It could be,' I said. 'But isn't her father alive – I'm sure that she said he could have given her a lift here?'

'Stepfather?' said Elsie.

'Yes, of course,' I said. 'He must be.'

'But that's not the most interesting part of it,' said Elsie.

'Go on,' I said.

'The last chocolate mousse had gone,' she said.

'Well,' I said, 'I'd assumed up until now that we were only dealing with murder, but I can now see—'

'Don't try sarcasm, Ethelred. You've got the wrong face for it. It's a good face for teaching fifth formers about global warming, but it's no good at all for sarcasm.'

'I'll try to remember that,' I said.

'You should. Anyway, my point was who took the last mousse?'

'You're sure you didn't miscount?'

'Ethelred, I have never, ever, in my entire life, miscounted chocolate mousse. It's just not something I could do. It would go against everything I stand for. Somebody, in between our going to bed last night and getting up this morning, sneaked into the kitchen and stole it.'

'Leaving behind a dirty dish?'

'No! They didn't! So, they took the mousse and the bowl. What does that tell you?'

'They took it somewhere else to eat it?'

'Precisely. Somebody is taking food from the kitchen.'

'And did they take anything else – salad, say?'

'How would I know that?'

'So, what is your theory?'

'What if Jenny hasn't made her escape? What if she is still in the house somewhere – she'd need food, wouldn't she? Something healthy, nutritious and easy to carry off.'

'But we've searched the whole place.'

'Not well enough, clearly.'

'Again, you have a theory?'

'I do. Father Speedwell hid here in this house, right?'

'Yes.'

'So, where did priests hide?'

'Priest holes?'

'Precisely,' said Elsie.

'But we checked it,' I said. 'It was empty.'

'Too claustrophobic to hide in.'

'I agree with Wendy that I wouldn't want to spend much time there, but they couldn't be too big or the search parties would be able to work out where they were by measuring the thickness of the walls. Too big was a complete giveaway.'

'But that one was also much too easy to find, right there in the hall. And Father Speedwell was supposed to have been arrested in the kitchen. If he'd left the hiding place in the hall, he wouldn't make a break for the kitchen where he had no escape route.'

'And?'

'It's just a diversion – like those false chambers in the pyramids. The searchers find it, see it's empty and conclude that the priest has gone. They wander off. Meanwhile he's actually hiding elsewhere.'

'Wendy would know if there was a second one.'

'Would she? Work on the house was more or less finished by the time she arrived here. She didn't see it being stripped out. The workmen had been told not to destroy anything that was old, just board it over or whatever if it had no use.'

'So a second priest hole could be here, but even more hidden than the other one? Somewhere even Wendy doesn't know about?'

'Yes. Jenny, on the other hand, played here when she was a kid. She might have found something like that. Maybe that's even where her father hid all those years ago. Maybe he was still living there secretly when she was young. Maybe the trips to the Hall weren't just to play dangerous games for children. She said she could still see the old house under all of the new work. So she could be the only one here who knows how to access the real hiding place.'

'It could be anywhere though.'

'Not anywhere. As I say, legend has it that Father Speedwell was arrested in the kitchen. We've been pretty keen to dismiss it, but why would that be the legend if there wasn't some truth in it?'

'So the second priest hole is there?'

'Couldn't be better positioned for a raid on the fridge – I mean now, not in the sixteenth century or whenever it was.'

'So how do we find it?'

'The same way they did then. We could measure to see where hidden spaces might be located. Then we could prise off bits of panelling.'

'I'm not sure Wendy would stand for that,' I said.

'Let's ask her,' said Elsie.

'I absolutely forbid you to do anything of the sort. The building is listed, grade one. I, not you, would be responsible to the relevant authorities if any original features were damaged beyond repair.'

'Ethelred would be very careful,' said Elsie. 'And he would take total blame for any infringement of regulations.'

'I'm not sure I would,' I said.

'Anyway,' said Wendy, 'it is impossible that Jenny is hiding in some priest hole that is unknown to me. For goodness' sake, I know this building better than anyone living.'

'Jenny knew it as a child,' I said, 'before the restoration work.'

'I'm sure she does have a vague memory of it as it was. I know it as it is. Scarcely a year goes by without having to commission some repairs – it's a never-ending job with a building this age. I have plans provided by the architects and have studied them minutely. Trust me, I'd know if there was another priest hole.'

'So where is she?'

'She's already gone down the valley. The snow's started to melt, if you hadn't noticed. If the thaw continues, I'll set off for Butterthwaite this afternoon, or tomorrow morning more likely, and summon help. Jenny might be willing to set off in these conditions, but there's no point in my doing so. She's got too much of a head start for me to have any chance of catching her.'

'Jenny's mother was involved in the Butterthwaite murder, wasn't she?' I said.

'Yes,' said Wendy. 'I thought you'd work that out sooner or later. I realised that I should never have suggested that as a topic for Claire's book. It was very wrong of me. I just wasn't thinking. I certainly didn't foresee Claire's murder as a result.'

'You think Jenny killed her?' I said.

'I didn't want to think so but you have to agree it's possible. Especially now she's gone.'

'We've read up on the case,' I said. 'The book in the library doesn't actually say so but Jenny's mother could have been the murderer. A successful retelling by Claire could have led to reopening the case. Of course, it would depend on how she wrote it.'

'I see,' said Wendy thoughtfully. 'I wasn't aware of that. Well, I can understand why she'd want to get away before the police could reach us, even at some considerable risk to herself. If all that's true, then at least we no longer have a killer in our midst.'

'Of course,' I said, 'we mustn't forget the possibility that she didn't do it but had worked out who the killer was and fled before she was the next victim.'

'But you've said Jenny had a very clear motive.'

'Yes, but Claire knew about the fraud at Jasper's bank,' I said. 'And she knew that Hal's masterpiece was actually a rip-off of another writer's work. I can tell you all about it if you wish.'

Wendy shook her head wearily. 'But couldn't they have just bought Claire off?'

'You think so?'

'Oh, yes. A cheap little slut like Claire. I spotted her for what she was the moment she came through the door. I doubt her price was that high. But nothing would have stopped her writing her bestseller – and certainly not the feelings of Jenny's family. I'm sure the others had something to lose, but cash was all that was required to buy her silence. Jasper wouldn't have even needed to have dipped into his investments; he could have done it from his current account. After all, he does drive a Porsche.'

'Perhaps we should still keep an open mind,' I said.

'If you wish,' said Wendy, 'but I think you've already successfully identified the killer. I'm standing you both down from any further investigations. The safety of the rest of you is no longer an issue. I think you'll find that Jenny's gone for good. I doubt the police will catch her any more than they caught her father.'

CHAPTER TWENTY-EIGHT

Elsie

In spite of Wendy's assurances, lunch was, in a very competitive field, the tensest meal so far. Even if Jenny was the killer, things had been said that could not be unsaid. Hal knew that Fliss had accused him of murder. Fliss knew that Hal had tried to fit her up. Jasper knew Fliss had grassed on him over a fraud that he very possibly hadn't even committed. Or not much. Wendy was aware that she had set off a series of events that had led to Jenny's flight into the snow, quite possibly to her death. And, in my mind at least, a small cloud of suspicion still hung over Dean, in relation both to his still-unexplained note to Claire and his conversation with Wendy by the stairs. Even if he hadn't actually killed anyone, he'd done something that he didn't want us to know about. Dean was aware of the small cloud and was anxious that it should not become a large one. Most of us merely toyed with Jasper's pasta bake, which in turn caused Jasper to sulk. We were all pleased when we could disperse again to our rooms.

'Wendy's forecast is spot on, however she does it,' said Ethelred, as we looked out of my window. 'The snow is melting. There are one or two places where you can see bare rock now. It wouldn't be worth the risk of trying to walk down this afternoon – not in my opinion anyway. But the road could be almost clear by late tomorrow morning. I've offered to help prepare tonight's dinner, by the way. Beef Wellington for those who eat meat – a nut version of it for those who don't.'

'Good,' I said. 'That's Wendy tied up for a couple of hours. It gives me a chance to search her flat in complete safety.'

'You have never searched anything in complete safety,' said Ethelred. 'In fact, I can't remember your ever searching anything without getting caught. I'd leave it if I were you. The sole reason for our investigation was to ensure that there wasn't a second murder. If Wendy is right, then the murderer has gone. And the police will be here tomorrow anyway. Let's just leave it all alone, shall we?'

'But there are so many loose ends,' I said. 'Why did Wendy suggest the Butterthwaite murder to Claire? She must have known what she was doing. Wendy plans everything – absolutely everything – and nothing gets in the way of her plans.'

Ethelred shrugged. 'She said she didn't think. I suppose we all do things without thinking, if you're tired or under pressure. Wendy finds running the courses quite stressful – the people side of it anyway.' His mind was on cooking Beef Wellington.

'Then there's the whole business of Dean and Wendy,'

I said. 'Why did Dean come here last summer? And that discussion you witnessed by the stairs was odd, wasn't it? And why did Dean write Claire a note – he's never explained that, has he?'

'I doubt that any of it is important. Dean could have been giving advice on the course – he's self-opinionated enough. And the fact that Dean wrote Claire a note doesn't prove much. We know he wanted to talk to her and advise her not to make a fool of herself. Doesn't it seem likely to you that Wendy's right? Jenny killed Claire to stop her writing about her mother. She's the only member of the party who has actually tried to get away before the police come. Everyone else has been pretty relaxed. Maybe Jenny didn't go to the woodshed intending to kill Claire. Maybe she arranged to see her, hoping to persuade her not to do it.'

'If Jenny was back in the kitchen by one-fifteen, as Jasper says, did she have time to kill Claire?'

'Just about,' said Ethelred. 'Maybe ten minutes, including a sprint back to the washing-up. Jasper saw Claire heading towards the rear of the house. He went off to look for a better place to have a cigarette. At some point during his smoke, he heard what he thought was Claire's voice in the kitchen.'

'An odd thing to do – kill somebody then do an amusing impersonation of them,' I pointed out.

'Perhaps for once it wasn't satire. Jenny may have actually wanted people to believe Claire was there and still alive, thus giving her an alibi – if somebody had seen her earlier, then Jenny was back in the kitchen and Claire was still alive at one-fifteen. And Jenny may have known

Jasper was there to hear her – don't forget he moved away from the open window because he thought she'd detect his cigarette smoke. Perhaps he was a bit late in doing so.'

I considered this. All agents have to manipulate the truth on behalf of their clients or, at least, on behalf of the sort of clients I have. 'I know you'll love this book as much as I do.' Yeah, right. Most agents could commit murder and you'd never know a thing from our expression. Had Jenny missed her true vocation in the book trade?

'Some of it seems likely,' I said. 'I mean, the complete destruction of her family is an adequate motive. As for getting from the woodshed to the kitchen, nobody would have been surprised to see Jenny running from one job to another, not with Wendy as her boss. Hal or Dean sprinting down the corridor would have been more memorable. And she could have faked the whole Claire asking for coffee thing. But, if I were her, I wouldn't have gone anywhere last night. She'd be better off waiting until tonight, when there will be much less snow. I think she could still be hiding here.'

'But where?' said Ethelred. 'Wendy insists she'd know if the workmen had stumbled across a priest hole. Even if there was one in the sixteenth century – and I accept your argument that the hiding place we were shown looks like a decoy – that doesn't mean it's still there. Wendy explained all of the changes that had taken place. The nineteenth century renovation seems to have been pretty thorough. Whole wings of the building may have vanished.'

But Ethelred had missed a key piece of evidence.

'So where did the last chocolate mousse go?' I asked.

'That's a major unsolved mystery.'

'You probably miscounted.'

I shook my head sadly. How could he even think that of me?

'All right,' said Ethelred, 'maybe Fliss took it or Jasper. You're not the only one who likes chocolate.'

'When are you going to start cooking?'

'Around four-thirty, I think. You're not planning to do anything stupid, are you?'

'No,' I said. 'Definitely not.'

Or not until four-thirty, anyway. There was a slightly more legal Plan B I could try first.

I tried Dean's bedroom, but got no response to my polite knock on the door, so I went back down to the sitting room to see if he was there. As I approached it, Wendy came out at some speed, glowered at me and headed off towards the kitchen.

'So, you've changed your mind?' said Dean, as I entered. 'Sorry, it's you, Elsie. I thought . . .'

'Changed my mind about what?'

'Oh, I was just talking to somebody else.'

'Wendy?'

'You saw her coming out?'

'Yes.'

'Right. So, yes, that's who it was. I was talking to Wendy. About the course.'

'She's not taking your advice, is she?' I said sympathetically.

'Not exactly,' he said, suddenly very much on his guard.

'And you're in a position to advise her?'

'Yes.'

'But you know nothing about courses or crime writing. Of course, you know a lot about the law. Human rights, wasn't it?'

'That sort of thing.'

'What are you doing here, Dean? You haven't come to learn how to write crime novels, have you? You walked up the valley in a snowstorm for some other reason entirely. And it was the same thing that brought you here last summer.'

'None of that is any of your business,' said Dean.

'Is Wendy your client?'

Dean smiled. 'No,' he said. 'Definitely not.'

'Are you with the secret service?' I asked.

This time Dean didn't laugh, even a bit. 'I'm a solicitor,' he said. 'A fully trained solicitor. Now, if you'll excuse me, I'm going to my room. I have some work to do. Solicitor's work.'

'I suppose I couldn't ask you a few questions?'

'No, you can't. And don't pretend that you're doing it on Wendy's behalf. She's told me you and Ethelred are off the case.'

Fine. Nobody could say I hadn't tried to do it legally. Back to Plan A, then. I knew where the spare keys to Wendy's flat were kept. I'd seen her take them out when we searched yesterday. And I'd noticed she hadn't locked them away properly, any more than she'd padlocked the shed first time round. She was getting careless. I just had to wait until after four-thirty.

At four thirty-one, I went to the still unlocked drawer in the sitting room and, from the various bundles there, selected the unmarked bunch of keys that I knew would give me access to Wendy's flat. I walked past the kitchen, pausing to check that I could hear both Wendy's and Ethelred's voices. They were discussing pastry. Bless.

I'd already searched the flat once, when looking for Jenny, and Ethelred and I had visited it together to talk to Wendy, so I knew my way around. I looked both ways down the corridor, inserted the key in the lock, and I was in. Raffles, eat your heart out.

I carefully locked the door behind me, because not doing so in the past had occasionally proved awkward. So, I was alone, with a couple of hours during which there would be no interruptions at all. I was well ahead of where I normally was in searches like this. Ethelred's fears that I might get caught hiding at the bottom of a wardrobe by the returning owner of the flat, say, were utterly groundless. This time everything would be fine.

The flat was noticeably less tidy than when I'd visited before, suggesting that even obsessive-compulsives can be a bit slovenly given the chance. There was a pile of newly laundered clothes on a chair. There was an empty rucksack. And Wendy had cleaned her walking boots and just left them out on the floor. I was struck again how anonymous the sitting room was and how few personal mementoes it contained. No photographs of friends or relatives or of Wendy herself. No university certificates. It was as if she'd deliberately removed anything that might have given me the slightest clue as to what she thought or felt.

Then I heard footsteps in the corridor outside. So that was:

1 Dean, doing some legal work or

2 The ghost of Father Speedwell, come to wish me the very best of luck or

3 Wendy.

I now re-evaluated the advisability of locking the door. If it was somebody with no business to be there, then the locked door would keep them out. I had however lost the excuse, if it turned out to be Wendy, that I'd gone to see her and just found the door unlocked and wandered in to see if she around and free to chat.

A key was pushed into the lock, suggesting it might be somebody who had a legitimate right to enter. Hiding in bedrooms has not been a great career choice for me in the past, but the options were either to brazen it out and explain what I was after on the one hand, and nipping into Wendy's wardrobe on the other. There really wasn't any contest.

I closed the bedroom door behind me just as the outer door opened. What I could only assume were Wendy's footsteps sounded across the floor. Would she come to the bedroom? People often did that when it was their flat. The problem with hiding in a bedroom, as you'll know if you've done it lately, is that it raises the stakes a bit – from a puzzled 'what are you doing standing there in my sitting room?' to a furious 'what the shit are you doing hiding amongst my clothes?' And I suspected I'd have even less time than usual to come up with a satisfying answer.

I heard another key in a lock and a drawer opening. Then I heard her open the French doors out onto the fells. There were some beepy-clicky noises I couldn't quite interpret. Then Wendy spoke to somebody in a whisper, which was odd because I hadn't heard a second person enter the room. Could somebody have been waiting just outside? I wondered for a moment if Jenny had been hiding in an outbuilding and Wendy was now letting her back in but what followed didn't sound like a conversation with Jenny. I heard Wendy say 'tonight if I can', then 'oh, will it?' then 'OK, that changes things a bit' then 'but you can still do it?' then 'thank you, I promise, this is the very last time'. Then I heard the French doors being closed, the drawer open and close, and the drawer being locked. Then footsteps echoed across the floor again, the outer door opened and closed. The key stuck briefly then turned, a delay which was neither good nor bad from where I was crouching. And I was alone again.

I returned to the sitting room and tried opening the various drawers. One, I wasn't surprised to discover, was firmly locked. Others had moderately interesting stuff – credit cards, bills in neat folders, receipts. But no codebooks, lists of agents or invitations to the CIA Christmas party. Then I noticed on the table some plans of the Hall. Wendy wasn't normally the sort of person to get things out and leave them lying around just to be untidy. Nor was she somebody to scribble on plans in pencil for no good reason. I studied them carefully. I couldn't risk taking them away with me, but I needed to remember one feature in particular – the one she'd put a circle round.

I had another look for the little black book but, if Wendy had it, it was hidden more cunningly than I hoped – possibly in the inaccessible drawer. I gave an inward sigh, unlocked the door, exited, locked the door and wandered off down the corridor. As I passed the kitchen I noted that Ethelred and Wendy had progressed from pastry to G. K. Chesterton. I moved on swiftly.

'Where have you been?' I demanded.

'Cooking Beef Wellington,' said Ethelred.

'With no time off for good behaviour? I've been waiting for an hour. It's freezing in here. You might have tried to get away from the kitchen.'

'I had no idea you were up here. I thought you were going to spend a quiet afternoon without doing anything stupid?'

'How do you know I did anything stupid? I might not have done.'

'So, which stupid thing was it?'

'First up,' I said, 'I spoke to Dean. I think he's giving Wendy legal advice of some sort.'

'Why do you think that?'

'Because he denies it. He refused to answer any questions. Wendy's told him we're no longer cops.'

'We never were. And that's it?'

'No, I then broke into Wendy's room, obviously.'

'And she caught you? No, she'd have mentioned it in passing as we made pastry.'

'I'm pleased to say the operation was a complete success. In future you should have more faith in me. She will never know I was there. Unless I dropped a pack of tissues or something in her bedroom.' I checked my pockets. 'Well, hopefully I dropped them in the sitting room. No worries. Anyway, you'll never guess what happened.'

'True,' said Ethelred. 'So why don't you just tell me.'

'Wendy came back to the flat,' I said.

'Yes,' said Ethelred. 'She said she had to pick up a cookery book she'd left there. She was away ten minutes or so.'

'Did she say she was going to make a phone call?' I said.

'No, because you can't. There's no signal.'

'Well, she did,' I said. 'I couldn't work out what she was doing at first – I just heard her open the French doors then speak. She'd gone outside to get a better signal before phoning somebody.'

'But there really isn't a signal,' said Ethelred. 'I actually did try in several parts of the house. There's nothing at all.'

'Unless she has a satellite phone,' I said. 'Much better coverage than an ordinary mobile but rubbish indoors a lot of the time. I can see why you didn't think of it, but I'm not sure why I didn't.'

'Because she's never said she has one,' said Ethelred. 'And she's gone out of her way to present herself as somebody who hates technology. But, with her stuck up here, it would be very sensible. If there was an accident, you'd want a way of calling an ambulance that didn't involve a four mile drive down the valley over a bumpy road. When you think about it, it would be irresponsible not to. I mean, none of

277

the guests have one because they're expensive to buy and to run. And you wouldn't want one in place of a normal phone anyway – they don't have the same functionality. So people who come here just take it for granted that they can't phone out or get the internet.'

'Why not just tell us she has it?'

'Because then everyone who came up here would constantly be asking for a lend of her phone. And returning it with germs on. She wouldn't like that at all. And if she made a separate one available to guests, it would spoil the whole creative isolation thing that is one of the course's selling points. So, she hides it away in her flat for emergencies. Very sensible.'

'Emergencies like one of the guests being strangled?' I said.

'Yes, a bit like that.'

For a little while we were silent, each thinking our own thoughts.

'We could have had the police here yesterday afternoon,' said Ethelred.

'If that's what Wendy had wanted,' I said.

'Which means that she probably doesn't want the police here,' he said.

'So, why delay the police coming here? If she knows who did it, then the police will still get them when they helicopter in,' I said. 'Unless of course the killer is Jenny and Wendy is hiding her in the second priest hole until she can get away safely.'

'Or giving her more time to get out of the country, having made her escape from here last night.'

'Wendy didn't like Claire,' I said. 'What did she call her earlier? A cheap little slut? So, Wendy must have already worked out the killer was Jenny. And she feels really guilty that she started the whole thing by suggesting the Butterthwaite murder as a suitable subject for a book. So, she tells Jenny not to worry – it's all her fault, not Jenny's – she won't call the police until Jenny's out of the country. That all fits together, doesn't it?'

'Absolutely,' he said. 'Jenny's already gone. Wendy is now trying to give her as much time as possible to get a flight somewhere before the search for her begins.'

'But in that case Wendy could tell us all about the second priest hole, couldn't she? It would be empty.'

'Except there may be only one priest hole,' said Ethelred. 'Wendy would know if there was a second one.'

'She does,' I said. 'I saw plans of the house when I was in her flat. Wendy had been studying them on her table. She'd marked a circle just between the two store cupboards in the kitchen. That's where it must be. The builders hadn't included it in their plans and I couldn't see how you got access – but that's always the clever bit. It's right there in the kitchen. Maybe Wendy discovered it recently and realised it was a really brilliant hiding place and the best way of concealing Jenny. If necessary, Jenny could stay there while the police search and conclude she's already gone.'

'What exactly did she say in this telephone conversation?' asked Ethelred. 'If Jenny's still here, then she can't have been talking to her.'

'It was difficult to hear. Something about doing something tonight or tomorrow. OK, so, Jenny isn't going to stay there longer than necessary. My guess is that the plan is to spirit her out of here once the snow allows. Maybe it was a call to Jenny's mother to say her daughter was in deep trouble and she'd need to . . . I don't know, do something. Get her a lawyer. Dye her hair. Buy her a ticket to São Paulo. Maybe all three.'

'Wendy didn't deny that Jenny might be the killer,' said Ethelred. 'So, she's not covering up for her that much.'

'She tried to at first,' I said. 'She even said she hadn't heard that Jenny's mother might have been the real murderer. How likely is that? She'd have read everything that had ever been written on a murder that took place just down the road. But she thought better of trying to cover it up in case it made us suspicious. It's so obviously Jenny that if she tried to claim otherwise we'd start to suspect what she was doing. Anyway, she doesn't want to get done as an accessory afterwards.'

'But we do suspect what she's doing,' said Ethelred.

'Because we're cleverer than she is.'

'We have to stop her,' said Ethelred. 'We have to stop Jenny getting away.'

'Do we?'

'Well, one step at a time then,' he said. 'First, we need to locate Jenny and question her.'

I nodded. 'Then, if we're right, we ask nicely for a lend of Wendy's satellite phone.'

'But you've no idea how we get into the hiding place?' said Ethelred.

'No.'

'And we can't start ripping the kitchen apart.'

'Wendy would notice.'

'Then we'll need to wait for Jenny to come out.'

'Will she do that?' I asked.

'I doubt that sixteenth century sanitation was that good. Not in priest holes. Jenny can't stay there for ever.'

'And then?'

'I think we move into the end game,' said Ethelred.

THREE UNQUESTIONABLE TRUTHS

CHAPTER TWENTY-NINE

Ethelred

I detected a slightly more relaxed atmosphere at the dinner table. Perhaps while Elsie was searching the flat, things had been discussed and patched up to some extent. Jenny's departure was spoken of as the escape of a suspect, no longer as a disappearance that threatened the rest of us. Everyone helped themselves to slightly more wine than usual and Wendy made no objection. Indeed, she seemed anxious that we should all drink as much as we could.

'Well,' said Jasper, 'this is our third dinner together. When we were sitting here that first evening, I doubt that any of us could have foreseen that we would have lost one of our number by now.'

'Two,' said Hal. 'I mean, we also lost Jenny last night.'

'I thought we were agreed she'd made it safely down the valley?' said Jasper. 'That seems likely, doesn't it?'

I looked at Wendy. If she knew anything to the contrary, she showed no sign of it.

'We're still two down,' said Hal.

In the silence that followed I decided I might as well say what the others would be thinking. 'So, the rules of storytelling demand that we lose a third member of the group tonight. And that the third loss in some way resolves the other two?'

'Unlikely in real life,' said Wendy. There was a note of weariness in her voice. 'By this time tomorrow, the snow should have melted, the police should be here and you should all have been able to get away.'

'All except you, Wendy,' I said.

'I suppose so,' said Wendy. 'But, for most of you, the plot seems to be Voyage and Return.'

'It's still Tragedy viewed from another perspective,' I said.

'The same story can be different things from different viewpoints,' said Wendy.

'Should you be staying here on your own?' I asked. 'I mean, after all that's happened?'

'A lot must have happened here over the years. I think many dark deeds have been committed up here, out of sight and sound of the rule of law that applies elsewhere. You feel it sometimes, wandering the house at night. But it's never frightened me. Things like that can't hurt you. Plenty of other things can, but not that. If you're worried, Ethelred, have some more wine. Have some more wine all of you. With luck, and I say that with the greatest respect to you all, this is the last time we dine together. And may this prove to be whichever type of story you choose.'

'Rags to Riches,' said Fliss. And she raised her glass.

* * *

We stayed in the dining room for some time, those who drank wine drinking wine, which was, incidentally, the best so far. The thought of a thaw gave the evening an almost end-of-term feel. But one by one we all made our exits, most fairly unsteadily. Fliss had decided in the end that she didn't need a change of room. The danger seemed to have passed and finding her old room was a sufficient challenge tonight.

'You're still sure Jenny is hiding somewhere?' said Elsie, once we had reached her suite.

'Wendy gave nothing away this evening,' I said, 'but, yes, I think we should go ahead with the plan. There are a number of things I am certain of. Things that should have been apparent to us a long time ago. The first was that Wendy must have had a satellite phone and therefore could have called the police any time since the murder. Hence, she's protecting somebody.'

'Not necessarily Jenny.'

'No, I agree. That doesn't prove it was Jenny in itself. But we knew Jenny was local. She dropped the bread basket when Wendy mentioned the Butterthwaite murders. She used to come up here and play in the ruins, when you'd have expected her to hang out with her friends. And she's put up with working for Wendy.'

'Why is working for Wendy significant?'

'Because she can't get a job elsewhere. She'd have to work with people who knew about her mother's past. It should have been obvious all along that she was connected in some way to what went on up here twenty years back.'

'Agreed. Two unquestionable truths that we should have

spotted,' said Elsie. 'What's the third?'

'There doesn't have to be a third.'

'Well, I think there is, and it's this. Over the past two days I've learnt that Fliss's baby isn't her husband's. I've learnt that Jasper was sacked for not bothering to check what his staff were doing. I've learnt the Hal's unique thriller is nothing of the sort. I've learnt that Dean is a solicitor specialising in human rights, who works out a lot and has an inexplicable interest in Fell Hall. I've learnt Jenny's mother could be a murderer. But I know nothing more about Wendy than I did the day we arrived. You'd have thought she'd have let her guard down once or twice, wouldn't you? Just a word or two about her days in publishing? I know a lot about Fell Hall, but she is still a complete enigma. She has no past.'

'Do you think she really *is* working for the CIA then?' I asked.

'I've no idea,' said Elsie. She gave a yawn. It was our second late night. 'You don't have any chocolate with you, I suppose?'

'No,' I said.

'So, we go down at midnight then?' said Elsie.

'A bit before,' I said. 'Say half past eleven to be safe. We don't know what time Jenny will choose to come out and we can't afford to miss her. Of course, she may be provisioned for several days, wherever she is. But, like we said, she'll need the loo. And she won't want to wake anyone.'

Elsie yawned again and looked at her watch. 'Half an hour to go,' she said.

* * *

At eleven-thirty we crept along the corridor and down the stairs. The ticking of the grandfather clock seemed loud enough to wake everyone anyway, but most were sleeping soundly in a contented alcoholic haze. There was a crispness to the air – the slowly spreading chill that always follows the shutting down of a boiler, a fact confirmed by the soft clicking from the cooling radiators. But, beyond all that, you could already sense the thaw that was taking place on the other side of the heavy-curtained widows. The thaw that would free somebody.

I had already been to the back door and secured one of the two remaining torches. The third had presumably been with Jenny, wherever she was hiding, since the previous evening.

We positioned ourselves just outside the kitchen and waited in the pitch-black stillness. The grandfather clock ticked the minutes away. It was an old clock that sounded only the hour and half hour. I suspected that she would use the midnight chimes to cover the noise of her exit from her hiding place. But it was in fact at quarter to twelve that I heard a scraping sound, then stealthy footsteps crossing the kitchen floor. The kitchen door, already open a little, swung slowly and silently and a dark figure emerged. I switched the torch on. The figure flung up its hands to shield its eyes and hesitated between going forward and going back.

'Good evening, Jenny,' I said.

'Oh, it's you, Ethelred,' she said. 'Well, that's a relief anyway.'

'And me,' said Elsie. 'And you're going to tell us everything.'

'With pleasure,' she said. 'But can I just go to the loo first? You can do a pee in there, but I'm dying for a crap.'

'Me?' said Jenny, when more urgent matters had been dealt with. 'I didn't kill Claire.'

'Well, somebody did,' I said, 'and Wendy is protecting them until the snow thaws and they can get away. She could have called the police on her satellite phone yesterday.'

'Wendy's got a satellite phone?'

'Elsie heard her speaking on it,' I said.

'Are you sure? She's never mentioned it to me. But I sometimes thought it was odd that she didn't get one. Some people just don't like technology of course.'

Elsie looked at me, but I ignored her.

'She was speaking to somebody and saying that she would have to do something tonight,' I said. 'But if that wasn't to get you down to Butterthwaite, then I'm not sure what it was.'

'Can we go somewhere safer?' asked Jenny. 'I'm beginning to think that she knows I haven't already gone.'

'I'm not going in that priest hole,' said Elsie. 'Not for any money. Unless you've still got the chocolate mousse there.'

'No, I ate that yesterday.'

'I told you I hadn't miscounted,' Elsie said to me.

'Look, I'm sure the mousse is very important,' said Jenny, 'but Wendy killed Claire and I think she knows I know, and what she's planning currently is to ensure that I don't get away at all – ever. She could kill me, dump me back in the priest hole and nobody would ever know that

I hadn't killed Claire myself and escaped across the fells.'

'We'll go to my suite,' said Elsie. 'We'll be fine there.'

'Ethelred will protect us,' said Jenny.

'I was thinking more that there was a strong lock on the door,' said Elsie. 'But three's always a good number to have. So I'm told.'

'You're right about the Butterthwaite murder,' said Jenny, once we were in the comparative safety of a locked room. 'When Wendy said to Claire at dinner that she should write about the murder, I couldn't believe what I was hearing. I mean, she knew all about it. She knew what it would mean to me if that happened.'

'And even more so to your mother.'

'Because she was the murderer? I don't think so. Or she never behaved as if she might have been. From the start my mother just brazened it out. She could have changed her surname or something. She could have moved away from the area. But she never did. Even when she married my dad . . . my stepfather . . . she kept her old name. But it was a bit of my past that I've always avoided if I could. You know that I spent a lot of time up here when I was young – yes, I loved it up here but in part that was because I didn't want to mix with the other kids, who knew all about it from their mums and dads, and called me the daughter of a murderer. The same with jobs. I've avoided interviews or anything where I might have to talk about myself. So, I work on my dad's farm when I'm not here.'

'But you applied for this job.'

'Yes. Well, when it came up, I couldn't resist it. I love it up here. It's funny, though. Wendy has been one of the few people I've felt able to talk to about the murder. I know she seems a bit harsh and difficult. But she's been really good about that, really supportive. That's why I was so shocked when she suggested Claire should write about it. It wasn't like her at all.'

'So, why did she do it?'

'I don't know. But, just before she did, there was this look of total panic on her face. You know Wendy – always in control of everything, always in control of herself. But just for a moment she seemed to lose it completely. And her reaction when I dropped the bread – that wasn't like her either. That's what really upset me.'

'And that was what convinced you that she killed Claire?'

'Oh no. That came later – a lot later. It was yesterday evening – about six-thirty. I was coming back to the kitchen after putting out the pâté and I heard Wendy and Dean inside, talking. Dean was saying to Wendy don't worry – we can represent you. And Wendy replied, no, it's too late for that.'

'And you think they were talking about the murder?'

'Well, it's obvious, isn't it? Dean had worked out it was Wendy and was offering to defend her at her trial.'

'How had he worked that out?'

'How am I supposed to know that? But there's something odd going on between him and Wendy, don't you think?'

Well, of course. Whatever else we'd missed, we'd spotted that. 'But Dean's not a criminal lawyer,' I said. 'He does human rights or something.'

'Couldn't he take on a murder case?'

'Yes, I guess he's qualified to do it in theory. But if I was accused of murder, I'd want the best criminal lawyers I could get. I wouldn't want a just-qualified human rights lawyer.'

'I suppose so. All I can say is that Wendy came out of the kitchen at that point and saw me standing there. So, she's like what are you doing there? And I'm like I'm in the middle of cooking dinner. She really was in another world. Anyway, she just says OK. But she's looking at me strangely. Then Dean comes out and he looks at me the same way. So, I thought about it for a few minutes and decided that if Wendy was the murderer and she knew I knew, the best thing was to disappear for a bit. I wasn't sure if it was safe to get down the valley yet, but I've played all over this building and I knew exactly where the second priest hole was and how to get into it. I got myself some food and water and took one of the torches from the back door. Then I hid myself away.'

'But Wendy could find you.'

'I've talked to her about the story of Father Speedwell. She only knows about the priest hole in the hall.'

'Well, she may have wanted to keep it a secret from you but she does know about the second one – at least she does now. It's marked with a circle on her building plans. She may not understand exactly how to access it, but if she thinks you're hiding then she'd know where to wait for you.'

'So, if you hadn't spotted me . . .'

'Wendy would have been waiting for you. We thought

you might emerge at twelve . . .'

From a distance we heard the clock begin to strike.

'I'll go and see if she's there now,' I said.

'I'm coming with you,' said Elsie.

'Lock the door after we've gone,' I said to Jenny. 'If we both vanish, it would be good if somebody knew in which direction we were last seen heading.'

'Don't worry,' said Jenny. 'Nothing will get me out of this room until daylight. Nothing at all. I've seen films where people go off on their own with a crazy killer in the house. It never ends well.'

CHAPTER THIRTY

Elsie

For the second time that evening, we crept down the stairs, wincing every time we made the slightest sound. We paused for a moment in the main hallway, just before the turning that led to the domestic quarters. Ethelred peered round the corner at the dark corridor towards the kitchen door.

'I think there's somebody there,' he said.

'Where?'

'Where we waited for Jenny.'

We stayed as still as we could. At the far end of the corridor somebody else was doing the same.

'Wendy?' I said.

'I can't tell. Whoever it is just moved a bit. If she is waiting for Jenny, she'll be pissed off that she didn't appear at twelve as expected. Wendy is fit, but there's a limit to how long you can crouch.'

'Let's go then,' I said. 'There are two of us.'

'She may be armed,' said Ethelred.

'That's fine. You go first,' I said.

Wendy's head turned suddenly as we approached.

'We've already got Jenny,' I said. 'And she's told us everything. The game's up, sister.'

In the light of my questioning of other suspects, I was expecting some smart-alec remark in response, but she just said, 'Yes, you're right. I suppose it is. Would you like a coffee or something? If so, we'll be more comfortable in the kitchen.'

We sat round the large kitchen table while Wendy fussed with a saucepan and milk. She eventually handed us both hot chocolate and made a coffee for herself.

'Where do you want me to begin?' she asked. 'With the Tomsitt case?'

'You could,' I said.

'So you know who I am?'

I paused for a moment and then said, 'You're Emily Tomsitt, aren't you? I mean, you have no past. And Emily had no future – she just vanished after she was released from prison. She became you.'

'Exactly. She became me. I'd had contact with Hiram Shuttleworth even before I left prison. A lot of people believed in my innocence and he was one of many who wrote to me, well before the successful appeal. We got to know each other. He paid for the appeal in fact. He was waiting for me when they freed me. He had a plan. He'd always intended to set up a centre like this. He suspected that, after prison, I'd just want to vanish. He offered me a way of doing it. I could take up residence here as warden of

Fell Hall. I could change my name, dye my hair. But I think it was being out, walking the fells in all weathers, that really changed my appearance. I lost a lot of weight. I gained the weather-beaten look that the farmers all have round here. For the first few courses I was afraid that somebody would recognise me, but nobody ever did. Of course, people thought that it was odd that I never strayed outside the fells – or as little as I could. I told them, truthfully, that I liked it. When rumours started to spread that this was a CIA operation, I didn't discourage them. It seemed to stop people asking too many questions. They drew conclusions about my past, but entirely the wrong ones.'

I took a sip of hot chocolate. 'And then Claire showed up?'

'No, the first thing was Dean. Of course, before Dean, there had been articles and books about the case, but the authors had never been able to track me down to interview me or get me to comment on anything. Then Dean did. You see, although the appeal cleared me, I'd still spent almost three years in prison. Dean's firm specialise in stuff like that. I don't know how they found my address, but I suspect they got it somehow from the firm that represented me at the appeal. I can't think of anyone else who would have had it. They said they could get me compensation. But I just wanted to forget it. I could see what was in it for them, but I had all I needed here and didn't want any of it taken away from me just so that a firm of solicitors could hog the spotlight. Anyway, there was a sense in which I didn't want to be compensated. I had killed my husband. And yes, I'd suffered years of ill-treatment, but in the end, I knew that I didn't *have* to kill him. I could have walked away. It was just that suddenly something snapped and a scarf was handy. It was right there. I put it round his neck and pulled and pulled and pulled . . . and then he was dead and I couldn't quite remember how I'd done it. I phoned the police and they arrested me. When Jenny told me somebody had been up here, posing as a walker and asking for me, I suspected what he was. But I wasn't certain of that until Dean fought his way through the snow on Thursday morning. He had a short time to work on me. He wrote me a note saying that he was on my side and could we meet? That was the note you found, Elsie, in my coat, the one Claire was wearing. He left it for me, and I just stuffed it in my pocket and went outside to check that the Land Rover was OK in the garage. But he cornered me anyway. He said a lot of people would know who I was, whatever I did, or would be able to work it out so I had nothing to lose. I told him to get lost – I'd say nothing more to him for the entire weekend.

'Of course by then Claire had shown up. I had no idea when she booked that she was planning to write about me. When she announced it at dinner . . . well, you saw I panicked. I suggested she tried something else – anything else. Unfortunately the first thing that came into my mind was the Butterthwaite murder. It was completely wrong of me – I mean, I knew that Jenny was Avril Cosham's daughter. In a sense we were sisters in crime – we both had things in our pasts that we wanted to keep quiet. She'd confided in me. I should have done better for her than that. But I panicked and just blurted it out. I tried to retract, but Hal pushed on with it – I suppose he thought it got him off the hook with the other book.

'When Claire and I took the glasses to the kitchen I tried to find out what she knew and whether she had the first clue who I was. She hadn't, I think, but she was bright. She started asking me questions, and I didn't answer them well. By the time we got back to the sitting room, I think she'd worked the whole thing out. She'd done the research – she knew more about the old me than I did. So, I did the only thing I could. I told her I wanted to talk to her and that we should find somewhere completely private after lunch. The woodshed would be chilly but safe. I said it would be better if we weren't seen going there together. She was to go out by the front door, while I left by the back door. But she was late, which gave me time to worry about what her intentions were. When she got there, she said very apologetically she couldn't get her coat and had borrowed mine. I wasn't quite sure what I was going to do, or whether she'd already read Dean's note, but I'd seen the rope hanging there and had had time to put it in my pocket, just in case I needed it.

'I asked her, straight out, if she knew who I was. She said I was Emily Tomsitt. I asked her what she was doing at Fell Hall. She smiled and said, "I've come here with blackmail in mind, Emily. Don't worry. It's nothing personal – I just need the cash." She turned for a moment to look out of the door, maybe to check we were really alone. It was then that something snapped. It snapped and the rope was in my pocket. It was right there. I put it round her neck and pulled and pulled and pulled . . . and then she was dead, and I couldn't quite remember how I'd done it. I ran back to the sitting room and announced that we would start the course.

But people said we couldn't start without Claire. I knew I had to form a plan quickly. There's no mobile phone signal here, so it surprised nobody that there would be a delay until the police arrived. What I had to do was to be ready to move at just the right moment – after the snow had melted enough, but before any of you thought it was possible to go down the valley and call the police. It would be a narrow window, but I know this valley better than anyone, except perhaps Jenny. I'd reinvented myself once. I'd go off and do it again.'

'And Shuttleworth would help?'

'I can't tell you that.'

'But it was Shuttleworth I heard you speaking to on your satellite phone?'

'I can't tell you that either. I'm surprised nobody guessed I must have a way of communicating with the outside world, but that's how stories work – you tell somebody something often enough and it becomes a fact. No phone signal. We were cut off without any way of calling the police. If I had a satellite phone, wouldn't I have said so?'

'Did Dean know you'd killed Claire?'

'He had the information that you lacked. He knew I was Emily Tomsitt. So, he knew exactly what my motive would have been. He made one last attempt to get me to agree that his firm should represent me, but I told him it was too late for that. Jenny overheard us. I don't quite know what she made of it all, but it didn't surprise me when she vanished.'

'Did she know you were Emily Tomsitt?'

'No . . . maybe . . . I'm not sure. She would have been quite young when it all happened. If she did, then she'd have known I'd now killed twice – the second time to prevent exposure. She also knew that I might just snap again and kill a third time. I suppose, if I'd been her, I might have made a break for it under the circumstances. I thought at first that she'd decided to walk down the valley in the snow – I noticed a torch had gone. I checked the priest hole of course – everything was in place on the shelves. But I'd always wondered if there could be a second one – the first just seemed fake somehow. So, I checked the plans again looking for any unexplained spaces, bearing in mind that Speedwell was supposed to have been arrested in the kitchen. When you looked carefully, knowing there must be one, it was obvious where it ought to be – it's just that I couldn't work out where the entrance was. I thought Jenny might decide she had to come out briefly. Midnight seemed a likely time – the noise of the clock, you see.'

'She needed the loo before that,' I said.

'Ah, on such small details our lives depend. Perhaps if I'd thought of that I could have caught her and persuaded her . . .'

'Or killed her.'

'Or killed her. Yes, I might have done that. If I'd decided I couldn't trust her. I could have returned her body to the priest hole that she'd been hiding in. Then later . . . what better place than the high fells to dispose of a few bones? And if anyone found them they'd just say well, she tried to get away and died up here in the snow.'

'You'd thought it out then?'

'Oh yes, I think everything out. Except for killing my partner all those years ago. And suggesting that the

300

Butterthwaite murder would make a good book. That's not many errors to make over forty-odd years.'

'So what now?' I asked. 'You've confessed to us. Are you expecting us just to let you go – to trek down the valley to freedom?'

'That would be very kind of you, if you've no objection. The conditions are finally right. The snow is melting fast. Any tracks I leave will have vanished by the morning. And I'd rather not go to prison again. I really missed decent wine and whisky when I was there last time. This story isn't Comedy or Voyage and Return. It's farewell to my old life – my second old life – the one that was never any more than a red herring. This story is Rebirth.'

'We can't let you,' said Ethelred. 'You'll get a fair trial and Dean's colleagues will, I am sure, make a good case for you. Claire was, after all, blackmailing you.'

I yawned. It was getting late. I took another sip of hot chocolate. 'That's right,' I said. 'You won't get away with it.'

'I had one thought for how I might,' she said. 'It would be plagiarism, but I'm allowed to do that. My plan was taken from one of Ethelred's own books.'

I looked at Ethelred, who was also now yawning. That wasn't good enough. We had to tie this up first, then we could get some shut-eye.

'What happens in the book,' Wendy continued, 'is that, towards the end, the narrator is confessing to somebody what he has done. He goes into every incriminating detail. Tells her everything. She says to him he'll never get away with it. He says he will. Can you remember why he does succeed?'

I turned to Ethelred for assistance, but he looked almost asleep. 'It's because he's drugged her hot chocolate,' I said.

'Exactly,' said Wendy.

I looked at the empty mug in front of me. 'How did you know the right quantity – I mean how not to give somebody so much that it kills them?'

'I don't know,' she said. 'That's why I didn't do it. I've killed two people. I really didn't want to kill a third, even if it did resolve the story very nicely. So, you're quite safe. Nothing in the mug except chocolate and milk. Relax. If I can't get away, then I'll simply have to give myself up to the police in the morning, just as I did the first time. And now, like Jenny, I need to visit the ladies' room for a moment. Help yourself to more hot chocolate or coffee if you prefer. Or you could check and see if you can find your way into the priest hole. I mean, if you're curious?'

I shook my head. She wasn't going to imprison us there by such an obvious trick.

She smiled. 'No, of course not,' she said. 'You're too smart for anything that simple. I'll be back in a couple of minutes.'

'So,' I said to Ethelred, as she closed the kitchen door. 'Case solved, eh?'

'Yes,' he said, though I could tell that he would have preferred to have been drugged, possibly to death, in homage to one of his own plots. He rubbed his eyes.

'She hasn't drugged us, has she?' I said.

'No, we've just had two very late nights in a row. We're tired and not thinking straight. That's all.'

'Good, I hate metafiction,' I said.

'The one thing I don't think we've cleared up is whether she's with the CIA,' said Ethelred. 'And whether that's who she was phoning.'

'We'll ask her when she gets back,' I said.

'You should have gone with her to the loo,' said Ethelred.

'Why? She can't escape. We're snowed in,' I said.

'Only Wendy, in touch with the outside world, knows how fast the snow is melting,' said Ethelred. 'She admitted that conditions are almost right.'

'Good point. I'll go and check.' I tried the door handle. 'She's locked it,' I said.

Ethelred, since he is a man and therefore contractually obliged not to believe anything a woman says, tried the handle as well. 'It's locked,' he said.

He looked at the door as if contemplating breaking it down.

'It's solid oak,' I said. 'Dislocate your shoulder on it by all means, but just remember we have no way of calling an ambulance. Dean says he knows a bit of first aid, of course, if you're happy with that.'

'We could call for help,' he said.

'Even if the others could hear us under normal circumstances, Wendy fed them all so much alcohol this evening that they'll snore their way through to the morning. And Jenny has sworn not to emerge from the room under any circumstances at all. Moreover if Jenny did come and try to find us, we have no way of communicating with the outside world.'

'True. How long do you think it will take for Wendy to get out of the house?'

'When I was in the flat she had a rucksack, that I now realise was about to being packed, and her boots were nicely cleaned. She would have needed only to throw the satellite phone and a passport on top of the spare T-shirt, then leave via the French doors.'

'She's probably gone already.'

'I'd think so. Gone and there's nothing at all we can do about it.'

'Well, I'm sure that one of the others will be down to make coffee in seven or eight hours, but otherwise I think it could be quite a long night. Do you know any good stories?'

CHAPTER THIRTY-ONE

Ethelred

The police helicopter arrived at ten, not because we'd called for one – Wendy had indeed taken the satellite phone with her – but because the melting snow had revealed Dean's car abandoned further down the valley, and that had initiated a hunt for the driver. They thought we might know where he was.

'So, it was murder mystery weekend, eh?' asked the sergeant. It was a fine day. The sun was shining. The snow had been reduced to a few irregular patches, except for where it hung on in thin, glittering sheets. The air smelt of the same spring that now bathed the lowland fields.

'Yes,' I said. 'That sort of thing.'

'Any dead bodies?' he laughed.

'Just the one,' I said. 'She's in the woodshed.'

He laughed again. Then he said, 'You're bloody serious, aren't you?'

'Go and look,' I said.

* * *

We told the police how Claire's body had been found and of Wendy's confession and disappearance. There was no need to mention the note in the coat pocket, which Elsie had in any case mislaid. Nothing needed to be said by any of us about Jasper's departure from his old job. Nothing needed to be said about Hal's latest book. Nothing needed to be said about Fliss's love life. These things did not concern the death of Claire Rowland, an accountant with literary ambitions, and the flight of Wendy Idsworth, sometime course director for the Golden Age Trust. The sergeant frowned when Jenny gave her name, as if it rang a bell, but restricted his questions to what Jenny could remember about Wendy's movements on the afternoon in question.

'You didn't notice anything strange about the operation here?' the sergeant asked me as he finished taking my statement.

'What do you mean?' I asked.

'Just rumours . . .' He looked at me as if trying to judge whether he could trust me with the information he had, then shook his head and closed his notebook.

We were fingerprinted as a matter of course. We were told that it might be necessary to speak to us again. We would almost certainly be required as witnesses at the trial. A forensics team would arrive as soon as they could drive up to us, but probably not before mid afternoon. It was Saturday after all. We looked at each other – yes, Saturday, so it was. The course would have ended tomorrow lunchtime.

The woodshed was firmly locked, and blue and white police tape placed round it. We were told to keep our hands off everything. Then the police flew out, on another emergency call, with a downdraft that scattered the wet leaves, slush and small stones. They didn't offer to give us a lift anywhere.

Dean had agreed to walk back down and get his car and, if it would start, transport us in a couple of groups down the valley. Now we were having a final, somewhat late, lunch together, cooked by Jenny and Jasper.

'The one thing that I don't understand,' I said, 'is what happened to the black notebook. Jenny didn't have it. Could Wendy have taken that with her?'

Fliss looked embarrassed and pulled a book from her tapestry bag. Well, of course – the one place we'd never searched. You could have got an entire library in there.

'Sorry. Claire had made quite detailed notes, some about me. I didn't want it to fall into the wrong hands.'

'So, what does it say about all of us?' asked Jasper.

'I think you know most of it,' she said. 'Any of you can take a look if you want. Then I'm going to throw it on the fire in the sitting room. That's the best place for it. What Wendy told Ethelred and Elsie is true. Claire did come here with blackmail in mind. I knew she was getting into something that was out of her depth. It was only after I got to read the notebook that I worked out which thing it was and how much she hoped to make. You see, she'd got to the stage in her work-in-progress where you look at it and decide it's all rubbish. She needed a new interest and blackmail seemed as good a one as any. She was enraged, Jasper, that you'd walked away from Harefoot with that

307

severance package. She had plenty of information from her investigations into your team. And the more she reread her notes from all those years ago, the more she thought you knew what your staff member was doing. To be fair, she hated almost everything about you. She'd have happily retweeted anything she could find, but she wouldn't have ruined the TV deal: she needed you as rich as possible. That way you could pay her just a little bit more.'

'But I thought she was also planning to blackmail Hal,' said Jasper irritably. 'And Wendy definitely told you Claire was planning to blackmail her.'

'I don't think so,' said Fliss. 'She admired you, Hal – I mean your early comic crime. It might have amused her to tell you she'd spotted similarities with Straw's book, but I'm sure she wouldn't have done anything about it. And, to the extent she knew about Wendy, she wouldn't have done anything about that either. She really sympathised with Emily Tomsitt. I think, once Claire knew who Wendy was, there was nothing she wouldn't have done for her. Unfortunately Claire seems to have mentioned her blackmail plans only in the most general way and Wendy – or should I now call her Emily? – just jumped to the conclusion that she was to be the victim. Hal also wrongly assumed he was being blackmailed, of course. Ambiguity is fine when writing a crime novel, but blackmailers do need to aim for clarity. Claire had nobody to blame but herself.'

'So, Wendy had no need to kill her?' said Elsie.

'That's the essence of tragedy,' I said. 'Though in one sense the hero's fall is inevitable, in another sense it could always have been avoided. I'll walk down to Butterthwaite with you, Dean. It would be good to stretch my legs after being cooped up here so long.'

Every step took us a little closer to spring. We felt the warmth on our faces and smelt the wet earth. Small streams of meltwater flowed down the sides of the road, but the sun had already dried a broad track down the centre. I noticed how whole sheets of snow still clung obstinately to the north-facing slopes, but grass and heather were pushing through elsewhere. Another day, perhaps two, and then only a few deep, shady hollows would still retain their wedge of snow – retain it perhaps well into May.

'Emily Tomsitt's was a case we've wanted to handle for a long time,' said Dean. 'They were too quick to accept her confession of murder without bothering to investigate the years of suffering that lay behind it. It was a miscarriage of justice and she deserved to be compensated for it. No win, no fee, obviously. Finding her was the problem. We got an address – I won't tell you how – and I tried just dropping in on her. That didn't work. Then, hearing she'd be talking at the Glasgow conference I booked to attend that. She cancelled at the last minute, but I met Claire, who told me she was writing a book on Tomsitt. I tried to get to know Claire better but she misinterpreted my interest and brushed me off. So, I came here. Well, you know the rest. Of course, the moment Claire's body was discovered I suspected Wendy. I had one last attempt to get her on board, but she said it was too late – I think we'd have got her a fairly short sentence for Claire's murder, in view of the blackmail.'

'Except there probably was no blackmail,' I said.

'We could have produced a lot of evidence to suggest there was,' said Dean. 'It wasn't unreasonable for Wendy to assume it. Claire *was* a blackmailer. It was just that the wrong victim killed her. There's the car ahead of us, on that bend. Let's hope it starts after being covered in snow. If not, we'll get help from the farm to give us a push.'

POSTSCRIPT

Ethelred

Hal's thriller continued to sell well for several months. His next book was a return to comic crime. He never really explained why. He just said that, in the end, he preferred it. He is still with Francis and Nowak, and he does a lot of tutoring to supplement his writing income. I asked Elsie once if she still planned to steal him, but she said pointedly that she had enough losers on her books already.

Jasper's television series made little impression. Some critics said that the scriptwriters had changed too much of the plot. Others said they hadn't changed anything like enough of it. There is no talk of a second season. But the books, with the new tie-in covers, sold well. Elsie was right about it all being in the cover. When I last saw Jasper, at Bristol CrimeFest, he told me he'd just bought a new Ferrari.

Fliss eventually showed her failed manuscript to Elsie, who got her to rewrite it and remove all the jokes. The book is out next year. She is still with Ollie. They have a second child on the way.

Though the police hunted for Wendy, first on the high fells then in broader and broader sweeps of Yorkshire and then of the whole country, they never found her. She had vanished as mysteriously as she had arrived at Fell Hall. There was speculation all that year, at crime fiction events that she'd been spirited out of the country. But nobody could quite say how or by whom.

Dean has represented several people in high profile civil rights cases. I often see his face on television, staring earnestly into the camera on his client's behalf. His suits look increasingly well-tailored. He has not found time to write a novel of any sort.

Fell Hall closed soon after the event on which I had been booked to teach. No reason was ever given, other than that the courses had never been financially viable. People pointed to the quality of wine and whisky that had been served and raised their eyebrows. And in any case, with Wendy gone, nobody else could be found who wanted to live there alone as resident warden – especially after Claire's murder. I walked that way recently, for old times' sake, trudging up the valley, in bright sunshine, through the neat fields of winter wheat, to the rough sheep pasture and into the steep, scree-covered hills beyond. Fell Hall had already started to look sad and dilapidated. At the farm in Butterthwaite, where I stopped to buy a drink, nobody knew what had become of Jenny. Somebody said they thought she'd moved away. London or Harrogate or somewhere.

I had of course looked up Hiram Shuttleworth on the internet as soon as I got back home to Sussex. As I expected, there was nothing on him at all, except as the founder of Fell Hall and of the Golden Age Trust, a body that has since been dissolved according to records at Companies House. I couldn't find any details of his previous career or of his other interests. There were no pictures of him. None at all. Like Wendy, he seemed to be somebody who disliked publicity of any sort.

But there are people like that. At least, according to rumour at crime festivals.

ACKNOWLEDGEMENTS

Since you've worked your way through the final explanatory chapter and a postscript, it seems unfair of me to inflict an acknowledgements section on you too. Writing is however a lonely business and it's nice to be able to remind myself that I did have contact with some real people during the past year, in addition to the fictional ones.

So, let me thank (yet again) Susie Dunlop, Kelly Smith and everyone at my publisher, Allison & Busby, for allowing me to give Ethelred and Elsie another outing. Likewise, my busy and multi-talented agent David Headley, his trusty and very efficient assistant Emily Glenister, and the whole team at DHH Literary Agency for their continuing support and advice.

In a year in which we were all intermittently locked down, I also greatly appreciated all of the people who emailed me to say they had enjoyed my books or engaged with me one way or another, or just made me laugh, on

Twitter or Instagram. (Not so much Facebook – I don't really do Facebook.) Even when COVID is over, please keep the emails coming in.

And finally my thanks and love to my family, Ann, Tom, Rachel, Catrin, Henry, Ella and Ieuan, some of whom enjoy my books and without whom writing would seem not only lonely but a bit pointless.

L. C. TYLER has won awards for his writing, including a CWA Dagger and the Last Laugh Award (twice) for the best comic crime novel of the year. He has also twice been shortlisted in the US for an Edgar Allan Poe Award. He is a former chair of the Crime Writers' Association and an Honorary Fellow of the Royal College of Paediatrics and Child Health, of which he was Chief Executive for twelve years prior to becoming a full-time writer. He has lived all over the world, but most recently in London and Sussex.

lctyler.com
@lenctyler

If you enjoyed *Farewell My Herring,* look out for more
books by L. C. Tyler . . .

To discover more great fiction and to place an order
visit our website
www.allisonandbusby.com
or call us on
02039507834